THE
FOURTH PHASE

EXTINCTION NZ BOOK 2

ADRIAN J SMITH

GREAT WAVE INK
PUBLISHING

GREAT WAVE INK
PUBLISHING

Cover Design by Deranged Doctor Design
Edited by Laurel C Kriegler and Alison Robertson

GREAT WAVE INK
PUBLISHING

Also by Adrian J Smith

Extinction NZ:

The Rule of Three

The Fourth Phase

The Five Pillars

This book is dedicated to all the daydreamers of the world.

And to my grandparents who fought and sacrificed so much so we could live the free life we do.

Thank you.

They shall not grow old, as we that are left grow old.
Age shall not weary them, nor the years condemn.
At the going down of the sun and in the morning,
We shall remember them.
–Laurence Binyon

Acknowledgements

When I set out to write these books, I never realised how many people help an author along the way.

First, I have to thank Nicholas for encouraging me in the first place. You have helped and inspired me from day one.

Frances, you have been there from the beginning, reading every single version of both books. I couldn't have done this without you. I hope I can repay your kindness in some way.

Rodger, like you say, it's probably good that we live far away from each other, otherwise we might cause a bit of chaos. Thank you for your encouragement and for keeping my spirits up with your humour.

To the Guardians of the Apocalypse, you are all wonderful people. Thank you for all your support.

A special thank you to Geoff Toni for helping me with the Maori aspects of this novel. Sadly, Geoff passed away before we could finish. I hope I got everything correct. Rest in peace, brother.

To all of my Beta readers: Col (Ret) Olson, Lisa, Shelli, Nathan, Frances, Cynthia, and Michael. Thank you for all your valuable advice and input. If you find any mistakes they are of my doing.

I tried to write these books from an everyman and woman point of view. Two people who find themselves in a crazy, chaotic world, each of them discovering new facets to their personalities.

Since the book is set in New Zealand, I've used UK spelling. I've also included a Glossary for any Maori terms that you may not be familiar. As always, I'm more than happy to answer any questions. You can contact me on the following platforms:

Facebook: Author: Adrian J Smith
Email: adesmithwrites@gmail.com
Website: adrianjonsmith.com

Come join our Facebook group:
Guardians of the Apocalypse

Thanks again,
Adrian

Foreword
by
Nicholas Sansbury Smith

Dear Reader,

Thank you for picking up a copy of The Fourth Phase by Adrian Smith. This is the second of a planned trilogy documenting Jack Gee and his struggle to survive in a post-apocalyptic New Zealand. Originally published through Amazon's Extinction Cycle Kindle World, The Fourth Phase became a reader favourite in the Extinction Cycle series side stories, and transcended to far more than fan fiction. Unfortunately, Amazon ended the Kindle Worlds program in July of 2018 with little warning. Authors were given a chance to republish or retire their stories, and I jumped at the chance to republish The Fourth Phase through my small press, Great Wave Ink. Today, we're proud to offer The Fourth Phase in paperback, audio, and to readers outside of the United States for the first time ever.

For those of you that are new to the Extinction Cycle storyline, the series is the award winning, Amazon top-rated, and half a million copy best-selling seven book saga. There are over six *thousand* five-star reviews on Amazon alone. Critics have called it, "World War Z and The Walking Dead meets the Hot Zone." Publishers weekly added, "Smith has realised that the way to rekindle interest in zombie apocalypse fiction is to make it louder, longer, and bloodier… Smith intensifies the disaster efficiently as the pages flip by, and readers who enjoy juicy blood-and-guts action will find a lot of it here."

In creating the Extinction Cycle, my goal was to use authentic military action and real science to take the zombie and post-apocalyptic genres in an exciting new direction. Forget everything you know about zombies. In the Extinction Cycle, they aren't created by black magic or other supernatural means. The ones found in the Extinction Cycle are created by a military bio-weapon called VX-99, first used in Vietnam. The chemicals reactivate the proteins encoded by the genes that separate humans from wild animals—in other words, the experiment turned men into monsters. For the first time, zombies are explained using real science—science so real there is every possibility of something like the Extinction Cycle actually happening. But these creatures aren't the unthinking, slow-minded, shuffling monsters we've all come to know in other shows, books, and movies. These "variants" are more monster than human. Through the series, the variants become the hunters as they evolve from the epigenetic changes. Scrambling to find a cure and defeat the monsters, humanity is brought to the brink of extinction.

We hope you enjoy The Fourth Phase and continue on with the next book in the Extinction NZ series, and the main storyline in the Extinction Cycle. Thank you for reading!

Best wishes,
Nicholas Sansbury Smith,
USA Today Bestselling Author of the Extinction Cycle

Prologue

The creature ran through the night. It leapt over rocks. Over tree roots. Through mud and bushes. Thorns and twigs stabbed at it, but the creature ignored it all. Its quarry was close. It scrambled up the steep hill, using its claws to dig deep into any crack, any crevice.

It was oblivious to anything but its prey. Its master had commanded that it track them. Follow them no matter where they went. It paused and sniffed the air, savouring the scents of the humans. Young humans. It could smell their blood. Young blood was different, newer, with a sweeter taste like it was fresh from the source. Full of iron and salts. The creature paused and smacked its sucker-like lips together. It crouched on a fallen tree and flicked its forked tongue into the night air, tasting for its game. No part of its brain was human anymore; it had evolved into something new, something different. Better and lethal. Now it hunted them with its kin and feasted on their flesh.

Not tonight, though. Tonight the master had tasked it with finding two young humans. They had fled into the interior of the island.

The creature threw its head back and howled into the crisp night sky. A chorus of howls answered. It had no trouble tracking the calls. Instinctively it knew the others' locations by the sounds of their shrieks echoing through the dark.

The beast tasted the air once more and grinned to itself. Other creatures were chasing the humans like sharks in a feeding frenzy. This beast knew better. It knew to wait, to hang back from the humans and their sticks that stung. No, the creature had picked up on a new scent. A musty smell, with dirt and odours like the sea. It tracked the mammal with four legs.

The creature spat. The four-legged mammal stuck to the humans, picking up on scraps. It didn't hunt for itself. It waited for them to feed it, something the beast found puzzling. It had limited thoughts, normally just:

Hunt…
Feed…
Mate… But above all, Obey the master.

The master was twice as big and so much stronger. With its own eyes the creature had seen the master tear ones like it in half and eat them.

The creature shook its body and tasted the air again. The humans were close. Another human and the four-legged mammal were closer.

It stayed on the tree and waited. It cocked its head as the bangs of the stinging sticks rang out. It hated that sound and the pain it brought. Its ears picked up on the noise of the humans' cries and the vibrations of their scrambling feet.

Finally the humans were moving towards it. The creature crept farther into the bush, ignoring every smell that surrounded it.

The master wanted these ones. It wasn't going to let a snack distract it. Turning, following the smells and tastes, the creature scampered into the undergrowth.

***

How? How did they find us?

Boss pondered this question on a loop as he ran his trembling hand along the smooth wall of the cave. If he was being honest, he knew the answer. Perhaps the better question was *Why? Why are they here?*

But he knew the answer to that as well.

Six weeks ago, the Hemorrhage Virus had swept across the world. No country was spared. Humans that became infected mutated into monsters, monsters the survivors had named *Variants*. And Variants reverted to the most animalistic of thoughts and actions: Food. They were now the apex predators. A few Variants had retained some of their intellect and now commanded others, as an Alpha leading the pack. Surprisingly, and tragically, a few humans collaborated with these Variant Alphas and helped them locate survivors.

Boss had been lucky. He had survived. Well, most of him had. No. *Why?* wasn't the right question either. He knew why. They all knew why. Besides the obvious *What did they hope to gain?* Boss paused and peered ahead.

He could just make out George in the dim light a couple of meters away and took a careful step forwards, wishing again that he could turn on his flashlight. But the fear of discovery stayed his hand. No, it was better to stumble in the dark than to alert the creatures to their location like a lighthouse warning ships.

In the distance, he could hear the faint sounds of gunfire, some single shots, a few rapid, close together. And the occasional boom of a shotgun. Checking that his own Mossberg was loaded, he hobbled along, his makeshift prosthetic clicking on the rock floor.

Boss strained his ears listening for them. A faint scurrying sound reached him, like a rat scampering across a wooden floor. With every sound his heart beat faster. Boss paused and took a moment to try to bring his nerves under control.

Something warm and soft nudged his good leg, pressing against him. Looking down, he saw Max, the New Zealand heading dog they'd adopted.

A conversation he'd had with Dee flashed in his mind, bringing a faint smile to his lips.

"A heading dog? Don't you mean herding?"
"No, Boss, it's heading. Google it."
"Google?" Boss laughed. "How?"
"Just believe me for once, then," Dee said, smiling at him.

Max pressed his nose into Boss's hand and gave him a quick lick, as if to reassure Boss that he was doing the right thing. Seeing Max calmly padding alongside helped him focus.

"How much farther?" he whispered. George pointed

down the tunnel. Boss could see a faint silvery patch of light in the distance. He hurried towards it, eager to leave the twisting and turning caves behind. At least out in the open he could see the Variants coming. The open would give them a chance to survive.

They exited the tunnel and Boss looked over at the dark patch that was the small island on the side of the crater lake, nestled against the eastern edge of the caldera. A lone pohutukawa tree stood, a ghostly sentry over the low scrub covering the island. Like some Maori guardian, it spread its twisting gnarled branches across the little island, protecting it. Beyond the island, the rim of the crater had eroded almost down to the height of the tree, allowing the sounds of the surf crashing on the rocks to reach him.

"Can you swim, G-man?"

George nodded.

"C'mon then, quick, dude. Take off your pack and push it in front of you. It's not far."

Checking to see that George followed his instructions, Boss took his own pack off and cradled it in his arms. Edging into the water, he was shocked at the cold that quickly numbed his foot.

A horrifying screech reverberated through the tunnel. Boss shrank inwardly. He hated that sound, and for the last few weeks he had been spared from it. He had thought he'd escaped from the horror that was the new world, fighting through hell to reach this island sanctuary. He'd even lost a leg to that evil abomination, the one with the severed heads spiked on each shoulder. He'd nicknamed him the "Trophy King". He'd said it so much the name had caught on amongst the other survivors.

Shaking away his thoughts, he prodded Max ahead of him into the frigid water.

Boss looked over his shoulder. George was still standing at the lake's edge. "G-man!"

George had his head turned, looking back down the tunnel. Boss treaded water, his teeth beginning to chatter. "George, c'mon!"

"I'm scared."

His heart sank at hearing those words. George had been so brave. Maybe he had reached his breaking point. They had all been through so much together. Dee had told him they were all suffering from something she called PTSD.

Boss remembered the conversation he'd had with Jack about the three phases of PTSD after a disaster.

"Phase one: Impact. Phase two: Recoil and rescue. Phase three: Recovery."

"So, what's this fourth phase that you talked about?"

"We fight back."

Looking at George, he knew Jack and Dee were right.

Another terrible screech echoed around, its pitch slamming into Boss's head, sending chills down his back.

Hell. That was really close.

He swam back to shore and hauled George into the chilly embrace of the lake. "I know you're scared. Shit, I am too."

George blinked rapidly but let Boss pull him out into deeper water. Soon he was swimming the few metres to the scrub-filled island alongside Boss, with Max paddling beside them.

Immediately, he searched for a place to hide from creatures. The island was covered in flax and manuka, offering limited cover. Boss groaned and looked up into the night.

Protect us now, Kaitiaki. We need you more than ever.

He rarely thought of his Maori ancestry, because his mother had tried to instil in him that ethnicity didn't matter. What mattered were your actions and your courage, the courage to fight on, fight for whatever you needed to fight for. Right now, he had to fight and protect George from the Variants.

He glanced over at Max, who was panting, his tongue hanging out, water dripping onto the earth, his tail wagging. Max was looking up at Boss, his eyes watching his every move as if to say, *"What now, human?"*

Boss continued his search. The only option he could see was the flax; it had grown together, creating a natural cave.

Sighing, he pushed George and Max inside and they nestled together, shaking. He didn't know if it was from the cold or from the fact that the Variants pursued them, wanting to tear the flesh from their bones.

Boss listened as the shrieking and howling intensified. He pumped his shotgun, ready to make a last stand, ready to fight until he drew his last breath. He peeked through the flax and up into the tree above.

Maybe I can get George and Max to the coast that way.

A booming bellow pulsed around the lake and Boss's breath caught in his throat. He closed his eyes and gritted his teeth, trying to shut the sound out. His left leg spasmed at its stump. He knew that bellow; he'd heard it as the Trophy King tore off his leg, nearly adding Boss's life to the millions of lost souls. That sound haunted his dreams and tormented his thoughts.

Now it was here, harassing him again. Boss flicked the safety off and tried to calm his nerves.

All right, you ugly bastard. Come and get it.

Well, Jack. So much for your four phases.

First phase: Impact.
Second phase: Recoil and rescue.
Third phase: Recovery.
Fourth phase: We fight back.

— 1 —

Jack tried to keep the cold autumn rain out of his eyes, but was failing miserably. Looking through the scope, he searched the dark bush, looking for any sign of Dee and the soldiers. After only a week of training with Captain Ben Johns, Jack, Dee and two others had flown with Ben to Great Barrier Island, located 140 kilometres north of Mayor Island off the northern tip of the Coromandel Peninsula. Colonel James Mahana had moved his Forward Operating Base here a week earlier as it had greater strategic value, more space and a larger natural harbour.

Ben had wanted to test what they had learnt in the thick bush and mountains that covered the island. The island was secluded and had a small population, vital factors for escaping the notice of the Variants. Ben called them his little Recon and Rescue team. Mahana had named them "The Renegades" after their rescue of Jack from the nest.

Jack adjusted his cap in a fresh attempt to stop the rain dripping into his eyes. So far he hadn't spotted anybody, and his patience was beginning to wear thin. The combination of little sleep, little food and this persistent rain was really testing his temper. Jack had worked hard over the years to keep his temper under control. It was only in times of great stress, and when he was tired, that it erupted these days. He took some calming breaths, practising the technique a Buddhist monk had taught him on his trip to Thailand. He concentrated on letting go of his anger and focusing on the task at hand. He could feel his muscles relax with each deep breath.

Jack glanced over to where Ben had set up camp. Ben had dumped Dee and the other two soldiers at one end of the island, and Jack at the other. Then he had set up camp at one of the trig points, high up in roughly the middle of the island, on Mt Hirakimata. Dee and the two soldiers' task was to reach the camp and claim the flag by midnight. They had been at this task for twenty-four hours now. He looked at his watch: 22:54. Just over an hour to go. His task was to find them and report their positions to Ben.

Where the hell are they? This is the only way to reach the camp.

All the hours of solitude for the past three days had made Jack think a lot about his lucky escape from the Variant nest. Subconsciously, he rubbed the scars on his leg. He wondered again, for about the hundredth time, why he had woken from his coma? No one else had. Well, apart from George. Why them? Everyone else stuck in that meat locker had been in a persistent state of unconsciousness. Back on Mayor Island, he had asked the doctors and nurses if they had a reason. No one had any idea. The not knowing annoyed him immensely. He hated not understanding something. With no Google or books to reference, it bugged the crap out of him. *Not that it will make any difference. This is a new kind of terror.*

Trying to focus his wandering mind, Jack scanned the track leading up to the camp. Ben had set his camp up well. It was high, on a rocky bluff, and out in the open, with only one way up or down. Jack had hiked through the interior of the island for eighteen hours straight to reach this spot. Most of the training he had received from Ben involved weapons. Guns — rifles and handguns. A small amount of knife work. Ben had thought Jack's bush skills and fitness were satisfactory to not need any other training.

A flash of red streaked across his scope. Scanning the area, Jack couldn't see anything. *Great, now I'm hallucinating as well.* His mind often played over the killing of the man in the red trucker cap back in that Variant nest.

Jack shivered at the memory. At the time he'd shrugged it off, but when everything had calmed down, it had made him sick to his stomach. That he had taken another human's life so easily, as if it meant nothing to him. Killing the Variants was a breeze, especially when they were trying to kill him or anyone he cared about. The doctor called it PTSD. Jack knew that he had it, but then everyone who'd survived had it. He wasn't alone, so why did he feel so alone? He'd discussed it with Dee. She seemed to be handling it better. She had been supporting him and talking about it with him.

"Time, laughter and meeting you is what healed me," Dee had said. *"You shared your love of nature, your love of movies, books, trivia and fun with me. You helped me forget about the monsters in the world. Sadly, now there are real monsters to deal with."*

Jack agreed, but he was struggling. He took some more deep breaths, wiped the rain from his forehead, and focused on finding Dee and the two soldiers.

Fourth phase: We fight back.

Seeing movement, Jack swung his AR-15 around and looked through the Nikon P-223 BDC 600 scope. Adjusting it slightly, he could see the two soldiers creeping up the track. They were about one hundred metres below Ben's camp. *So, where the hell is Dee?*

He reached for his radio. "Ben? Do you copy? Over."

"Receiving. What have you got for me, Jack? Over."

"Two bogies approaching from the north. It looks to be Eric and Tony. Approximately eighty metres out, over."

There was a pause. Jack assumed Ben was searching the area.

His radio crackled back to life. "Got them. Good work, Jack. Now find me Dee, over."

"Wilco, out."

Jack watched Eric and Tony for a bit before turning his attention to the hillside below.

***

Dee squirmed her way up the steep ravine, under rotting logs and through thick vines. Metre by metre, she crept on. She had spent the last day and a half slowly wriggling her way around the rocky bluff, and now she was heading up towards the camp. Her small frame was suited for this type of exercise. She leant against the rock and risked a glance up. The bright yellow flag that was her goal fluttered above her in the chilling sea breeze. Inhaling, she savoured the pungent but pleasant smell of the forest undergrowth. Dee pulled her woollen cap down over her ears. The cold May air was stinging her exposed flesh.

Cupping her hand around her watch, she checked the time: 22:58. She had just over an hour to reach her goal.

It hadn't taken her much to convince Eric and Tony to follow the obvious route up to the camp, allowing her to circumnavigate Jack's position.

She had settled well into military life. She loved the routine and the sense that she was part of something bigger, a machine. A way to fight for their freedom, to not be afraid of the Variants.

Perhaps we deserved it?

Humans are like a virus. Feeding, devouring everything. Depleting all before moving on.

It took a virus to destroy another virus. *If that's even possible.*

Dee shifted her weight, trying to relieve her cramped, tired muscles. She hadn't had any sleep for the last twenty-four hours. And the persistent rain made this climb extremely perilous.

She strained to hear any sounds above the pattering of the dripping water, for any sounds of discovery. Satisfied, Dee glanced around one more time. She checked her rifle and secured it. Reaching above her, she gripped her next handhold and hauled herself up another metre. After several more aching metres, she paused again. She was so close now.

A couple of voices filtered down to her. She could just make out what they were saying.

"C'mon. The All Blacks would have won the Rugby World Cup, for sure."

"I don't know, bro. We're good, but the Aussies always rise to the occasion."

"Maybe, but we won the last one, bro."

"True, too true, cuz. 'Spose we got that monkey off our back?"

"One word, bro: Richie!"

"Richie!" they chorused, their laughter echoing out.

Dee grinned, her cheek muscles twinging with the effort. *Man, I'm exhausted.* Those idiots were at least giving her the chance she needed. Using the distraction, she gripped the wet rock above her and, with her last bit of energy, hauled herself up and over the shelf. Rolling, she looked up, expecting to see the yellow flag above her. Instead, Ben's eyes stared down, dark and wide, his rifle held over her, to one side.

A tight grin spread on his face. "Nearly, Dee. Very close."

"Damn it. How did you know?"

"I knew these two were the bait you sent ahead, so I let them talk. Plus, this is the only other climbable route up here." He reached down and gripped Dee's hand, hauling her to her feet. "We'd better let Jack know. Do you want to radio him?"

"Yeah, thanks."

He handed Dee his radio, turned to his camp stove, and ignited it. Dee watched hungrily as the flame sparked to life. She dearly looked forward to getting some food into her growling stomach. She pressed the talk button. "Jack, this is Dee, over."

"Dee? How the hell?"

"Thought you had it all covered, eh?"

"Yeah I did. How?"

Dee shifted her weight from foot to foot. "I came up the other side. Up the ravine. It's okay. I didn't get the flag. Captain spotted me before I could, over."

"Yeah, look, sorry Dee, I'm just tired. Congrats anyway. Should I come to camp, over?"

Dee looked at Ben. He nodded.

"Affirmative Jack, out."

"Wilco, out."

***

Jack slid the radio back in its pouch and busied himself breaking camp. It didn't take him long, as he had kept himself ready to go at a moment's notice, as per Ben's orders.

Be ready, at all times.

He adjusted the pack on his back and secured the waist belt so that some of the weight lifted off his shoulders. Jack glanced out at the grey Pacific Ocean, blanketed in rain. A silhouette looming on the horizon made him peer through the gloom. It looked like a large ship, perhaps a container ship? He lifted his rifle to his shoulder so he could look through the scope. Scanning left to right, he couldn't see any running lights on the port or starboard sides. On closer inspection, Jack frowned, perplexed: a large Navy vessel was steaming directly for the island.

That's too big to be one of ours! If it isn't ours, then whose? Australia? America? Two smaller vessels slid out of the rain, looking more like NZ Navy ships. A cold shiver ran up Jack's spine, the tingles webbing across his head.

He unhooked his radio and raised it to his lips.

— 2 —

Staff Sergeant Maggie Liontakis watched the dew drip off
the wire mesh fence. The water formed droplets and
then, with the pull of gravity, stretched off the metal and
fell to the ground. She shivered, her body still
acclimatising to these weird, back-to-front seasons she
now found herself in. Sighing, she looked to the bush-
clad mountains far in the distance, marvelling at the
greens mixed with browns, the odd outcrop of rock
jutting out into the early morning light. *I need to get out of
here. I need to go home.*

Maggie stared into the pine trees surrounding her
prison. She focused on one particular tree, letting the
corners of her eyes do the work, just like she'd been
taught in the army. She waited patiently. There! The guard
walked through her line of vision. Dressed in red
coveralls like painters' wear, she saw him stop and light a
cigarette. The smoke billowed above him, and he looked
around before carrying on his path. Cursing herself again
for not being more cautious a few weeks back, she leant
back against the post, gritting her teeth.

Maggie had been taken prisoner by humans, humans
who were helping the Variants. She, along with several

other women, had been brought to this makeshift prison. Children and men were also brought here, but neither stayed long. Maggie suspected something sinister was happening and she had a theory, something that frightened her to admit.

"Hey, Maggie."

She turned to the source of the voice and smiled when she saw its owner. "Morning, Alice. Sleep well?"

"Not bad, considering. You dreaming of freedom again?"

Maggie looked down at the warm cup of coffee she held in her hands. Even after three weeks of being in this prison, she still had trouble with the Kiwi accent. To the untrained ear it sounded like the Australian accent, but to her it was totally different: not as nasal. The Kiwis tended to mash up their vowel sounds, so an "i" became a "u", making "fish" sound like "fush". The Aussies said "chance", where the Kiwis made it sound like "Charnce". Regardless of what she had learnt, she still had to give herself time to process what she heard. They also spoke so fast, while Maggie was used to that southern drawl of Houston, Texas.

Her eyes glinting with memories of home, she looked back up at Alice. "That is an affirmative. It's every captured soldier's duty to escape."

Alice grinned, a small laugh escaping her lips.

Maggie indicated the seat next to her. Patting Alice on the leg, she lowered her voice. "How many guards have you seen?" Pointing into the trees, she added, "Out there, beyond the fence."

Alice stared out into the trees. "I'm not sure. Four, maybe five?"

Maggie nodded, taking in the information. She took a sip of her coffee, savouring the bitter taste. "Yeah, that's about what I think. Any luck with your guard friend?"

"A bit. You said slowly, right?"

"Yeah, we have to be subtle about this. We have to act defeated, compliant. But we need information. We need to know their movements. They'll have a routine. It's human nature. So just observe for now."

Maggie looked up from her cup, watching Alice's face. She could see fear, real fear. But she could also see a determination to survive, and that was what she'd spent the last three weeks looking for. Someone willing to risk it all to get out of this place. To risk it for a chance at freedom. Maggie had already put a plan in motion. She felt a pang of guilt for not telling Alice, but she needed to wait until the time was right.

Alice tucked her blonde hair back behind her ears. "Okay. I'll keep on him."

"Thanks. I better get to my garden before Ian comes looking for me, swinging his police baton."

The two women grinned at each other. Maggie thought Ian, the warden of this camp, was a joke. He liked to wander around keeping an eye on everyone. Always swinging that baton.

"See you after?" Maggie said, still grinning.

"Yeah, I'll see you after," Alice said.

Maggie stood and stretched out the kinks in her back. She gave Alice a reassuring pat on the shoulder and headed off towards the gardens. All around her, the prison camp was coming to life. She estimated about a hundred people were here. Mainly women, but a few children were allowed to stay. Maggie walked across the dew-laden grass between the weatherboard buildings. The whole camp reminded her of a school, with the buildings laid out in two rows and an asphalt courtyard in the middle. To the east lay two huge machine sheds, and in the direction she was headed, she and the others assigned to gardening had created some large plots. Winter was coming, so all they had planted were some lettuce, cabbage and other winter crops. A two-metre-high chain link fence enclosed the complex. Maggie sighed. The fence wasn't the problem, and neither were the red-clad guards. It was the monsters from hell. Variants, Alice called them. Variants of humans who had devoured all but a lucky few.

Then why are we here?

Maggie reached the gardens and collected the tools she needed for weeding.

"Morning, y'all," she said, waving to the others already hard at work. Some murmured greetings but most didn't. Maggie was fine with that.

She wanted to be alone today; she needed to think. She busied herself with the task at hand, running the hoe through the soil, being careful not to get too close to the vegetables they had planted. As she worked, she let her mind drift.

She remembered the heat and sand of her two tours of Afghanistan and one of Iraq. Feelings of guilt took hold again. She had been a medic in the army and had learnt quickly that you couldn't save everyone. She didn't miss the heat of those sun-scorched dens of hell, nor did she miss the constant sounds of war around her. Explosions, screams, guns, shouting. Men bragging, trying to get her into bed one day, bleeding and dying in her arms the next.

She didn't miss the gore of trying to stem the flow of blood from missing limbs, soldiers screaming in agony, gripping her hand as the life left their eyes. No, she would never miss that. But she did miss the sense of belonging, the camaraderie. When she was enlisted, she had belonged; she was fighting for the greater good, to protect her homeland from the threats to democracy. She missed the night she had spent with that army ranger. She'd liked him; his wisecracking friend not so much. Maggie wiped away a tear.

Like all veterans, she'd struggled with life after the army. She had decided to tick an item off her bucket list and travel to New Zealand. Visiting all the *Lord of the Rings* sites had been top of her list. As soon as she arrived at Auckland International Airport, she'd fallen in love with the green rolling hills, the bush-clad mountains. As she travelled, there had been some new joy around every corner. A dazzling blue lake here, forests dropping down to a perfect white sand beach there, and snow-capped mountains rising up into the clouds. She had enjoyed the rough and wild west coast of the North Island, and had travelled down to Wellington via New Plymouth, enjoying the friendly people all the way. She admired the Kiwi can-do attitude, which she attributed to their isolation. They were involved in world politics, but not aggressive. Not as heavily as her country was.

Lost in her thoughts, Maggie ran her hoe through the rows of lettuce. *The apocalypse would have to come now, and me without my rifle.*

Maggie paused from her work and wiped the sweat off her brow with her sleeve. The day had become warm but pleasant. Glancing around, she could see the other gardeners hard at work. No one wanted to look like they were slacking; the guards took pleasure in reminding them who was in charge. Maggie let out a laugh. *They may guard us, but the Variants rule the world now.*

Stretching, she headed to the beach umbrella with the ice box — or chilly bin, as the Kiwis called it. Maggie smiled to herself as she drank the cool liquid. They certainly had funny words for things. She used the time to look at the main gate, watching the guards. During her time here, she had observed two things. One, they didn't seem to be frightened of the Variants, and two, they were becoming complacent. A fact she intended to take full advantage of. *Traitoring bastards.*

— 3 —

The fall sun crept across a sky dotted with puffy clouds. Maggie worked tirelessly weeding her rows, enjoying the monotony of the work, distracting herself from her worries. Her stomach began to rumble just as she heard the dinner bell ring out. Packing up her tools, she headed to the courtyard, her mouth watering.

As she walked between the buildings flanking the courtyard, a shadow loomed from behind the wall.

"Hey, Yank!"

Maggie stopped and stared into the brown eyes of Ian, the warden of the prison, the movement of his swinging police baton flicking in her peripheral vision. It looked comical, as his arms and legs were so skinny. Clenching her teeth at the insult, she stared at him. "What?"

Ian glared at her, spittle forming at the corner of his mouth. "Enjoy your day in the sunshine?" His mocking tone was clear.

Maggie forced herself to remain civil and not let him see her rising anger. Men like Ian purposely taunted and antagonised to get a reaction. When you did react, it was a victory for them.

She glanced up and held his gaze. "Yes, I did. Reminded me of working on the ranch."

Ian's mouth upturned into a snarl. "Ranch? Pfft. You Americans don't know what a farm is. Anyway, I want to see you after your meal."

Maggie tensed her arm muscles. She wanted nothing more than to punch him in the windpipe and ram that baton where the sun don't shine. But now was not the time.

"In your office?"

Her skin crawled as Ian reached out and stroked her arm. Holding it, he smiled, showing his teeth. "Yes, in my office. Don't make me wait. I don't like being made to wait. Anger me Yank, and I'll leave you out in the forest. I'm sure the monsters would like my offering."

Maggie forced herself to remain calm, calling on all her training. Keeping her face void of emotion, she looked at Ian. "Sure, see you there."

He released her arm and Maggie stepped around him, letting out a breath.

Looking around the mess hall, food tray in hand, she spotted Alice sitting in the corner with a couple of other people, a male and a female. Newbies, by the looks of their ragged clothes and the way they were shovelling food into their mouths. She walked down the centre gap, murmuring greetings to some of the women she saw. Many of the tables still lay empty, with everyone congregating at the middle ones, closest to the kitchen.

Maggie stopped at a table and crouched down next to a little girl with red hair and sparkling green eyes. "Hey, Becs. Did you have a good day, kiddo?" she smiled, watching as Becs twirled her fingers, nodding her head.

Maggie reached over and patted her on the leg. "That's good, Becs. I'll see you for story time, okay?" She stood up and leant over Becs to shake the hand of the woman sitting next to her. Feeling a piece of paper palmed into her hand, she turned and walked over to Alice, sliding the paper into her pocket as she did so.

Reaching the table, she plonked herself next to Alice and squeezed Alice's hand. "Hey, so who are your friends?"

Alice squeezed back and laid her fork down, nodding in the newbies' direction. "Tracey and Dean, this is Maggie."

Maggie watched as the pair barely stopped eating to voice a greeting. Leaning in close to Maggie's right ear, Alice lowered her voice, her eyes glancing at the four red-clothed guards watching the women and children eat. "I thought you might want to talk to them. They were brought in this afternoon. Unhooded."

Maggie furrowed her brow and leant against the backrest of her seat. "Unhooded?" she mouthed.

Alice picked up her fork and started eating the rice on her plate. "Yeah, exactly."

Maggie looked over at the two newbies, eating as if this was going to be their last meal. Tracey had dark hair and light-brown skin, her broad nose typical of the people of Polynesia. She could see the traditional Maori koru-style of tattoo on her forearm and a smaller one behind her left ear. Dean was a fine specimen of a man. Muscular, tall and dark haired. He too had Maori tattoos on his arms. *Brought here without a hood?* Dean was the first male prisoner she had seen for over a week. They didn't keep the men here. Some stayed to carry out physical

24

labour, but they were all shipped off eventually.

Maggie busied herself eating. With this new information and the piece of paper in her pocket, she didn't have much of an appetite. But that old army training kicked in. *Eat when you can, sleep when you can.*

It was time to advance the last part of her plan.

Rejuvenated by thoughts of escape and her long-term quest of getting home to Texas, Maggie ate the rest of her meal in silence. Better keep the peace with Ian and his baton.

— 4 —

Boss turned the detent dial, moving slowly through the frequencies, scanning for any chatter. He glanced at the clock to one side: 5:45, or 17:45 as he was supposed to say now.

Yes! Not long to go.

He had enjoyed learning all the details of radio operations, but for the last few days he had heard limited chatter. His orders were to continuously scan, searching for any survivors. His last success had been yesterday, when he had found a couple on a boat. After giving them the coordinates of Mayor Island, they had relayed that they were running low on fuel and were heading off to look for more. Since then, Boss had heard nothing. Worry was beginning to creep in. Leaning back in his chair, he rubbed the bandage on his stump. Hell, it was itchy. Glancing over at the ledger of contacts, he searched out the name of their boat. *Sea You Later*. Running his finger down the page, he read the frequency next to the name and turned the detent dial to the correct number. He adjusted his headphones, listening to the static hissing in his ears. Pressing down the talk button, he reached out.

"*Sea You Later*, this is Falcon 7, over."

Hissing and static buzzed in his ear.

"*Sea You Later*, do you copy?"

Boss frowned and tried a few more times with no success. He reached up and rubbed the ridges of skin on his forehead. *Damn it!* He made a note on his ledger. Turning his attention back to the radio, he dutifully turned the dial, listening for anything, any sign of more survivors. So few had made it to the outlying islands. Mayor Island had a population of just 120, Motiti Island, a few kilometres south, a mere 45. But, thankfully, it was a working farm with a thousand head of sheep and 350 dairy cows. Last Boss heard, Mahana wanted some army personnel sent there, to secure the island. Great Barrier Island, where Jack, Dee and Ben were, had just under 800 people. So few, from so many.

Boss looked at the clock again hoping for the end of his shift. It flashed 18:03. Grinning, he reached for his crutches. Hoisting himself up with a grunt, he looked down at where his lower leg used to be. The doctor had warned him about phantom pains. Boss still caught himself trying to use that leg. Embarrassingly, he had fallen over a few times. Grabbing his ledger, he headed over to Sergeant Brian Haere sitting at a desk in the far corner. It was a simple room; two stacks of radio equipment lined the left-hand and back walls, with Haere's desk on the right-hand wall, next to the door as you entered. A couple of maps of New Zealand and the surrounding islands had been pinned to the sheetrock wall, white marker pins locating the pockets of survivors. Boss couldn't help but glance at the mainland. Only three white markers remained there: Auckland, Wellington and a pin in the South Island. Someplace called Waihopai.

He'd never heard of it.

Boss remembered all he'd been through just to reach this island. How he had hidden in the attic with his mother. His father's return as one of the flesh-eaters. His flight. His rescue from the hounds of hell by Dee. Hiding in that stinky basement with her. She had become someone he cared about dearly and, when he admitted it, had a huge crush on. He thought about the guilt he still felt for running: running to save himself, leaving his mother to his once-father. He liked to think that karma had been paid when he lost his lower left leg to that hideous Alpha.

Frowning at the memory of that beast, Boss glanced over to the other RO. He waved at Signaller Geoff "Six" Austin, getting his attention. "Game later?"

Six pulled one of his headphones off his ear, like DJs do when mixing dance music. "For sure. See you in a bit. You better bring it tonight."

Boss barked a laugh. "I'm 10-6 up."

"Yeah, yeah. I'll catch up with you tonight, bro."

Boss shook his head as he walked the last few metres to Sergeant Haere. Pool was his game. It was all about angles and placing the ball ready for the next shot. All those hours practising at home, playing his dad, had paid off.

Reaching Sergeant Haere, he put his weight on his remaining leg and handed over his ledger. "Nothing new to report, Sir."

Sergeant Haere looked up from the report he was reading and stared straight at Boss. Boss found it difficult to hold his gaze. He knew it was Haere's way of measuring him, to see what sort of man he was. Boss hated that aspect of masculinity. Men and boys trying to prove to each other just how macho they were. Surely being here on this island was proof enough?

He couldn't hold the stare any longer and glanced away, looking out the window. He could see the few lights of the camp dancing on the water of the natural harbour. The sounds of children playing reached him, bringing a smile to his lips. He was looking forward to seeing George.

"Nothing new in your report, Shepard?" Haere said.

Boss looked down at his feet, heat rising up through his body, flushing his cheeks.

"Look at me, Shepard." Haere pointed first at himself, and then back at Boss. "When an officer speaks to you, you look him in the eye. It's all about respect, Shepard."

Boss ground his teeth together. He hated how Sergeant Haere talked to him. He was still getting used to the chain of command.

"Yes, sir, nothing new to report, sir."

Haere raised his hand and rubbed his chin. "Very well, Shepard. You are dismissed. See you here at 0800." .

"Thank you Sir."

Boss turned and caught Six's eye, grinned, and raised his head in acknowledgement.

He walked down a short corridor and into the common area that was once the lounge bar, back when the building was a hotel, back before the Variants ate everyone.

Boss hobbled down the stairs and out onto the concrete boardwalk that hugged the shore of the bay. Max bounded over, playfully nudging his head into Boss's leg. He reached down and scratched behind the dog's ears, savouring the familiar touch. Max had adopted them in a way. He had started sleeping on the deck of the villa and had never left. Jack had asked around the village, but nobody claimed him. Dee said that sometimes animals find their own forever home.

Boss liked that. Forever home. That would be nice. He looked out at the small settlement he now called home. Before the Hemorrhage Virus, it had been a camping ground, hosting people over the summer months. A few cabins were dotted around the hills, some bigger summer houses mingled between, with the hotel — now Operations — in the middle of the bay. The large, older-style villa sat on the hill overlooking the bay and the mainland. It was the house he shared with Jack, Dee, George and Ben. A small laugh escaped his lips as he remembered Jack calling it the Walsh Villa, from some movie back in the 80s. *Jack and his movies.*

Boss stood on the stairs overlooking the beach and glanced around, looking for George. He smiled. Maybe Beth would be there too.

A few of the kids had a game of touch rugby going, eking out every last minute in the fading autumn light. Boss searched out the red hair of George and watched him dodging around a couple of older boys, heading for the try line marked in the sand. One of the boys slammed his shoulder into George, sending him sprawling.

"Oi! It's touch, you dickhead," Boss shouted.

The older boy looked over at him. "Oh look, it's hopping Virgil. Come to save your little boyfriend?" he said, his tone laced with sarcasm.

"Leave it out, Tyler. He's only eight."

"Whatever. Game's finished anyway," Tyler scoffed.

Boss looked left and right, taking in the other players. A couple of them were shuffling their feet. He spotted Beth striding over to George. She bent down and hauled him up, brushing off the sand. She looked at Boss, smiling. Her sparkling blue eyes sent a flutter through his stomach.

Beth turned to Tyler and whacked him on the arm. "He's just a kid. You always have to ruin the game, don't you?"

"Yeah, whatever, you guys are all soft anyway."

Boss was relieved to see Tyler storm off, his two cohorts following. They feinted a couple of punches at the other players as they left, their cackling laughter echoing out over the water.

Boss shook his head. What was Tyler's problem, smashing into George like he was some big South African rugby player? Bullies always got on his nerves. Bigger kids throwing their weight around, physically and mentally torturing everyone around them. Did they have to make everyone's lives as miserable as theirs? He had hated school for that reason. All the cliques with all their little rules and dramas. Always so much drama.

Tyler was the only one who called him by his given name, Virgil. He cringed whenever he heard it. Boss often cursed his parents and their love of all things NASA.

Sighing, he pushed himself off the concrete wall.

"Hey G-man, you okay?"

George brushed some of the grainy-gold sand from his hair. "He's so mean."

Boss leant down and helped get more sand off George's clothes. "I'm sorry, G-man. Some kids are just like that. Probably best to stay away, okay?"

"I guess. But I like playing rugby with the other kids," George said. He kicked at the sand.

"I know, mate. Let's go get some dinner, eh?" Boss glanced up at Beth, and his heart leapt in his chest. Plucking up courage, he smiled at her. "Umm, do you like… I mean would you…ummm—"

"I'd love to. Thanks," Beth cut in, saving Boss from further embarrassment. Boss grinned at her. "Ah, thanks for your help back there, by the way."

"No probs. Can't have that idiot doing that."

The trio made their way over to the mess hall nestled next to the hotel. Boss could see the old restaurant name, "Obsidian", painted across the facade. The smell of frying fish made his stomach rumble. He licked his lips.

Boss leant back in his chair, stretching out his tired back muscles. Ever since he'd recovered from his injury, he found it difficult to sit for very long. Doc had explained that it was to do with him relying on his good leg all the time, and that once he fitted the prosthetic it should improve.

Prosthetic! Bugger.

Boss looked around the restaurant for the doctor. He couldn't see him. He waved at Beth, getting her attention. "Can you watch George? I've got to visit Doc. He wants to test my prosthetic tonight."

"Sure, no probs. See you in the games room after?"

"Yeah, definitely. I've got to keep my streak going with Six."

Boss hobbled along the path his crutches clicking on the concrete. Movement out in the bay caught his eye. A large luxury yacht was churning its way past the moored boats, and he could see a dozen or so other motor boats strung out behind it. *Survivors?* Six must have found some survivors and directed them here. He stood watching for a bit before entering the infirmary, admiring the sleek lines of the silver and black yacht.

The smells of antiseptic and disinfectant filled the air as he scanned the room.

"Ah, there you are."

Boss smiled at the doctor. He was a kindly man with glasses perched on his nose and his receding hair combed back. A keen birdwatcher, it was a crazy bit of luck that he was on the island during the early days of the Variant outbreak.

"Hey Doc, sorry I'm late. Went to dinner and forgot."

Doc looked over his glasses at him. "Beth?"

"Yeah," Boss said, his eyes cast at the floor.

Doc patted him on the shoulder. "No harm, no foul. You're here now, eh? Now let's see if this fits."

Boss watched, intrigued, as Doc removed the bandage on his stump, checking his handiwork. "A little red, but that's normal."

He rolled a soft, fluffy sock-like bandage over the stump, causing Boss to wince slightly. Then Doc grabbed the prosthetic, nestled the leather cup onto Boss's stump and tightened the straps.

"How does that feel, young man?"

Boss looked down at his prosthetic. One of the soldiers had welded a couple of metal pipes together from an old bike. Three smaller pieces of metal tubing were welded to it as support struts. "Okay, I guess. Can I try it out?"

"Yes, yes, of course," Doc nodded.

Boss slid off the examination bed and tentatively put weight on his new leg. The leather cup pushed into his stump, and tingles raced up his spine.

"It's going to take a while to get used to," Boss said. He gestured to his crutches. "But better than those things!"

"I think we'll give your leg a bit more time to heal, then you can wear it for short periods. It will take a while young man."

"Okay. Thanks, Doc," Boss said.

"You're welcome. I'm proud of you, son. You've done a remarkable job recovering from such a horrific injury. I can only imagine the horrors you saw out there."

"Yeah, it was bad. Dee helped me a lot."

"Yes, yes. Good company and friends always help."

Boss made his way around the infirmary, gingerly testing his prosthetic. He glanced out the window towards the games room, eager to meet up with his friends.

The bark of gunfire stopped him in his tracks. More gunfire answered, gathering in urgency. Boss frowned. The wail of the siren wound up, echoing around the bay. He shivered as he realised what was happening.

The camp was under attack!

He exchanged a look with Doc. Boss saw the fear in Doc's eyes.

"Get to the bunker!"

Doc nodded and gathered a medical kit before racing out the back door. Boss flung open the front door and looked out at a scene of utter chaos.

The luxury yacht had moored at the jetty, easily

dwarfing the other boats in the harbour. Hundreds of Variants were pouring over the sides, flinging themselves at the soldiers, who were firing into the rolling mass of terror. More Variants swarmed off the smaller boats, fighting, tearing, scrambling over each other to get onto the yacht and beyond, to their human prey.

Boss pulled the Glock 17 from his holster and looked up at the villa, cursing himself for sleeping in and forgetting his go-bag that morning. He looked left and right down the boardwalk, indecision freezing him. Would Beth have taken George to the games room? Boss hobbled down the boardwalk, his new leg clicking on the concrete as he gathered pace.

Only one way to find out.

— 5 —

Dee stirred the soup in the aluminium billy, watching the thick red liquid bubble. The acidic smell of the tomatoes made her lick her lips. She hadn't eaten a decent meal for a couple of days. She could hear Ben and the gunners Jones, Eric and Tony, rustling about as they packed up the rest of the camp. What were the odds of Eric and Tony having the same surname? Even at the end of the world, it was common. *Well, at least I don't have to keep up with them.* Dee smiled to herself at her little joke. Jack would have liked that one. Thinking of Jack, she hummed a few bars of their favourite song, *Freebird*. On a normal Saturday, she and Jack would be settling in, watching a movie, with Jack adding little facts as she enjoyed the warmth of his body pressed against hers. She loved watching movies with Jack; the sheer joy they brought him amazed her. His eyes would light up as each scene played out on the screen. He would grin and look at her, watching to see her excitement. He would cheer as Ripley swung her flamethrower over the xenomorph eggs, cooking them. He would cry as E.T. left Elliot and soared into the sky, leaving a rainbow. He would laugh as Baby learnt her dance moves. Movies were his thing, and now they were gone.

Dee sighed, stood up and stretched. She was looking forward to getting some sleep tonight. Ben's radio squawked. He flicked his eyes up at her, a flash of surprise dancing across his face.

"Ahh, Ben, receiving? Over," Jack said.

"Receiving."

"Possible bogies spotted. Bearing north north east. Over."

Ben glanced at Dee before turning and looking out to sea. She followed his gaze and strained to peer through the falling drizzle. She gasped. Three ships were cutting through the choppy sea towards the island.

What the hell?

Ben spun around. "Dee, put that fire out, now! Jones, lights out!" Dee could tell from the stern tone that he meant business. Gone was the friendly, wise man. The hardened former NZ SAS soldier took over. The joking and backchat from the Joneses vanished as they quickly switched off all the lights and crouched down behind their gear. Ben raised the radio back to his lips. "Jack?"

"Receiving."

"Go dark. And stay put. Maintain radio silence. Over."

"Wilco, out."

Ben crouched down next to Dee. "Eric, get me eyes on those ships. I want to know whose they are. They're not allies, that's for sure."

Eric nodded. "Yes, Sir."

Ben turned his attention to Tony. "Get Colonel Mahana on the horn. Let him know what's going on and tell him that damn radar still isn't operational."

"Yes, sir."

"Dee, break camp. We're going to have to hightail it back to the FOB."

She gave him a curt nod and started packing away the camp stove. She shovelled a few spoons of soup into her mouth and tipped out the rest. Dee hated seeing the food go to waste, as it had become an ever-increasing luxury. She listened as Ben spoke softly to Eric.

"What do you see, Gunner? Give me details."

There was a pause, so long that Dee thought Eric hadn't heard Ben.

"Two frigates and one cruiser, maybe a corvette. No markings, no numbers, no lights, Sir. They're sailing dark. Bearing straight for us."

"Tony, give me that radio." Ben walked the few steps to him and spoke into the long-distance radio. The rain was getting heavier, making it difficult for Dee to hear the conversation.

Eric helped take the tarpaulin down. Some of the collected rain tipped over Dee, running down the inside of her raincoat. The icy water made her shiver. Thoughts of standing under a nice warm shower and a decent sleep, were now forgotten.

Dee snapped the last clasps shut on her pack and checked that her rifle was loaded and safety on. She patted her side, feeling for the Glock and knife. She looked at her katana tucked into the back webbing of her pack, and smiled. There was no way she was going anywhere without it. That katana had saved her life many times over. Something deep down inside told her that it had a bigger role to play.

"Jack?" Ben said. He turned and eyeballed Dee as well as Eric and Tony.

Static buzzed, mingling with the noise of the rainfall.

"Receiving."

"Right. Listen up, Renegades. Radar is down. We have unfriendly ships coming in. I suspect from the class they are Indonesian. Why they are here, we don't know, so for now they are to be treated as hostile. Colonel Mahana has ordered us down the mountain. We are to proceed to Kiwiriki Bay where a chopper will extract us. We shall then proceed to Mayor Island where we are to improve the fortifications in case of hostilities. Jack, stay put. We are coming to you. In the interim, plot the most direct route to the LZ. We have 90 minutes. Understood?"

A chorus of "Yes, sir" answered.

"Move out, soldiers."

Dee gave Ben a tight-lipped smile as she hoisted her pack onto her shoulders and positioned her weapons. She tried to adjust her raincoat to keep the cold rain from dripping down her neck, but after a few attempts she gave up and concentrated on keeping her feet from slipping on the rocks scattered along the mountain pass.

Here we go again.

***

Jack stretched out his tired legs as he waited for the other Renegades to reach his position. He watched the approaching Indonesian Navy ships warily, their silhouettes looming ever closer to the island. The whole situation bothered him. If it was indeed the Indonesians, why the hell were they here in New Zealand? The mainland was gone, overtaken by the Variants. He had heard rumours of failed operations the Americans had attempted to eradicate the Variant hordes from the vast landmass of the continental United States. Jack tugged on his ear and wiped some of the rain off his neck.

Musing over his concerns, Jack pulled out his map of the mountain and double-checked the route he had found. He remembered a hiking trip to Great Barrier Island some years ago. Some gloriously sunny days had been spent exploring the old timber trails. The island had a rich history in logging kauri trees, and the hardy loggers had left some long-forgotten trails snaking their way down rocky valleys. The kauri tree was a much-prized piece of timber. Tall, straight, and strong, it soared above the other trees in the forest. Now only a few pockets remained, standing as they always had, sentinels, watching the world. Jack could just imagine when Captain Cook and his crew first saw the majestic trees. They'd immediately valued them for masts on their tall ships. He shook his head at the short-sightedness of the early settlers and their relentless pursuit of the timber.

So few of the trees remain…a bit like us.

Jack risked a quick flash of his light to check he had the correct compass bearing. He secured his map away and took up a covering position, overlooking the trail.

His heart skipped a beat as he recognised the petite frame of Dee emerging out of the darkness, her katana poking out from her pack and her rifle slung on her shoulder within easy reach. Their eyes met, and Jack couldn't help but grin. Those eyes gazing at him always softened his mood, picking him up when he needed it most.

Dee grasped his hand. "Hey."

"Hey yourself." Jack drew her into an embrace, kissing

her on the nape of her neck. "I'm sorry about being a grumpy."

"Doofus. It's us till the end, remember?" Dee said, kissing him back.

"Yeah, I know." He smiled at her as he disengaged from the hug.

Jack gazed back down the track as the Joneses joined them. Ben brought up the rear, his long beard slinking out of the night like a glow worm waiting for its prey. Jack tilted his head in acknowledgement, meeting his gaze.

"What have you got for us?"

"I found us an old logging trail. It cuts down through the valley before meeting up with that river we crossed. That should take us to Kiwiriki Bay and the LZ." Jack used his elbow to indicate the direction he was talking about.

"Nice work," Ben said. He clasped Jack's shoulder. "You'll make a good ranger yet."

Ben faced the other Renegades. "All right. We maintain radio discipline and keep our torches off. When we get to the valley floor, we can switch them on. Tread carefully, Renegades. I don't want any injuries or delays. And be ready for any hostiles, human or Variant."

"Yes, sir."

"Do the lovebirds want to get a nice room first?" Tony said, smirking.

Dee punched him on the shoulder. "Leave it."

Tony grabbed her arm and twisted it. Dee pivoted around, sweeping her leg out. The muscled soldier tumbled to the ground, surprise on his face. She stood over the now-prone gunner. "I know you and Eric want one, but it will have to wait."

Jack barked out a laugh and grinned at his wife. The other Renegades joined in. The muscled Tony was no match for Dee's speed.

Still chortling at Dee's witty remark, Jack adjusted the rifle on his shoulder and moved past the Joneses to the front, with Dee following behind. He turned his head, looking Ben in the eyes.

Ben gave him a quick nod. "Lead on, McDuff."

Jack turned and trudged into the gloom. The Renegades followed silently.

— 6 —

The chaotic sounds of the battle bounced between the buildings as Boss raced towards the games room. He scanned left and right, searching for Variants, his Glock 17 held up like Ben had taught him. He reached a corner and peered around it.

A square of light shone on the ground and shadows of figures danced in the open window.

Boss peered through the darkness towards the front of the building, hunting for the Variant threat he knew was there. So far the creatures had eluded him.

The constant booms of gunfire were rattling him. He took some deep breaths and adjusted his new leg, trying to find a comfortable spot. It was throbbing after only a few moments. He should have grabbed his crutches; now was really not the time to test out his prosthetic.

Boss looked once more at the window and went through the actions in his mind. He pushed off with his good leg and ran to the window. He knocked the gun against the glass and peered in. One of the figures, a little girl, turned and, seeing him, ran over. Boss mimed for her to open the window, but the girl looked back at him, terror across her cherub face. She shook her head.

Peering deeper into the room, he saw Beth's blonde hair. He rapped louder on the window, praying she would hear.

As he waited, Boss struggled to grasp what was happening. After a month of peace and solitude, his world had come crashing down again. He thought he'd left the monsters behind on that mountain. He had paid for his escape with his lower leg cruelly ripped away. If the chopper hadn't arrived, and if courageous George hadn't stabbed his little screwdriver into the Trophy King's eye, he wouldn't be standing here now.

Boss looked up and slammed his gun against the glass, cracking it. Finally Beth heard and grasped the shoulders of the children next to her, guiding them towards the window.

A screech echoed out, distracting him. Three Variants scampered down the small alley, their reptilian eyes glowing in the night. Boss raised his gun, aiming for the head of the middle beast. It glared back at him as if daring him to fire. Boss squeezed the trigger. A black arc of gunk sprayed out behind it as the bullet tore through its skull. The other two Variants sprang off the ground in opposite directions. They used the buildings on either side like springboards and bounced off, leaping at Boss, shrieking.

He raised his Glock and got off a round, killing one of the creatures. Pain raced up his good leg as he was lifted off the ground and slammed into the building behind him. The children inside screamed. The Variant on top of Boss howled and spat thick gobbets of sludgy goo onto him. He desperately tried to bring his gun up and fire it, but the Variant knocked it aside, howling.

The force of the blow had stunned Boss, stars and colours swirling in his vision. Trying to focus, he looked into the eyes of the beast, waiting for its sucker mouth to latch onto him and tear at his flesh.

He flicked his eyes towards the window of the games room, hoping to get a last glimpse of George so he could apologise for failing him. The window was now open. *What did that mean for Beth and the others?*

The Variant hissed and dug its claws under his shoulders to pull him away. Boss shut his eyes, ready for death. He heard a wet thumping sound and opened his eyes. The creature on top of him was staring past him, its eyes bulging. It looked down at the jagged piece of timber speared through its torso before reaching up with clawed hands to grasp it. It let out a muted gurgle, blinked rapidly and slumped to the ground, dead.

Beth stood, looking down at the dead beast. She flicked her eyes to him, her mouth opening and closing. Boss pushed himself up and retrieved his Glock. He put a round through its grotesque skull.

"Thanks. I thought I was a goner for sure." Boss grinned.

"I killed it," Beth said, gawking at the creature slumped on the ground. Black blood had begun to pool under its body.

"You sure did. C'mon. We have to get these kids to the bunker."

He turned back to the window and saw George staring out at him.

"G-man? C'mon, let's go." Balancing on his good leg, Boss reached up and lifted him out. The crushed shells on the path crunched under his feet.

He handed Beth his Glock. "Cover us, just like Ben taught us. George, you keep watch up that way." He pointed up the hill towards the villa. They both nodded.

Boss lifted out the remaining kids, his muscles straining. The sweaty smell of fear permeated the smaller children. He got a few wafts of urine too as he lifted the two youngest down.

The gaggle of frightened kids huddled around Boss and Beth. Gunfire smoke hung in the air, the constant flashes and bangs strobing through the night like some crazy discotheque.

"All right. We're going to run as fast as we can up this path to all those tents up there, okay?"

He indicated the shell-strewn path and a couple of the kids nodded. Boss did a quick head count. Five, including George.

"Good. And then we are going to run for the bunker, just like we practised, okay?"

He reached down and grabbed a couple of hands and as quickly as he could, headed up the path.

Beth pushed a few of the kids in front of her, and the little gang raced for the tents.

They ducked down behind the first tent just as a huge explosion boomed around the bay. The concussion wave caused the tent to buffet as if a sudden tornado had sprung up. Boss pulled the kids down, covering them with his body. Several of the children started to cry as his ears began to ring.

Shaking his head, he hauled up two of the kids, urging them on. He crawled behind the row of tents, hoping the thin nylon fabric hid their getaway. At the last gap, Boss got a glimpse of the harbour. The luxury yacht was a raging ball of fire. He paused, stunned.

Someone had managed to fire an ATGM at the yacht. Variants writhing in flames leapt into the ocean.

The remnants of the army left on this outpost were fighting their "Gallipoli". They were mowing Variants down in their dozens, but Boss could see more pouring out of the boats behind the burning yacht, filling the jetty in a rolling black wave. The machine gun nests and gun placements were fast becoming overrun by the Variant horde. Soldiers, mothers, fathers and children were being torn apart. He could hear their terrified screams, even over the gunfire.

Boss looked at the old hotel, to where the bunker was. Ben had commandeered the old cellar and repurposed it. He had run the camp through drills, getting them to practise again and again. Children and medical staff were to be evacuated, everyone else was expected to fight. Boss peered into the chaos. He could just see the stocky figure of Sergeant Haere moving guns into position to protect the bunker. Seeing this gave Boss new hope. He took some deep breaths and checked that his gun was loaded. He ran his hand around his belt, feeling for his extra magazine.

"Lead them to the bunker, just like we practised. I'll bring up the rear with George, covering you. Run, and don't look back," Boss said, holding Beth's gaze.

"Okay."

He moved to one side and ferried Beth and the four kids in front of him. "Go!"

Boss pushed up, getting his good leg under him. But his new prosthetic caught on the ground and he stumbled and fell, landing heavily. George turned at the noise, glancing down at him. Boss waved him on, but George stopped and ran back to help him balance on his good leg while he adjusted his prosthetic. *Bloody thing.*

He nestled his stump back into the leather cup and tightened the strap. Boss looked at the entrance of the bunker and saw the soldiers ushering the kids in. He let out a sigh of relief. Beth stood at the door, beckoning.

Screeches and howls tore through the night above the chaos. A group of a dozen Variants prowled into the gap, screeching and hissing at the retreating humans. They were cut off. The soldiers at the bunker door pushed at Beth, but she spun out of their grasp and sprinted up the hill and into the bush.

Beth, NO!

Sergeant Haere and the soldiers opened fire on the Variants.

"Get out of here, Shepard!" he yelled over the sounds of the battle.

Boss was still reeling from the sight of Beth dashing into the bush. He shoved George in front of him and hobbled towards the villa.

— 7 —

Maggie paused outside the yellow door, her hand raised ready to knock. Absently, she read the sign stuck on the door. Manager. The guard posted outside stood a few metres away. She narrowed her blue eyes as she followed his gaze sweeping over her curves. He didn't even try to hide it. She pushed an errant strand of hair behind her ear and rapped on the door.

"Come in," called a muffled voice.

Maggie took a deep breath to calm her building temper and pushed through the door. The skinny frame of Ian waited, leaning against his desk, a smirk planted on his face.

A sour tang formed in her mouth. "You wanted to see me?"

Ian motioned to the free seat on her side of the desk. "Please, sit. Would you like a drink? Some tequila arrived today."

Ian moved around the desk and eased himself into the chair behind it.

"No. I'm good."

Ian swivelled in his chair, turning his back to her. He grabbed a bottle of tequila from the shelf, the glass clinking against the tumbler as he spun back around. His eyes narrowed.

"I know you hate me, Maggie, but I want to offer you a job. Better rations for you. I might even spare you. Look at this like an opportunity."

"Spare me?" Maggie said, scrunching her eyes together.

Ian placed the tumbler down and poured a couple of fingers of tequila.

"What? Did you think this was a nice little holiday camp where you could all live out your lives and the creatures would leave you alone?" Ian smirked again.

Heat rose through Maggie's stomach and up her neck. She clenched her fists under the desk, her nails cutting into her palms. "Of course not. Tell you what. You tell me what's going on here and I'll consider it."

"I can't tell you that."

"Why not? Is it that bad?"

"Listen, Maggie. We all did what we had to do, to survive. I might tell you later. When you are on board with the programme."

Maggie stared at Ian as he sipped his drink.

He swirled the liquid around the glass, watching her through the sloshing liquid. "So, do you want to know what the job is?"

Maggie thought about her work, about how most of the children never stayed long. Her suspicions regarding their fate angered her.

"Whatever the job is, you can shove it up your ass!" Maggie pushed herself out of her chair.

Ian followed her up and slammed his glass down on the desk, spilling his drink.

"You're going to regret that, Yank! And your little friend Becs? I'll send her out on the next tribute. Oh, and Alice? They have special plans for her. Yes. Special plans for her."

Maggie could see spittle forming at the corner of his mouth. She cast her eyes down to the tequila bottle. It was within easy reach. She could grasp it. Break it. And jab it into his throat.

"Go on, Yank, do it. You'll be dead within moments, and your friends too."

She spun around and flung open the door. Ian's cackling laughter followed her down the hall.

Maggie exited the building and strode out over the grass, heading for the gardens. She needed some space and time to calm down. Breathing in the cool night air always helped. She reached the gardening shed and sat down on some bags of potting mix. So many questions swam through her mind, each bobbing to the surface, demanding answers. Questions she didn't have answers to.

Why were they here?

What was Ian talking about? Tributes?

To succeed at warfare, you needed intel. She had very little of that. She remembered reading *The Art of War*. It was full of wise quotes. The plan she had put into motion for their escape was based around her favourite: *"In the midst of chaos, there is opportunity."* She smiled. *Yes, Ian. I have a special plan for you. But first, I promised a little red-haired girl a story.*

Maggie rose and made her way to their sleeping quarters. She could see a dim light shining through the window. Good. She still had time. She sniffed and wiped her nose, memories of her own daughter rising to the front of her mind. As unwanted as the memory was, she welcomed it. To relive any memory of Isabella was a treasure. Laughter, hugs and tears. Falls, running around the park, swinging from trees. Baking in the kitchen, flinging flour around, making a mess. Sitting on the sofa, snuggled in watching *Toy Story* for the hundredth time. Isabella's delight at school and making friends. Her sixth birthday party, stuffing so much sugary food into herself she was sick for two days afterwards.

Maggie couldn't believe one could love another human being so completely. Izzy had become sick not long after her eighth birthday. Frantic visits to doctors, and many tests later, it was discovered that Izzy had a rare form of leukaemia. They tried everything, but only a year later her baby had passed on. And Maggie's world crumbled into a chaotic mess. She buried herself in her work as a nurse. Maybe if she could help others in their hour of need, the pain would go away. But as hard as she tried to forget, the pain remained.

She and her husband grew apart slowly. It began with them sleeping in separate rooms. The excuse was her shift work. It led to them hardly speaking to each other. When they'd needed each other the most, they'd each abandoned the other.

Maggie had never felt so alone and directionless. She'd popped a few pills one day, to try to bury the way she was feeling. Within a few months, she was an addict. After one night of bingeing, Maggie sat watching the TV in a stupor. Show after show of mindless drama. Amongst the haze, she saw a recruitment ad looking for more medics in the army. She'd joined the next day; anything to escape the hell her life had become.

In the army, Maggie had found a new purpose in life. Defending her country by helping others when they were having their worst days ever.

The shadow of the sleeping quarters snapped Maggie out of her teary memories. She smoothed down her shirt and walked up the stairs.

As Maggie entered the room, the fragrance of the rose-scented candles burning lifted her mood. Becs was sitting cross-legged on Maggie's bed, a pile of books around her.

"Hey kiddo."

Becs smiled up at her. "Hey."

Maggie returned the smile, and her eyes flicked to Alice, who was brushing out her long blonde hair.

"What story is it tonight?"

Becs held up one of the books.

"*The Witch in the Cherry Tree* by Margaret Mahy? Looks good," Maggie said, taking the book from her.

"It's my favourite."

Maggie sat down on the edge of the bed. "Scoot over a bit."

Becs snuggled into her as she began to read, and Maggie enjoyed the warmth emanating from the child. Reading to Becs stirred more memories of Izzy. She pushed them aside for now and read on.

Later, Alice helped Maggie lift the sleeping Becs up off the bed. They gently placed her on her own mattress and tucked the blankets under her chin.

Maggie motioned with her head towards the two chairs next to a small table before moving over and sitting herself down. She waited for Alice to get settled, mentally going over the plan she had to get them out of this prison.

"So, what did Ian want?" Alice said, dimples forming as she smiled.

Maggie mulled over what to say.

"Not much, He offered me a job."

"Job? Don't you already have one in the gardens?"

"Yes, exactly. We didn't get to the job description though. I stormed out, telling him to shove it."

"About time someone did," Alice said. She grinned. "What did you say exactly? I want details."

"I told him to shove it up his ass."

"I'd loved to have seen the look on his ratty face at that," Alice said. "Do you think he knows you were in the army?"

"I think he suspects but doesn't know for sure," Maggie said. "How did you get on with your guard friend?"

Alice dropped her gaze, looking to the door and back to Maggie. "Ah, good. You were right. They leave the keys in the vans."

"I thought so. This is good news. That's one less thing to worry about. And the red jumpsuits?" she said.

"Kept with them in their rooms. Jill from the laundry said she can get us a couple."

"Good, good. What about those newbies? Do they know where we are?"

"Yeah, they did. They said we're just south of Putaruru."

Maggie raised her eyebrows. "Which means what, exactly?"

"It means we're close to the coast and a boat."

Maggie nodded, contemplating this new information. Remembering the piece of paper she had been palmed earlier, Maggie pulled it from her pocket. "*New gas in today, 10.*" She gave a sly grin, some air escaping her lips in a whisper.

"More good news?" Alice said.

"Yes definitely. Do you think you can get us those jumpsuits tomorrow?"

"Should be able to, yeah."

"Good. Excellent." She patted Alice on the leg. Giving her a squeeze, she lowered her voice. "I want us gone by the day after tomorrow. We leave at 0400, and we're taking Becs."

Alice stared back at her before turning away and looking out the window.

"What about the others?"

"We have to save ourselves first. Let's get Becs to safety. Try to find some semblance of an army. Then we can come back and free everyone."

"The newbies. They said they were on their way to Mayor Island. They were in contact with someone there. They went looking for fuel to make the journey and were ambushed by these bastards."

Maggie sat up straight and stretched out her legs. This was excellent news. It was the break she had been waiting for. For three weeks she had played along, done her work. Today was the first time she had let her anger and frustration get the better of her. Ian and his baton made her skin crawl. She smiled to herself. *We're getting out of here, Ian. I have a surprise for you.*

Maggie sat, enjoying the silence. Nothing moved outside. She could hear the occasional screech of a

Variant, but they sounded far in the distance. She had heard them closer before, but normally much later in the evening. Their presence intensified in the early hours before dawn. Maggie decided she needed to do some recon tonight to find out why.

"Why do you think these guys are helping the Variants?"

Maggie leant in closer. "Because they are scorpions."

"Scorpions?"

Maggie smiled. "Yeah, scorpions. You see, one day, a scorpion was walking through the jungle, looking for his next meal. After a while, he came to a raging river. The scorpion looked around for a log or some rocks so he could get across, but found nothing. He needed to get across that river. After a while, a frog came along and the scorpion yelled out, 'Hey, how about a lift across?' The frog turned to the scorpion. 'No way. You'll just sting me.' So the scorpion says, 'Why would I do that? We'd both drown.'

"The frog thinks about it for a while. 'All right. Jump on. Let's go.' About halfway across the raging river, the scorpion stings the frog. The frog turns his head and asks, 'Why did you do that?' to which the scorpion replies, 'I couldn't help it. I'm a scorpion'."

Alice let out a small laugh and giggled. Maggie couldn't help but laugh with her. It felt good to laugh after all her frustrations. She stood up and rolled her shoulders.

"I'm going to turn in. Big day tomorrow."

"Yeah, good idea. Night," Alice said, still giggling.

Maggie walked over to her bed. Pulling off her boots, she tucked them under it within easy reach. She lay still, staring up at the ceiling for a few minutes, mulling over her plan. It was simple, but simple plans were the best; less to go wrong. She glanced over to Becs, sleeping peacefully. Satisfied, she let sleep pull her into its embrace.

— 8 —

The crack of the wooden door smashing into the wall of the room jolted Maggie awake. She threw back the covers and instinctively reached for her rifle. Cursing, she focused on the four figures bursting into the room.

Ian stood behind one of his muscular goons, swinging his police baton. "Wakey wakey, ladies!" He eyeballed Maggie. "Don't worry, we're only here for one of you."

He lifted his baton, pointing it at each of the now-standing women in turn. "Not you, not you. Oh, I like you, I'll save you for later."

Maggie stepped closer to Becs and clasped her hand, pulling the shaking child into her side.

Ian spun around. He swung his baton and let it thump onto the wooden floor.

Raising it, he leered at Maggie, a cruel glint in his eye. "Yes. I'm here for Becs. Did you really think I was going to let you get away with that? What did you say? I could shove my job up my arse?"

Becs started sobbing, pressing herself closer into Maggie.

"If you touch her, I'll end you!" she said, glaring at Ian.

Ian cackled, his laughter echoing around the room. Several of the women in the room moved away, putting distance between themselves and the men.

Ian indicated to his goons and they moved towards Maggie. She backed up closer to the wall. One of the goons pulled out a Glock and grasped Alice in a headlock, pushing the gun against her temple.

"I'll give you a choice, Yank. The girl, or he'll splatter your friend's sexy head all over the wall."

Maggie glanced at Alice. She focused her eyes on Maggie's and nodded, accepting her fate. Distracted, Maggie didn't notice the other two goons flanking her. She turned at the movement, jolting her head to one side. A meaty fist slammed into her head, followed by a blow to her side. The strikes were powerful and strong, and pain exploded up her spine. She dropped to one knee, losing her grasp on Becs. The other goon picked up the squirming girl.

Maggie gasped for air, each breath hurting. She glared at Ian who was staring at her, an amused grin on his face.

"There. That wasn't so hard, now was it?"

Maggie could feel heat rising through her body. She pressed one fist to the floor as she struggled for breath. "This isn't over, you skinny little bastard."

"Oh, but I think it is, Sergeant."

Maggie struggled to keep her face neutral.

"Yes. I know what you did before. That's the problem with women. You talk too much. You can't help it. Talk, talk, talk. You never shut up." Ian swung his police baton up and pointed it at Alice. "Bring her too. My bed needs warming tonight." He turned and raised an eyebrow at Maggie crouched on the floor.

"Sleep well now, you hear." Cackling, he stomped out of the room.

Maggie rubbed her throbbing side.

Stay strong girls. I'll come for you.

— 9 —

Colonel James Mahana stared at the vodka bottle sitting on his cheap flat-pack desk. He wanted to reach out, unscrew the cap and down the burning clear liquid in one gulp. He imagined the fiery sensation as it made its way to his rumbling stomach, dousing his hunger and, for a moment, clouding his mind, making him forget this nightmare, if only just for a time.

James pushed back his chair as he stood, hearing it thud against the wall. He rubbed his temples with the fleshy part of his thumbs, trying to expunge some of the tension. Sighing, he glanced back down to the report in front of him. Another stronghold gone. Auckland had gone dark, and to add to matters, his attempt to get the Prime Minister out from the bunker under Government House had failed miserably. It had been four hours and there was still no word from NZ SAS Team Kehua. A garbled radio message was the last communication he'd received from Major Ken Hind. He and his remaining team had been heading for the harbour, the bunker overrun by Variants. The Prime Minister and all those who'd sheltered within were dead.

And now I have a foreign navy heading this way. Where did it all go wrong? I should be relaxing on the East Cape, maybe doing a little fishing.

He knew where it had gone wrong. Those damn-fool scientists had played God once too many times, trying to create a super-soldier. *Idiots.* James rubbed the back of his neck, trying to ease the knots. His gaze flicked to the vodka bottle once more. The liquor sat there, taunting him.

He pulled a red binder from under a pile of paperwork and looked at the report he'd written for the Brigadier, shaking his head in frustration. How did the Brigadier expect him to beat back the Variant hordes? The Americans had failed at so many attempts. First with the bombing of the cities, Operation Reaper, Depletion and Kryptonite had all failed. They had reached out with Kryptonite, but with no air force to deploy it, the Brigadier had ordered him to come up with an alternate plan to rid the land of the monsters. It was time to fight back. They were on their own, and they weren't going to leave the mainland to the Variants.

James had fought hard and long to get to the position he had. He came from a poor, forgotten and downtrodden neighbourhood, rife with domestic abuse and drug and alcohol dependency. He had shivered and coughed his way through many cold, damp winters, huddled under blankets with his siblings as his mother and father partied, smoked and drank their way into oblivion every weekend. The parties always ended with a fight. Some were brutal and quick, others long and full of screaming and shouting.

As the eldest, he'd done his best to protect his brothers and sisters, often taking beatings from his enraged mother and father. He'd learnt to protect his head and vital organs from the fury of the blows.

A deep rage had seeded in his belly, and as he grew older it festered, and had eventually bubbled to the surface.

As James had grown into his body, he had worked out and taken up martial arts, learning Karate, Judo and Kung Fu. When he was sixteen, his life changed. Cleaning up the room his sisters shared, he'd found his youngest sister's diary. It had fallen to the floor. James had flicked through it and been horrified at what he read. One of his uncles had regularly abused his little sister. The deep-seated, festering rage exploded. James stomped down the road to his uncle's house, barged in and attacked him. He'd smashed the man's face with all his anger and fury. Everything that had built up over the last ten years came out. He didn't stop until the police arrived and hauled him off his uncle's lifeless body.

James had pleaded guilty and was tried as a minor. He served five years in a juvenile detention centre. He joined the army soon after getting out and channelled his anger into forging a career.

A knock at the door pulled James back to the present. With a last look at the vodka, he smoothed his receding hair down.

"Enter."

A private swung open the door and met his gaze. "Sir, the Indonesians are making their way around Miner's Head. ETA in one hour."

James scratched at the stubble on his chin. "Inform the men to go on high alert." He held the private's gaze. "Is that radar operational yet?"

"No, sir. The team you sent to fix it is still working on it."

"Very well," James said. "Dismissed."

The private shut the door with a thud.

James pushed back his chair, turned and gazed out into the darkness. A few lights around the settlement twinkled through the falling rain. He could see soldiers walking briskly as they prepared, moving mortars into position, moving vehicles. He had ordered all civilians indoors as soon as he'd received word of the approaching ships. He wanted to wait until he learnt what the Indonesians wanted before letting them out. The fact that the radar was down bothered him. It had been working fine. It was as if someone had sabotaged it just as the Indonesians were sailing in. *Who? And more importantly, why?* The timing was too convenient.

Normally HMNZS *Te Mana* was anchored in the harbour and they'd been using its radar. But it had sailed north three days ago to support HMNZS *Taupo*, forcing them to erect a new radar.

James caught his reflection in the window. His brown eyes stared back at him. He could see black bags forming under his eyes. Letting out a breath, he entered the head room.

He stood for moment on the threshold, taking in the action. To his left, a long desk with computers lined the wall. On the opposite side of the room, through an open door was the radio room. It was narrow, and against one wall ran a desk with several radios. Four operators were chattering into microphones attached to headsets. In the centre of the head room sat a large square table covered with maps, a few chairs around it. Second Lieutenant Jay

Badminton looked up and gave him a curt nod.

"Lieutenant, SITREP?" James said.

"Sir, the three Indonesian ships have rounded Miner's Head. At current speed, the ETA is one hour. Eyes on have reported that they are slowing their speed."

James looked at the map of Great Barrier Island and located Miner's Head. "I want any available ships to be deployed out here to Maunganui Point, but tell them to keep their distance. I want wheels on the ground shadowing them. Have the guns on Kaikoura Island and across the channel been set up?" He raised an eyebrow.

"Yes, sir. Four ATGMs have been positioned."

James ran his finger down the map, through the narrow channel of water. *If they want to invade, they're going to have to come through here. The rest of the shoreline is too rocky.* Their behaviour hadn't indicated as such, but, so far all attempts at communication had failed.

"What about our ANZAC brothers?"

"Nothing to add from them Sir. They haven't detected any foreign ships encroaching on their islands."

"Very well. Keep vigilant."

Badminton nodded. "Yes, sir."

James turned his attention back to the map, scanning for any weakness in his defences. They were on their own in this fight. HMNZS *Te Mana* and *Taupo* were twenty-four hours away.

A shout from the radio room shifted his attention. James turned as one of the operators strode over, waving a piece of paper.

"Sir, this just came in for you. I don't know what to make of it."

James glanced at what was written and frowned.

Mayday, mayday. Require immediate evac from GL-426. Power is failing. This is code black. Repeat, this is GL-426 requiring evac. Please advise.

"Signaller, advise GL-426 we are en route, ETA fifty minutes. And get me Captain Johns on the line."

Well, Johns, it's time to test your Renegades. You're not going to like it.

The door to the radio room banged as the signaller rushed back in.

"Sir, it's Falcon 7. They're under attack."

"Is Captain Johns on the line?" James asked, clenching his jaw.

"Patching it through now, Sir."

James pulled down the shirt of his fatigues and picked up the headphones.

What next?

— 10 —

The rotor blades of the NH-90 helicopter loomed out of the darkness. The pilot had nestled it between the cabbage trees dotting the beach. Dee moved out from the bush and onto the dunes. The white sand squelched under her boots as she swept her rifle up and down the beach, checking for hostiles.

Jack gave her a nod and she peeled off left while he went right. She took up a covering position next to the chopper door and made eye contact with the pilot as he slid it open.

Dee let out a shrill, quick whistle, and watched as the Renegades exited the bush at a light jog. The Joneses jumped in and turned, covering Ben as he jogged the last few steps. He gave Dee a reassuring pat and hopped in, making for the vacant co-pilot seat. Jack turned and climbed in after him, with Dee bringing up the rear. Eric, stationed to one side, slid the door closed with a thud as the whine of the powerful Rolls-Royce engines fired up.

That was a smooth transition.

Ben had made them practise it for a whole day and night. Again and again, he'd timed them, shouting that they could do better, had to do better. That their lives would depend on it.

"Nice one guys," Dee said. "About time we got that right."

"Don't you mean you?" Eric said, smiling.

Dee shook her head at him. Eric knew that his clumsiness had been holding them up.

She felt her stomach drop as the chopper lurched off the ground and swung out over the Hauraki Gulf and back towards Mayor Island. Dee was looking forward to seeing the boys and finally having a shower. Spending some quiet time with Jack would also be welcome. Maybe he would get the solar panel working better so they could watch a movie with Max and George snuggled between them, and Boss sitting in his chair pointing out all the plot holes while Jack argued with him. She smiled, a comforting tingle buzzing in her chest. The argument they'd had about the eagles in *Lord of the Rings* had lasted three days. Jack had become quite animated, gesticulating wildly as he explained why the fellowship couldn't use them to fly the ring directly to Mordor. That argument had then morphed into why the Star Destroyer hadn't fired on the escape pod in *Star Wars*. Dee shook her head, remembering how Jack had stormed off and gone into the bush for a few hours.

She was surprised at how much she loved Boss and George. Seeing them each day made her happy. She'd thought she had found pure happiness with Jack, but a sliver of the puzzle had always remained unfinished. Amid the terror and the chaos of their flight, she'd found that last piece. Dee knew the fight was far from over, and now, with this new threat from the Indonesian Navy, she worried that they would never have any semblance of a normal family life.

Jack moved over and plonked down beside her. Dee shifted, giving him some space. She met his gaze, watching his blue eyes twinkle, then nestled in to him, enjoying his warmth and comfort. No words were needed. She knew he felt the same. Had the same fears and worries, the same doubts. He was just as determined as her to not let the Variants get them. Dee felt for her necklace. Rubbing the metal and diamond between her fingers comforted her.

A squawk in her headset brought her back to the present.

"Renegades, listen up. We've got our first mission. It's a straight pick-up. A scientist from a lab has called in for an immediate evac. ETA twenty minutes. I want everyone prepped and ready. Understood?"

"Affirmative," Dee said. Her mind raced. They were barely trained. Were they even ready? She exchanged a glance with Jack. His brow was furrowed and he was fiddling the stock of his rifle. Dee was struggling to grasp that anyone was left alive on the mainland. And a lab? She looked at Ben, hoping to learn more.

"Renegades, let's do this quick and clean. I want to get…"

Dee turned towards the cockpit at Ben's pause. He had cupped his hand around one headphone and his head was tilted, looking out the side window. He shouted something into the microphone. Ben untangled himself from the co-pilot's seat and moved between the seats to join them. He remained standing as Dee watched his face for any clues. It was grim. Her heart sank.

What was going on?

"All right, Renegades. I've just received word from Falcon 6. Mayor Island is under attack."

"What?" Dee said. "Who?"

"All I know is it's collaborators and Variants. Mahana has ordered us to proceed with our mission. Picking up this scientist is deemed a PRIORITY ONE. He's sending two squadrons to Mayor Island as reinforcements."

Dee stood up, grabbing the bar above her. "Are you serious? I don't care about some scientist! That's our home. The boys are there!"

"She's right, Ben. Screw the scientist. It's the friggin' boys we're talking about! Our family!" Jack shouted, standing beside his wife.

Ben looked at Dee and Jack, his face softening. "I'm with you guys. I want to get home and fight too. But this scientist, she may hold the key to ending this. So, I know how you feel. I love all those back on Mayor too. But we have to trust the soldiers to do their job. If we have a chance to find a cure for this madness, then we have to take it. If we do our jobs right, we'll be back in the air within minutes."

Dee's head swam as the thumping of the chopper blades pounded in her head. She squeezed Jack's hand and felt him squeeze back, trying to comfort her as she sat back down. She couldn't believe Ben was choosing the mission over her family. She loved Ben. After all, he had saved her, and helped Jack too. But now he was obeying orders rather than dashing home to fight? "Dee!" Ben shouted, getting her attention.

"Sir?" Dee said, brushing aside her emotions.

"I want you locked and loaded, and eat something. Understood?"

"Yes, sir."

She busied herself, going through the motions, trying to take her mind off her swirling fears. Jack nudged her and handed her an energy bar.

Dee clicked bullets into her magazines as she swallowed the food and secured the loaded magazines into her pouches.

She stared out the window at the Coromandel coastline whizzing by. The chopper was flying low over the Firth of Thames, hugging the coast. All was dark, and Dee wondered if anyone had escaped the scourge and headed for the bush-clad mountains of the interior. She knew just how littered it was with valleys and gorges, trails and old huts.

The NH-90 helicopter flew up the coast, skimming over the town of Thames, lying silent and dead. It followed the Waihou River south for twenty kilometres before turning south east. Dee recognised the blunt, rocky cliffs of Mt Karangahake emerging out of the dark.

She raised her eyebrows. *They built a lab, here? Where?*

"All right. We're two minutes out. I want a clean exit, just like we practised. We've got a five-minute hike from the LZ to the entrance. The scientist is a Doctor Katherine Yokoyama. She should be there waiting for us, just inside the lab entrance. We grab her and go. Stay frosty. Possible Variants in the area," Ben said, joining them in the hold and grabbing his gear.

"You two lovebirds ready for some real action?" Tony said, grinning.

She shook her head at him as he made thrusting pelvic motions. Dee knew he was just blowing off steam, acting all brave.

The hold fell silent as each of the Renegades prepared themselves to enter a night that was full of terrors. She felt the bump of the chopper as it hit the ground a moment before she jumped out and spun left, checking for Variants. Leaves and dust whirled around them, agitated by the wash of the blades. She stared over the sight of her rifle, ignoring the debris. Dee risked a glance back and saw the muscular frame of Ben bringing up the rear. He waved her on. She took a few breaths to calm herself and jogged along the gravel road leading up the mountain.

— 11 —

Jack strode up the narrow gravel road, the sharp bits of rock crunching under his feet. He swept his rifle left and right, looking for any contacts, his ears straining for any noise. He had the route to the lab plotted in his head, so had no need to consult his map. He struggled to grasp the fact that there was a secret government lab hiding in this mountain. He and Dee had hiked this area extensively over the years. Once a source of coal, and more importantly, gold, the landscape was a warren of valleys, rivers and soaring andesite cliffs veined with quartz. The quartz had brought the early settlers, who'd had a tendency to dig mines, hunting for treasure like dwarves.

A few buildings emerged out of the gloom; they looked like barns to Jack. He could see two to his left, and there was a large vehicle shed with a couple of tractors and a 4x4 sitting dormant inside, waiting for their owners. Owners who would never return. Directly ahead lay their target. A large corrugated iron shed, its dark paint blending with the bush behind it. The shed was nestled against the mountain, with its back end hard up against the earth. The people who had built this lab had been clever; they'd hidden the entrance within a working farm, so any strange vehicles coming and going wouldn't raise an eyebrow. Jack wondered what was so important that the government had gone to all this effort. Pausing, he glanced to his left, checking Dee's and Tony's positions.

Jack crept up alongside the building. It bothered him that they hadn't heard any Variants yet. It was too quiet. He couldn't even hear any of the birds that frequented the area. Jack took a deep breath, savouring the smells; the farm, the rusting iron, the long wet grass mixed with old manure. A strange chemical smell from inside the building reached him. He scrunched his nose at its pungency.

Ben flashed the "Go" hand signal for him to proceed. Taking a calming breath, Jack sprang around the corner, keeping his rifle up and searching for hostile targets. He saw the sliding doors a few metres ahead and jogged to the far side.

Dee ran up, and Tony and Ben crouched in front of the doors.

With everyone in position, Jack pulled the door, straining with the weight. The door slid along a well-oiled runner, silently gliding open. Dee, Ben, and Tony disappeared inside.

Jack searched into the gloom, looking for any of the horrors he knew waited out there. He sighed, struggling to keep his growing apprehension from bubbling to the surface. He needed to keep focus. Ben had said this scientist could hold the key, the key to their salvation.

Did she have a cure?

A soul-destroying screech shattered the silence, followed by a cacophony of howls and screeches. Jack glanced over at Eric, meeting his fearful eyes before thumbing his radio.

"We have company. Over."

"How many?"

"No visual yet. Over."

"Hold position, we're on our way. Out."

"Wilco. Out."

Jack's hand tightened on his AR-15 as he felt along and flicked off the safety. He'd known the bastards had been out there waiting, but he had hoped they could just do this one thing without being harassed.

Bloody Variants.

He heard muffled footsteps thumping onto the concrete floor as Ben, Dee and Tony emerged with the scientist, joining him in the doorway. Jack looked at Katherine. She was petite with toned, wiry muscles. Small-framed glasses perched on her nose, and her blue eyes stared back at him as if she was assessing him. He saw fear in her eyes, but also determination. He glanced down at the small metal case she gripped tightly in one hand. Was this the cure?

Another screech tore through the night, grating on his brain as the thumping of the chopper reached him. Jack watched in horror as it lifted off above the trees, banking sharply away from the mountain.

"LZ is hot! I've got multiple direction hostiles. Renegades, get out of there. I'll extract you from somewhere else. Protect the asset. Find me a new LZ," squawked his radio.

Ben spun around. "Back inside the lab. Now!"

The Renegades fled into the barn. It was piled high with fertiliser and drums containing God knows what.

The stench was making Jack's eyes water. He pulled up his buff.

Up against the back wall was a smaller shed that reminded him of a cool storage area. Once inside, Katherine spun a wheel attached to a door, granting them access to an alcove. She raced to a keypad that was still glowing and punched in a code. A final internal door hissed open, revealing tunnels behind. Emergency lighting lining the walls threw out a warm orange light, illuminating the smooth concrete walls and ceilings. The floor was lined with a hard rubber mat. The Renegades crowded into the corridor and Jack was happy to hear the door slam with a hiss, locking out the Variants.

His head swam as he stood apart from the other Renegades, looking around the inside of the lab. The concrete tunnel-like corridor stretched away, and Jack could see multiple doors on both sides.

What the hell were they doing down here?

"Jack," Ben said, his voice sharp.

"Yes, sir?"

"You've got point. I need you and Doctor Yokoyama to find us a way out."

Jack nodded and turned away, looking down the long corridor. Find a way out? Where? He felt a hand on his shoulder and looked into the calming eyes of Dee, his rock. She gripped his shoulder, kneading his tense muscles. She didn't say anything. She didn't need to.

Jack clasped her hand, thanking her with his eyes, and smiled at her.

Right okay, a way out? Where are we? Karangahake Gorge. What's here? Mines, trails, bush and rivers. So, how's that going to help? How? It's just trees and more trees. Those things out there will catch us before we can get anywhere. Trees! Yes, that's it! Trees!

Jack spun around, searching out Katherine. "Do you have another entrance to the lab? Like a back door on the other side?"

"Yes. A maintenance entrance. Why?"

Jack flicked his eyes to Dee and Ben, smiling. "There's a treetop zip-line in the next valley. It goes right across to Dickey Flat."

"Yes, of course! But It's new. Let's hope they finished it before the chaos." Dee smiled.

Katherine was staring at Dee, her mouth hanging open, gaping like a fish. Dee turned towards her. "What?"

"I can't…I can't believe it. Diana? Is it really you? After all these years?"

"How do you know my name?"

Katherine let out laughter short laugh, a grin spreading across her face.

"It's me, Katherine. Katherine Yokoyama. Doctor, if we are being formal. I'm a friend of your mother's. I haven't seen you since you were little. Look at you, all grown up!"

Dee shrugged her shoulders. "Okay. I'm sorry I don't remember you. Mum died a long time ago."

"Died?" Katherine took a few steps towards Dee. "Maybe now, after all this, but I spoke to her just as the Hemorrhage Virus took hold."

"What?" Dee backed away, reaching out for Jack.

The shrieking, tearing sound of metal being torn apart preceded the desperate thumps of the Variants trying to get into the lab. Jack pivoted. The door shuddered as the Variants slammed into it, rattling the hinges. He glanced around at the metal framing, praying that it would hold.

"We need to leave, NOW! Renegades, combat retreat spacings. Let's go!" yelled Ben.

Jack gave Dee a reassuring embrace. She hugged him back, before breaking away and fiddling with her carbine, checking the magazine. He knew from experience that she would be troubled by the scientist's revelation. It pained him to see her in distress, but right now they had creatures hunting them. Her eyes met his, and she gave a nod that she was okay. Satisfied, he took his place at the front.

Striding along the tunnel, he glanced back to the Renegades. A seed of doubt was gnawing at Jack. Where was everyone else? It seemed strange that Katherine was the only one here. This lab was huge. A place this size would require a large number of people. Not just scientists, but support staff too. Janitors. Computer technicians. Electricians. Cooks. All kinds of people would be needed to keep a place like this going.

Jack reached a T-intersection. A door labelled Stairs lay directly ahead.

How many levels does this lab have?

He swept his rifle around, searching for targets. Satisfied they were safe, he looked back at Katherine. "Which way?"

Katherine pointed right and Jack strode on, eager to escape the lab. He held his rifle up and walked heel to toe, eyes sweeping over the doors as he passed them. He read a few of the labels on the doors. Genetics. Biosecurity. Behavioural Lab. Staging Area. He shook his head. The names meant little to him.

They reached another sealed door. Katherine moved past him and punched in a code. Before she pulled open the door, Jack grabbed her arm. "Wait. There's something bugging me. Where's everyone else?"

Katherine pulled her arm from his grasp and turned her head to look first at Dee, then back to Jack. The ghastly sound of tearing metal echoed down the concrete tunnel, followed by the howls of the Variants. They had broken through. Katherine brushed past Jack, opening the door. "They all left, okay, to be with their families."

"So why not you?" he asked, his tone sharp.

"To find a cure. Why else would I stay?" Katherine replied, a defiant look in her eyes.

"Keep moving," Ben said. "Don't stop."

Jack could see another intersection up ahead and looked back at Katherine, his eyebrows raised. She indicated left, not meeting his gaze. On they went. Down long corridors, twisting left and right. Down several flights of stairs. All the while the Variant screeches were getting louder. Jack took some deep breaths, trying to calm himself. He remembered what his grandmother had taught him: "Keep calm and carry on." He had to do that now. Now was the time to stay calm. They had to escape with Katherine and whatever was in that case of hers. Mahana thought it more important than Mayor Island. Important enough to risk the Renegades, untried in combat as half of them were.

Jack reached the end of another tunnel. Doors stood to his left and right, both marked with the biohazard symbol. A door directly in front of him was labelled Maintenance. The Variants following them screamed out. Louder. Jack caught a whiff of the tangy, rotten fruit smell that always hung around them as it drifted down the tunnel. A sudden flashback of the corridor in the dam flickered through his mind. He shuddered, shaking away the memory.

"Hurry," Ben said.

Katherine punched in the code and pushed the door open. A hideous screech rang out behind them. Jack turned with the others, searching for the source. Seeing nothing, he spun around and passed into the maintenance room. Movement to his left caused him to jolt his head up. Several Variants were scampering over the pipes lining the walls. Katherine let out a blood-curdling scream that rang in Jack's ears. He flicked his eyes to Dee. "Go back! Hostiles!" He turned and grabbed Katherine's arm.

"Multiple targets coming from our six," yelled Tony.

Jack watched as dozens of Variants poured down the tunnel in a wave of hungry terror. He pushed Katherine back into the maintenance room and raised his rifle, getting a bead on the lead Variant.

"Watch your backs. They're on the walls," he warned.

Jack moved in front of Katherine, protecting her, and fired, aiming for the nearest creature's head.

"Inside!" Ben yelled.

Jack fired and ran, heading for the door at the far end.

The Renegades fought their way into the room and Ben slammed the door to the corridor behind him as the mass of horror slammed into it, shaking it in its frame. He spun quickly, taking down a Variant running along the pipes.

"Move it! Protect the Doc."

Dee pulled Katherine into the middle of the group, and the Renegades moved on as one. Firing, reloading and firing again. Within a couple of minutes, they had dispatched the Variants.

"Jack! Go, before these other bastards break through," Ben said, slamming a fresh magazine into his rifle.

Jack turned at Ben's instructions. Tony was wrapping an arm in a bandage, blood seeping through it. The body of a Variant stared up at Tony, its torso riddled with bullets. Jack sprinted the short distance to a big grey door. It had several bolts and a keypad on it. He looked at Katherine.

"Code?" he yelled as he started to fling back the various bolts.

"NZLV-8675309," she yelled back.

Jack punched it in and tried to open the door, but it wouldn't budge. "Doc?"

She looked at him, eyes scrunched. "That's the master code. It should open everything."

Dee pushed him aside, racking her shotgun. "Screw this!"

She blasted the keypad, sending pieces of metal, wood, electronics and plastic everywhere.

Jack stared in admiration as she then kicked open the door. He grinned at her and ran into the rock-strewn tunnel beyond, running towards the pinprick of light.

Emerging into the early morning glow, he glanced left and right, trying to get his bearings. He saw the Kaimai mountains stretching away to the south. He could see Mt Te Aroha peeking through some low cloud, its antenna soaring on top. Looking left, he could just make out the farmland stretching towards the Pacific Ocean.

Ben caught up and grasped him on the shoulder. "Where's this zip-line."

Jack nodded towards the farmland. "This way, about a kilometre."

"Keep going. Lead us to safety. I know you can."

Jack nodded and took a breath, he jogged into the awakening world as the hideous screeches of the Variants echoed around the Karangahake Gorge.

— 12 —

The chilled breeze blew off the sea. It did little to cool James's growing frustration. He stared out into the darkness, watching the foreign ships. With each passing minute, his anger increased. He tightened his grip on the binoculars and planted his legs wide on the wet soil, trying to gain a better purchase.

Every attempt to make contact with the vessels had failed. The three Indonesian Navy vessels had anchored in Port Abercrombie and were just sitting there, dark, silent and confronting. Not a soul moved on the decks. It was as if three ghost ships had sailed themselves into the calm waters of the harbour and stopped.

The warrior in James wanted to open fire and destroy these pesky invaders. He could think of no other reason for their incursion into New Zealand waters. If they sought refuge, wouldn't they just ask, instead of all this cloak-and-dagger stuff? The Brigadier had ordered him to exhaust all possibilities of contact before responding with force. If there was a possibility of capturing the ships, then great. If not, then he was authorised to use deadly force. James struggled to remember if New Zealand had ever fired on a foreign ship? Maybe during World War Two? Well, now they might have to.

The sound of boots crunching on the gravel road alerted him to Badminton's approach. He turned and made eye contact. He glanced at the short, stocky man who strode alongside Badminton. James swept his eyes up and down, getting a better look at Lance Corporal Qasim Hassen. He had jet black hair and high cheekbones and his muscular frame strained the buttons on his fatigues. Hassen met his gaze and stood to attention.

"You wanted to see me, Sir?" said Hassen.

James let the question hang in the air for a moment. "You were part of the communications detail, were you not?"

"Yes, sir."

"What can you tell me about the mobile radar you set up?"

Hassen paused and pulled on his ear. "Well, it was…I mean, we adapted it from one of the luxury yachts. It took us a bit to get going, but it was working fine yesterday."

James glanced at Badminton, getting the barest of nods in confirmation.

"And you were the last person on duty, were you not?"

"Yes, sir." Hassen stared at the ground and shifted his weight from foot to foot. James waited for him to look up. He wanted to look this Benedict Arnold in the eye as he confessed to his transgressions.

"So tell me, Lance Corporal, why didn't you report any faults in the radar. Can you tell me why it conveniently happened to go dark just as these ships sailed within range?"

Hassen frowned. "Is this because of my name? Have you just picked out the only Muslim-sounding person and brought him to trial? This is crazy! Bloody racists!"

"Being Muslim isn't a race, Lance Corporal, it's a religion. The term you are looking for is sectarianism or religious discrimination. But the fact of the matter is, you were on the work detail that installed the radar. You, Lance Corporal, were on duty and failed to report a fault. Are you telling me it's just coincidence that three Indonesian ships show up a short time later?" James could see Hassen's cheeks flushing, and his left eye was twitching as he continued to hold James's gaze.

"No, sir. I'm not denying those facts. But I'm not a traitor. My family has been in New Zealand for fifteen years. We love this country, but the racism I've had to endure, the hatred... People tell me to go home, go back to my country. They call me a terrorist. All because I'm from Kuwait. No, I didn't report the fault in the radar, Sir. It's been glitchy ever since we installed it. I don't know who these people are. Why would I?" Hassen flung his arms out, gesturing wildly.

James stood there watching, his hands clasped behind his back. "You're talking to me about racism? Let me give you a quick history lesson, Lance Corporal. My people have occupied this land for over twelve hundred years. Then the Pakeha show up with their 'culture', with their alcohol, tobacco and guns. Once, my people were warriors. Once, we were a proud race, looking after the land, living with the land. Before *them*. The Pakeha turned my people soft. Oppressed us. Banned our language.

Tried to beat our culture out of us. Stole our land. You dare stand here telling me about racism!" James glared at Hassen, daring him to retort, but the Lance Corporal refused to meet his gaze, his head lowered, eyes staring at the muddy clay underfoot.

"You want to know something else, Lance Corporal?" James spat out between clenched teeth. "I'm from the East Cape of this country. My people were amongst the first to make contact with Captain Cook in 1769. His ship sat out in the bay, much like these ones. Our elders had a meeting that night to discuss this invader. He was allowed to carry on and trade. I often wonder what would've happened if the elders had decided to burn his ship to the waterline, how different it would have been for my people."

"You may fire when ready, Lieutenant," James said, nodding at Badminton.

Badminton raised the radio to his mouth.

James watched Hassen out of the corner of his eye. He saw his eyes flick to the three ships, saw the twitch on his cheek speed up.

Hassen raised his hand. "Sir, please, they have women and children on board."

James eyeballed Hassen and handed him the radio.

"Get their captain on the line."

James could smell the slight scent of diesel over the salt air. It lingered in his nostrils, stirring memories of summers spent with his grandfather, hunting for lobster, kina, and his favourite, paua.

I'm glad you didn't live to see this, you silly old paka.

He could hear Hassen chattering into the radio, speaking Arabic. James recognised the language as he'd been to Iraq on a couple of peacekeeping missions. The heat, sand and squalid conditions had made for an unpleasant experience. He'd spent most of his tour training new police recruits.

It had stunned him when the Sunni fought the Shia over everything. They continually blew each other up. James could never get his head around how, within a war-torn country, people of the same religion hated each other. Where was the working together? He had gladly left, despondent, not sure if he'd helped in anyway. Flying back into New Zealand, seeing the green land surrounded by turquoise water, his worries had evaporated. Now, staring back at him, were three ships full of Muslims. Yes, Muslims they may be, but still human. Still men, women and children. If the Variants hadn't taken over the world, his actions may have been different, but with so few humans left, they needed every possible one.

James weighed up his options. Should he disobey a direct order and fire upon innocent people, people whom he suspected would be trouble in the future? He sighed, forcing down the darkness in him. No, he was better than that. He turned. Holding out his hand, he took the radio off Hassen.

"This is Colonel James Mahana of the New Zealand Army. Who am I speaking to?"

A slight pause of static and hissing crackled out of the speaker.

"Colonel, this is Captain Arif Koto. We come in peace and beg your forgiveness."

"Then why all the smoke and mirrors, Captain?"

"Smoke and mirrors? I'm not familiar, please, my English is limited."

James pulled the radio away from his ear, cursing inwardly. *Of course your English is limited, it always is.* He raised the radio back to his lips. "Why are you here, Captain, and why shouldn't I just send some missiles your way?"

"Please, Colonel, we just want refuge. These creatures are everywhere. And where they are not, it's crazy. We are just peaceful Muslims wanting help."

"I can understand that, Captain, but why not radio ahead?"

"We tried that around the Pacific but were chased away every time. We reached out to our Muslim brothers. One heard, praise Allah, and led us here. We came in the dark, hoping and praying. He heard us."

James shook his head and glared at Hassen. He was going to have to deal with him later. He made eye contact with Badminton. "Take him out of my sight. Put him in the brig until I can deal with him."

He raised his binoculars up to look at the bridge of the Sigma-class corvette. He could see dim lights shining on the bridge, figures moving about. The decks still remained void of any activity.

"All right, Captain Koto, listen carefully. You are to remain anchored where you are. Any sign of intrusion, and you will be fired upon. Are we clear?"

There was a slight pause before Koto answered. "I understand, Colonel. But please, we are out of fresh water and have very little food."

James clenched his jaw. These Indonesians were really testing his patience. "I'll get you some water, Captain. You can fish from your boat. And when it's light, you are coming ashore to have a little chat."

"Thank you, Colonel. Peace be with you."

James clicked his radio off and hooked it into his belt. He turned and walked briskly to his vehicle, parked on the gravel road. He sat behind the wheel, staring at the bush-clad mountains rising up inland, mountains his people had lived on for generations. He turned the ignition. Revving up the engine, he jammed the accelerator down, spinning the tyres in the gravel as he tore up the road.

Bloody Variants.

— 13 —

Maggie lay in her bed, the covers pulled up to hide the fact she was fully clothed. There was no way she could sleep after Ian had come storming in, tormenting her by taking Alice and Becs. It was now early morning and light shone through the windows, making little orange squares on the wooden floor. The old building where they'd put her and the other women had very little insulation. The rooms creaked and groaned as the timber expanded beneath the sun's rays.

The frostiness of pre-dawn chilled Maggie, even with all her clothes on and blankets on top. She strained her ears, listening to the sounds of the others breathing. She could hear their steady inhales and exhales. In the growing light, she could see their breath fogging the air. She stretched her legs and pulled back the covers. As silently as she could, she slid under her bed and pried back the floorboard she had loosened. Quickly, she pulled up the boards. Once she'd made a hole big enough, she slipped through, landing with a dull thud beneath the building. She froze, waiting for the guard posted at the door to shine his torch under, exposing her escape. Hearing nothing and, more importantly, seeing nothing, she wriggled forward in the soft dirt, its musty smell threatening to make her sneeze.

Reaching the edge of the sleeping quarters, she peered out. She could see where the guard stood sixty feet away. She watched for a few minutes, waiting for him to move, but he didn't. Maggie smiled to herself. People said the witching hour was midnight to 1am., but she thought the true witching hour was that hour before dawn. If you have been on watch for the last few hours, your mind naturally wanders to thoughts of your bed, of food, of coffee. The yawning kicks in, your eyes droop and before you know it, you've nodded off.

Maggie pulled herself up into a crouch, getting her bearings. Spotting the laundry building, she dashed across the dew-laden grass. Her footprints marked her path.

Her plan was simple. Steal some red coveralls and a vehicle, make for the coast, find a boat and find that island. She hoped she could find a yacht and someone willing to sail her across the Pacific and back home to the USA. Maggie thought of that as her quest; a near-impossible quest. Like her favourite hobbit's difficult quest: take the ring to Mordor and destroy it. Okay, yeah, right. Sail across the vast expanse of the Pacific Ocean and then make your way across deserts, mountains and urban wastelands to Texas. She could only imagine what was happening in her home country. She was alone and cut off in this land. Now it was time to leave this prison camp and find out about her family. She had to know if they were still alive. As much as she loved this beautiful country, she longed for the big open countryside of Texas.

Maggie reached the laundry building and peered

through the window. She could see Jill, already hard at work washing the guards' clothes. She tapped on the glass, praying the sound didn't echo. Jill looked up from her work and smiled. She reached under the counter and dug out a package wrapped in brown paper.

The window creaked open and Jill handed her the package. "Good luck, Maggie," she whispered. "I hope you find what you're looking for."

Maggie grasped her hand, feeling the warmth. "Thanks Jill. Keep safe."

She spun around, a tear forming in her eye. She hated to leave these people behind. Most of the guards behaved themselves towards the women, but Maggie knew that was only a temporary measure. Soon that animal instinct would take over. The power of their positions would corrupt any morals they once had.

She sighed, jogged over to the gardening shed and ducked inside. The pungent smell of compost and peat made her wrinkle her nose. She quickly undressed and pulled on one of the red coveralls, then struggled to pull her own clothes over the top of them. Searching under the potting mix, she pulled out the cloth parcel Becs had hidden there earlier. Unwrapping it, she checked to see if the items were all there. Grinning at the lighter and the blue rag, she wrapped it back up and shoved it down her front.

Maggie checked herself over. Satisfied with her disguise, she tucked the package under her arm and cracked open the shed door. Seeing her path was clear, Maggie headed through the garden. She skirted around the sleeping quarters, being careful not to walk where the guards posted at the gate could see her.

The large maintenance shed stood beckoning in the growing light. Off to one side sat a small steel cage. Sunbeams bounced off the white surface of the gas bottles inside, making them shine like beacons. Maggie glanced down at the wooden pallet the bottles were sitting on. Pausing, she looked around. Seeing no movement, she crouched, pulled the parcel out from down her front and unwrapped the lighter and rag. The fumes of the petrol soaking the rag made her eyes water. She got a slight whiff of gas as she leant through the steel bars to wrap the rag around the pallet. Flicking the lighter, it sparked to life, its little flame dancing in her eyes. With one last look around, Maggie lit the rag and watched as the flame spread quickly. She took a moment to see if the wooden pallet caught, then stood up. Checking the coast was clear, she took off across the camp at a sprint.

Next to the guard's quarters was a small prefab building with two guards posted at the door. Maggie hoped this was where Becs was being held. She dashed up behind it and slid under the building. Holding her breath, she waited. She checked the guards. One set of feet moved, jogging in place. Maggie wriggled farther under the prefab. The fire, three hundred feet away, was taking hold. Waiting, her muscles tense and ready for action, Maggie prayed this was going to work. She was still confused by the camp's exact purpose, but she guessed it was a breeding farm. It was the only way to explain the nearly all-female population, a few of them pregnant. The bastard traitors were helping the Variants by breeding them food. The thought turned her stomach. Was this what the human race had become? Mere animals. She would have thought that in a crisis like this, all humans would band together, fight the common enemy and destroy it. *It happened in movies, right?* She sighed inwardly, watching the growing fire. Apparently not. How could people like Ian turn against his own? It shocked her. Maggie shook the thoughts from her head. Right now, she needed to concentrate on getting Alice, Becs and herself out. Hopefully she could come back and save them all. *If we live that long.*

Thick black smoke poured out from the maintenance shed. It billowed up, drifting into the pine trees surrounding the prison. Maggie grinned as she watched the flames dance their flickering, darting recital. She turned to look at the jogging feet of the guards. Their panicked voices reached her.

"What the hell?"

"Where's that smoke coming from?"

The feet turned and ran around the side of the building. As each of the heavy footfalls hit the ground, they vibrated the ground beneath her. Maggie took a deep breath, centring herself. The guards, shouting to each other, ran off towards the flames.

"Get the bloody hose!"

With one last look at the fire, Maggie crawled out and jumped up the steps.

She rattled the door handle, trying to wrench it open, but it was stuck fast. She banged on the door. "Becs! Are you in there?"

Maggie peered through the window, trying to catch a glimpse of the girl's red hair. She could see some movement deeper into the room. She banged again. "Becs, c'mon baby!"

The figure moved, pulling back bed covers. Maggie's heart leapt as she saw her hair gleam in the sun. Becs eyes went wide as she recognised Maggie, and quickly ran to the door.

"Maggie, get me out of here," she pleaded.

"I will, baby. Stand back from the door, okay?"

Maggie waited until Becs had moved back a few feet. Movement from the other beds caught her eye as several more children started raising their heads, rubbing the sleep from their eyes.

Maggie glanced around the building towards the fire. Several of the guards were standing near it now. Two of them had pulled a hose over from the garden, and a pathetic gurgle of water dribbled out. The guards were trying to direct it at the fire but were not making much headway. She smiled. Her diversion was working. She had banked on their fear of fire, and her gamble had paid off. Now she needed to get this damned door open or it would all be in vain.

Shouting from the direction of the flames made her look back around. She saw Ian striding across the camp, his dressing gown billowing behind him. His long skinny legs looked so comical, a small laugh escaped her lips.

Refocusing, Maggie searched for something to break either the glass or the door handle. Spying some bricks next to the stairs, she quickly grabbed one and, with all her strength, smashed it down on the silver door handle. The handle flew off, clanging against the concrete steps and spinning away into the dirt.

Maggie leant back and kicked the door a few inches below the handle where she knew it would be weaker. It shuddered but held fast. She forced down her rising panic and looked around. Desperately, she tried to remember anything about breaking down doors. She searched the whole door, looking for weak spots. Maggie let out a grunt, spotting the hinges. Hinges took a lot of punishment, and the screws holding them in become worn and brittle. Maggie said a silent thank you to the home improvement show and raised her leg. She aimed for the bottom hinge and gave it a kick. A crack appeared, splitting up the door. She kicked again, making the crack bigger. After a few more well-placed kicks, the door splintered and swung open, tilting haphazardly to one side. Becs ran to her, wrapping her small arms around Maggie's waist, gripping it tight. Maggie returned the embrace, enjoying this small moment of comfort and normality. She wanted these few seconds. She knew the next few minutes, hours and days were going to be a mad trip through hell. Reluctantly she let go.

Maggie looked up to meet the curious looks on the other children's faces. One small blonde girl wrenched at her heart. She reminded Maggie of the children she saw on TV from war-torn countries. Of those she'd seen in Iraq. Her hair was matted and knotted, dried tears and mucus covered her face, and she clutched a small stuffed animal tight against her chest. Her lips were pulled tight, into a thin line. Eyes wide, she stared at nothing, yet those same eyes seemed to be pleading with Maggie. Pleading for her to be kind.

This little girl had no one. She was locked away, to be used for God only knew what. Crouching down, she beckoned for the little girl to come to her. Not surprisingly, the child hesitated, her large blue eyes searching Maggie's face, looking for someone to trust.

She took a few small steps, then leapt into Maggie's outstretched arms and nestled her head into Maggie's chest, sobbing. A few of the other children started chattering, firing questions at her.

"Who are you?"

"Can we go now?"

"Where's my Mum?"

"Why are we locked up, like jail? Have we been bad?"

Maggie put her finger to her lips, shushing the questions. "I don't know any of those answers, except that we're going to get out of here. But you need to be quiet and run behind me, okay?"

The children nodded.

"Good. Let's play a game. Who can get dressed the fastest? Ready? Go!"

Most of the children scrambled and pulled on their clothes.

"Don't forget your shoes!" Maggie walked Becs and the little blonde girl to their beds. Then she crouched to help the blonde girl dress. "What's your name, darling?"

The blonde girl twisted her fingers together as Maggie pulled on her shoes. She remained silent.

"I'm Maggie. What's your name?"

"Leela," she mumbled.

"Leela? That's a lovely name. We're going to get out of here now, okay?"

"Mmkay."

Maggie patted her on the leg. When she looked around, all the kids had dressed themselves and stood watching her. She was amazed at their resilience, and pleased with how they had accepted her orders. It would make her task that much easier. She did a quick headcount. Six, including Becs.

"Okay, we're gonna go out and run over that way, to the fence." She pointed south, away from the fire.

The children murmured their acknowledgement and followed her out of their prison.

Maggie herded the children towards the forest, risking a glance at the raging fire as she jogged. The guards were too busy to notice her and the children.

Perfect.

She scanned the fence surrounding the camp and spotted the white plant label jammed into the ground. Maggie grinned. It hadn't taken much to convince Becs to help. She had pretended they were doing a treasure hunt and had asked Becs to plant the label here as it was out of sight from all the guards.

She had set her plan into action a little earlier than anticipated, thanks to Ian's late-night incursion.

*To succeed you must adapt to your surroundings…*or something like that.

The motley crew of would-be escapees neared the fence. Maggie searched above the white plant label. If Alice had done her bit, it should be cut. Within moments she found the cut and smiled. With a quick yank, the thin wires slithered out like eels from a sack. Once the wire had come loose, she managed to create a gap big enough for them to squeeze through.

"Hurry, kids. C'mon," Maggie said, her voice as loud as she dared. She counted the children as they passed her, checking them off mentally.

"Are the monsters still out there?" Leela whimpered, her lip trembling.

A lump caught in Maggie's throat. She knew she had

to lie to this innocent little girl just so she could have a chance at saving her. Doubt crept in as she looked down at Leela.

"No, darli—"

Kaboom! The shockwave slammed into them, pushing Maggie, Becs and Leela against the fence. The LPG bottles had finally exploded. The heat that followed reminded her of that sandy hell-hole that was Iraq. The shattering of glass echoed, mixed with the panicked screams of the guards caught in the fireball.

Maggie grimaced. She hadn't wanted to injure anyone, but those men had chosen their side.

"Go!"

A screaming figure ran towards her. She squinted into the sun and smoke and could just make out Alice.

"Go!" she cried again, urging them on.

Maggie looked at the fire and saw the skinny frame of Ian sprinting towards them, baton raised and dressing gown open, exposing his naked chest. Quickly, she hauled herself off the ground and pushed Becs and Leela through the gap before ducking through herself.

Alice bolted the last few metres as Maggie held open the fence.

"Thanks," Alice panted, gasping for breath.

With a quick look towards the charging Ian, Maggie pulled out the parcel from her front. "Take the kids into the trees and put this on. Look for an access road. There should be a van."

"What about you?"

Maggie met her eyes. "Ian and I have a date. Go! I'll catch up."

Alice grabbed Becs's hand and guided the children

deeper into the trees.

Maggie pursed her lips and watched as Ian ran the last few feet to the fence.

"C'mon, Ian. If you want me, come and get me."

Maggie spun around and headed away from the kids. She wasn't interested in his reply.

"I'm going to fucking kill you, you American bitch!" he screamed after her.

Maggie smiled to herself as she jogged through the trees, their fresh pine scents clearing her sinuses. *That's it, Ian. I need you angry. Anger clouds your mind.*

— 14 —

The shell path crunched under his foot as Boss ran for the villa, Glock held ready. George sprinted ahead. Finally Boss reached the deck that wrapped around the 100-year-old house and glanced around, scanning the immediate area for Variants. Thankfully the vicinity remained clear. From the noise coming from down in the village, the battle was still raging, concentrated where most of the survivors were.

Boss hobbled the last few metres and climbed the stairs. The pain from his throbbing stump made him grimace. He should have been only fitting the prosthetic, not running around on it fighting monsters. But Boss was grateful just to be alive. He had seen some horrendous things since the Variant outbreak. Tonight simply added to the trauma.

As he entered the house, a flash of red caught his eye. Jack's red-handled machete was leaning up against the wood box. He picked it up and strapped it to his thigh. Something told him he was going to need every weapon he could carry, even this rusty old thing.

Boss ran through the small galley-like kitchen, past dirty dishes stacked around the sink. George had reached the coat rack and was lifting down his small backpack. Next to the coat rack, Ben had installed a gun cage.

Boss clicked the release button and pushed open the wire-mesh door. He stared for a moment at the two shotguns and his AR-15, trying to decide whether to take all of them or just his rifle.

Ben's voice echoed in his head. *You can never have enough…*

Boss sighed and shoved his shotgun into his pack before removing his AR-15.

He grabbed a magazine and clicked it in. Checking the safety, he slid it over his shoulder. Boss turned to George, the boy's blue eyes watching him while he waited. Boss could tell he was afraid and he was doing his best not to show it. He knew how brave the kid was.

"Ready?" Boss said.

"Yeah."

Boss scooped up a few more boxes of ammo and shoved them in his pack.

Never have enough, eh Ben?

A plan formed in his mind. He looked down at George. "We're going to go to those caves, to the lake you found. Okay, buddy?"

George nodded back at him.

"Jack and Dee will come for us, G-man," Boss said, grasping George's shoulder. He wasn't sure if he said this more to himself than George. In truth, he was doubtful. Even if the Renegades had been alerted, would they get here in time? They were over 100 kilometres north. Boss clenched his fists. No. He had to keep George safe. Haere had given them a chance. He needed to honour that and get George away from danger. Away from the madness down in the bay.

A screech blared out, and a couple more answered, closer. Boss threw open the door and stepped out onto the deck, keeping George behind him. He had hoped to escape detection, at least for long enough to hide.

Three Variants bounded up the path, shrieking. They spotted the humans and paused, sniffing the air. Their yellow eyes stared.

Slowly, Boss unslung his rifle and sighted the lead Variant, trying to get a bead. With a savage cry it leapt towards them. It zigged and zagged, leaping left and right.

Boss took a punt at where it would go next and squeezed the trigger. Watching over the sight, he saw the bullet enter its sucker mouth. Big chunks of gunk flew out as it crumpled into a ball of flesh and bones. Boss spun to his left, letting off a couple of bursts just like Ben had shown him. He aimed for the centre mass and took down another one. The third Variant screeched and leapt onto the roof of the covered verandah, its claws scraping the corrugated iron. The metal moaned as the Variant dug its claws in, the sound reminding Boss of a ship rubbing against the poles of the jetty. Boss desperately watched as it walked across, making dents in the thin metal. With a hideous howl, the Variant bounded off the roof, hooked its claws into the gutter and swung over the edge of the verandah, flinging itself at Boss. Its legs slammed into him, launching Boss off his feet and smashing him against the cladding. The sharp weatherboard edges dug into his back.

The breath wheezed out of his bruised chest and sparks of orange light danced in his vision. The Variant straddled him, its powerful legs pinning him down. Claws dug into his remaining leg, while others grasped his shoulders. George screamed at it. It turned its head and shrieked at George. Boss used the distraction to pull the machete free and swing it, yelling with frustration. He drove the sharpened edge deep into the Variant's neck. The beast cried out in anguish and yanked the blade free. It leant back, howling, holding its claws to the gushing wound, trying to stem the flow of black blood pouring out.

Boss scrambled free and stood up. He pulled his Glock from his holster and looked into the monster's eyes. The reptilian slits stared back at him, its nictitating membrane flicking. Boss raised the gun and pointed it at the Variant's head. The creature that was once a human grasped his leg. Recognition grazed across its eyes. Boss felt a fleeting moment of sorrow for the monster as he squeezed the trigger, ending its nightmare.

Without looking back, he grabbed George and scrambled up the bank, heading into the bush. Branches scratched his exposed arms.

Once he was far enough away, Boss looked down on the once-idyllic bay. Flashes from muzzle fire sparked out like a fireworks display gone wrong. The luxury yacht tied up at the jetty was still burning, throwing out plumes of thick white smoke. The huge flames licked the wooden jetty, threatening to consume it. Boss's eyes darted left and right, catching glimpses of fighting all over the bay. Soldiers ran, turning and firing. Variants bounded and chased after them, tearing apart those fleeing. The bulk of the Variant infestation had crowded around the old hotel and the bunker behind. Sergeant Haere had rallied the troops to protect those inside. A steady stream of monsters threw themselves at the thousands of bullets spewing into them. Boss shook his head, the sounds of the battle rattling around in his mind. So much death, so many lives ended. The Variants would kill until no one was left. Until humanity was but a memento etched in stone.

Boss shrugged his shoulders and hauled himself up the clay bank, ducking under the scraggy manuka. He breathed in deep, savouring the trees' oily scent. George was scrambling through the leaf litter up ahead, disturbing pebbles and little rocks that hit and bounced off Boss as he followed. The pain in his stump was becoming unbearable. He was desperate for the painkillers in his pack, but the ever-closer screeches forced him to push the pain aside. Instead, he pulled on the leather straps, tightening the prosthetic.

After thirty minutes of climbing, they reached a clearing and Boss looked around, searching for the white crushed-shell paths that ringed the island. Screeches chased them up the hill, getting louder with every passing moment.

"Where's that cave?" Boss said, trying to get his bearings.

"On the big hill." George gestured. Above them soared the island's tallest peak. Up past the treeline was craggy volcanic rock. Now that Boss could see the rocks, he remembered.

"Keep going, don't look down," he whispered.

George pulled himself up the slope, his little hands grabbing onto whatever roots he could find. Up they climbed, away from the terrifying noises of the battle below, away from the sights of limbs being torn off, of intestines sloshing onto the ground. Away from the Variants sinking their sucker mouths into flesh, tearing off chunks of muscle. Boss hated to run; he felt like he was betraying all those fighting down in the bay. But he and George were running away to save themselves.

The lactic acid burned in his tired leg, and it felt like jelly as they finally reached the path they were searching for. If they stuck to this route, they should reach the cave within minutes.

"This way," George said, tugging on his arm.

"Go."

A crashing sound of branches snapping behind them rang out. Boss pivoted, his rifle raised, searching for a target. A blur of black and white burst from the undergrowth. Max! And there was someone dashing after him.

Boss slid his finger off the trigger guard, ready to put a bullet into the figure. But his eyes went wide as he saw blonde hair.

"Beth! I nearly shot you."

Beth dusted some white shells off her pants and top. "We need to go. They're not far behind me."

"Here, take this," Boss said, handing her his rifle.

"Thanks, what about you?"

"Say hello to my boomstick," Boss grinned, pulling free his shotgun.

"Idiot." Beth smiled and flicked her eyes to George. "Hey kiddo."

Boss sighed inwardly. He *would* find a girl he liked in the apocalypse. He looked over to George who was hugging Max.

Boss rubbed the dog's head. "Aye, Boy." Seeing the

dog calmed him somewhat. He could still hear the sounds of the battle down in the village and the shrieks of the Variants, but the simple act of petting Max calmed his banging heart.

Max snarled, teeth bared. Boss frowned and turned.

Beth grabbed Boss's arm, yanking him away. "Go! They're coming!"

Screeches and howls followed her warning.

Boss cursed. He was tired, stressed and angry. He could feel the fury building in his gut. Angry at those monsters that had caused this nightmare, angry at the collaborators helping the new apex predators. But most of all, angry at himself for not being able to do more. Losing half his left leg had scarred him mentally just as much as physically, maybe more so. He felt useless, not whole. A piece of him was missing physically, and a piece was missing on the inside. Without Dee here to help centre him, he struggled. She had a way of calming him. Jack had told him it was Dee's greatest latent quality: she could calm you with a smile, assure you with a simple touch or look. He'd said some people have that gift, as though a calming aura emanated from them. Boss smiled to himself. He looked ahead to Beth and George running. He was going to get them to safety or die trying.

A screech jolted him back to reality. He stopped. Spinning on his good leg, he searched for the source. A couple more screeches sounded out, this time from above. Boss glanced up. Several pairs of reptilian eyes flashed back as figures scrambled down the rocky face of the volcano. Beth was a little ahead of them by a few metres.

"Run!" he warned.

She glanced up and saw the creatures. Two of the Variants leapt down in front of her. She raised the rifle and fired a couple of shots, hitting each of the beasts in the torso. They dropped to all fours and let out horrifying screeches. Beth turned, horror plastered on her face. Her lips trembled as she looked first back at Boss, then out to sea. Boss watched, stunned, as she took a few steps back and then sprinted off the cliff, her body vanishing from view.

"NO! Beth!"

He stared at the point where Beth had vanished. A swirl of conflicting emotions flashed through his mind. Why had she done that?

George yelled something at him, but all the noise around him became a blur. His emotions were threatening to overtake him and render him useless. He screamed, squeezed the trigger and pumped the shotgun again and again, unloading into the gathering knot of Variants. He hit a few, dropping them.

George grabbed his leg, getting his attention. He pointed at a path to the right. Boss could see the cave entrance. He took a deep breath and let it out through gritted teeth. Shoving George ahead, he whistled for Max. The dog growled and barked at the beasts. He whistled again. Max obeyed and they sprinted for the cave, the howls of the man-hunting monsters chasing them. As they reached the entrance, Boss pulled the red-handled machete from his belt and jammed the blade into the clay bank adjacent to the cave. On they ran, fleeing into the darkening maw.

— 15 —

Jack ran down the wide, muddy track. Once it had been a mining road, back in the days when men shifted tonnes of earth and rock to get a few precious ounces of gold. As he jogged, he looked out at the vista. The sun was beginning its climb up from the horizon, spreading its life-giving glow to the world. Jack snorted. *A very nearly dead world.*

The valley cut through the landscape, intersected by the river gorge. He scanned the tree line ahead, searching for the dull metal of the zip-line tower. The steady thump of boots behind him comforted him, knowing the other Renegades shared his fears. He still thought it was crazy they had been ordered to collect this scientist. Out of all of them, Ben was the only real soldier. The Joneses were privates barely out of boot camp. He and Dee were still learning. Hoping to help. Now here he was, running from these eternally hungry beasts.

Thinking of Dee, Jack glanced back and smiled. She was covered in sweat from their flight through the underground lab. She smiled back before scanning around, searching the trees for the beasts. The howls of the Variants were getting closer as Jack leapt over a creek, its muddy water gushing over the track and down into the valley.

After twenty minutes Jack spotted the metal tower he was searching for. A ladder clung to the side, and five metres above the ground sat a small platform. Hooked up, attached to the tower, were two metal cradles similar to the ones rescue choppers use to ferry injured people off cliff faces.

Jack spun around. Raising his rifle, he covered the other Renegades as they made up the last few metres to his position. He caught the pungent smell of sweat mixed with the peaty smells of the forest. It didn't matter who you were, the fear was the same.

Ben called out his instructions. "Dee, take Yokoyama across to the first platform and keep going. Eric, you pull the cradles back and then go with Tony. Jack and I will follow last."

Jack nodded and turned to help Dee and Katherine up the first few steps.

Screeches rang out and Dee bounded up the ladder, pushing Katherine ahead. Jack pivoted, scanning the track and bush, waiting to catch sight of those yellow eyes. Eyes that haunted him. Eyes that meant death and loss. He kept his finger on the trigger guard, waiting. He heard the whirring of the zip-line and risked a look to see Dee racing across with Katherine.

"Multiple targets!" yelled Tony.

Jack looked down the track, searching for a target. A dozen Variants were sprinting up the muddy old road, water, leaves and soil spraying out behind them in an arc, like water behind a speeding motorboat. Jack flicked off his safety and aimed for the nearest charging hound of hell. He hit it in the shoulder sending it sprawling face-first into the mud. A few Variants behind tripped over it. Jack would've laughed if it wasn't for the charging pack behind. He went into battle mode, aiming, firing. Just trying to take them down. His ears were ringing with the proximity of the other Renegades' gunshots. A couple of the Variants broke away from the pack, sprinting around the sides to flank them.

"Flanking! Take them down!" Jack yelled.

Eric spun to his side and tried to get a fix, but the Variant was too quick. With a terrifying howl, it leapt the last couple of metres, smashing into Eric who managed to get his rifle up to protect his neck. Tony screamed and shot it in the chest. The Variant swatted at the bullet as if a wasp was stinging it. Tony ran forwards. Pulling out his knife, he stabbed it in the head. The knife stuck fast. The Variant reached up and swatted Tony aside.

Eric used the distraction and kicked the beast off him.

The Variant thudded down next to Tony, who was scrambling up. It grabbed his arm, latched its sucker onto Tony's bicep and tore off part of the muscle. Tony screamed and desperately tried to pull away, but the Variant held fast and pulled him closer.

Jack put the last charging Variant down with a shot to the neck.

"Ben!" Jack shouted.

Ben took a few steps and pivoted on his left foot, raised his leg and, with a roundhouse kick, smashed the knife deeper into the Variant's brain, killing it.

A multitude of howls and screeches echoed around the trees.

Ben reached down and yanked Tony to his feet. "On your feet, soldier. We have to go." He glanced at Eric. "Help your mate. C'mon. Go!"

Eric pulled the buff from around his neck and wrapped it around Tony's torn arm. Together, they climbed up the tower and pulled the cradles back across.

Dozens of Variants charged out of the bush and tore up the track from both directions. Jack glanced up. Eric and Tony were halfway across. He felt a strange calm wash over him as he realised they were out of time. There were too many Variants, and no way would he and Ben make it up and across to the next platform.

"I don't think we have time," Jack said.

Ben met his eyes. He gave him a curt nod and clicked in a fresh magazine.

"Probably not. Let's kill as many of them as possible though. Give the others a chance to survive." His eyes were sorrowful.

"Thanks for saving me at the beginning, Ben. You gave me hope when I had given up."

"I couldn't resist helping a pretty lady," Ben murmured, raising his rifle.

Jack lifted his eyes at the advancing horde of death as his radio squawked.

"Jack, what are you doing? Run!"

Tears welled in his eyes. Jack could barely get out what he had to say next. "I'm sorry Dee, I love you. You saved me. I'll never forget that."

"Jack! No! There is always a way out. You told me that. Think!" Dee's voice crackled over the radio.

He sniffed and looked around, trying to catch a glimpse of the woman who had saved his life, showed him how to live. He saw her standing on the tower on the opposite side of the valley. The sun was hovering over the horizon, bathing the valley in light. Her hair shone. Jack smiled. He turned, looking at the bush around him. Photographing the memory of Dee and the native forest. If he was going to die, he wanted to remember his two favourite things in life. The sun coming up over the steep hills reminded him of Gandalf's return in the *Two Towers*. He looked over at Ben, his rifle raised up as he fired at the fast-approaching beasts. Jack saw the nikau palms surrounding him, their frond casings scattered around the trunk. *Wait a minute! The frond casings!*

Jack whacked Ben on the shoulder and sprinted over to the fronds. "Ben! C'mon!"

He grabbed a frond and flung it out in front of him, over the bank. With a thud, he landed on top of it and skidded down the muddy bank, riding it like a sled. Ben grunted to his left, followed with a curse, before he crashed through the undergrowth beside Jack. The pair bounced and slid faster down the banks of the valley. Jack grabbed the sides of his makeshift sled, trying his best to steer it around trees, his shoulders glancing off a few. He flew off a small bank and splashed down into the creek at the bottom.

Ben sailed through the air. Missing the creek, he thudded into the clay bank, spraying mud and coating a nearby tree. The frustrated howls and shrieks of the Variants chasing them frayed Jack's already-shot nerves. *Bloody things never give up.* Jack clicked his talk button on the radio.

"Dee, guys, cover us. We're nearly at the tower."

Hiss and static belched out over his radio. "There's

too many of them. They're climbing over the zip-lines," Dee shouted. "Run for the river."

"Take Yokoyama and go. Get to the LZ. Eric, set some charges and blow those fucking things to kingdom come. We'll catch up. Dee, it's vital you get Yokoyama to safety," Ben said.

Jack helped the old SAS soldier to his feet and glanced up the ravine. Variants were tumbling down the steep sides towards them.

"Copy that. Affirmative. Hurry, guys."

Jack grinned as he took off at a run down the creek, jumping over moss-covered rocks and splashing through the brackish water. His movie obsession had saved him again. He loved that.

He led Ben down the valley and out into a small clearing. He recognised the river gorge ahead; Jack had taken Dee through here on many trips, enjoying the history and the way the sun bounced off the iron-rich quartz that lined the cliff faces. He was aiming for the campsite nearby. Thoughts of their cabin flashed through his mind. It was only three kilometres away. He knew there were several weeks' supplies there. Jack desperately wanted to see if his family had escaped the Variant purge. He glanced to his right, and his heart soared as he watched two cradles zipping across the valley. Two figures crawled out at the final tower. There was no mistaking the petite frame of his rock helping Katherine out.

The river he was searching for emerged out of the morning light, mist swirling over its surface. Jack leapt off the small bank and plunged into the water, enjoying the chill. The sweat, mud and frustrations washed off him as he kicked to the surface and pushed himself out onto the rock-strewn sand bank in the middle.

Dozens of Variants poured down the valley towards them. Several had climbed up the zip-lines and were hauling themselves over to the other towers. Jack shook his head. He had never seen them climb before.

He glanced over and watched Dee help Tony off the last tower, Katherine hovering nearby. Eric bounded down the ladder and pushed the Variants away. A few of them were scrambling their way across the last zip-line, eager to taste the fleeing man-flesh. Jack's radio crackled.

"Fire in the hole," yelled Eric, and three huge explosions tore through the once-peaceful landscape.

Ben grabbed Jack's shoulder, shoving him down onto the sandbank as the shockwave thumped into them. It felt like someone had reached into his brain and split it apart. Jack pressed his hands over his ears, desperate to lessen the pain. Heat washed over him. It was like the first time he'd hopped off the plane onto the tarmac of Sydney Airport and was hit with the heat of Australia. A shock after the milder temperatures of New Zealand.

Ben hauled him to his feet and yelled something at him. Jack signalled he couldn't hear anything above the ringing in his ears. The light from the sun seemed to strobe around him. Ben grabbed him by both shoulders, getting his attention. He pointed towards Dickey Flat and signalled a chopper. Understanding, Jack took a couple of unsteady steps after him.

Nothing like a movie explosion at all.

Acrid smoke blew over the gorge, invading his olfactory nerves, filling his nose with the stench of burning flesh. He had no sympathy for the wretched beings as they lay scattered, screaming and burning.

The ringing in his ears was beginning to fade and a cacophony of noises filtered through. Howls, shrieks, the thumping of the chopper. At last, they reached Dee and the others. Jack threw open his arms and pulled her into a hug. Squeezing her tight, he didn't want to let go for fear of never being able to hold her again. He nuzzled her neck, kissing it, enjoying her comforting embrace.

"Don't do that to me again, you bastard!" Dee whispered, whacking his arm. "I thought I'd lost you."

"Sorry. I thought we were finished."

She kissed him. "Till the end, remember."

"Until the end."

The howls of the gathering Variants reminded Jack of the danger they still faced. Reluctantly he pulled away from Dee and raised his rifle. The beasts were beginning to amass on the opposite side of the river, shrieking and spitting.

Ben yelled into his radio as the chopper hovered above the clearing.

"Hurry. Get us out of here."

"It's too hot. I can't land. I'm running on fumes. I'm sorry. I'll come back for you."

Jack looked up into the morning sky, horrified to see the chopper banking away.

"Don't you leave us! You piece of shit!" Ben screamed.

Jack spun towards the Variants. There were dozens, if not hundreds, now, lined up and ready to attack. They jumped up and down howling, but waiting. Waiting, for what?

A deep baritone bellow echoed up the gorge, bouncing

off the steep cliffs.

Katherine Yokoyama cowered behind Dee. Even from where Jack stood, he could see her trembling.

Another bellow sounded and the horde parted. An Alpha Variant lumbered into view. It stood at least seven feet tall with huge, bulky muscles. Its skull had distorted into an oblong egg shape, giving it an alien-like appearance. But that wasn't what chilled Jack. The Alpha had a swollen, deformed left forearm ending in a huge pincer-like claw. It reminded him of a cross between Hellboy and a crab. It glared at Jack and the Renegades. It raised its deformed arm and slammed it into the ground, bellowing.

This was the signal the Variants had clearly been waiting for. They split and ran down the banks towards the two foot bridges spanning the river.

Still afraid of the water, then?

Jack pivoted, scanning the grass clearing behind them. Variants streamed out of the thick bush, snarling and hissing as they leapt over each other, eager to taste flesh.

"Renegades! Into the river! Head south into deep water," Ben yelled.

Jack reacted, pushing Katherine ahead of him. He fired off a burst into the charging beasts. Katherine had stopped in the knee-high water, terror etched on her face. Jack urged her farther into the river. "Keep going!"

He caught up to Ben. "Sir, our cabin is three kilometres upstream."

Ben nodded, his eyebrows rising. "All right. Let's hope we make it."

The Renegades waded into deeper water, rifles raised, watching as the Variant hordes streamed across the bridges. The deformed Alpha led a squad of beasts up the far side, tracking their movements.

Jack kept glancing upstream, looking for the deep swimming hole he knew was coming up. The swarm of Variants had reached their side of the river, joining the other beasts. They were now surrounded, with only the river remaining clear.

Some Variants had stayed on the bridges, howling and shrieking at the group of humans. Several jumped up onto the suspension cables, clinging to it with their claws.

Ben let out a curse. "Clever bastards."

Jack turned and caught a glimpse of Tony. He stood in the river, barely managing to hold his rifle out of the water. He could see sweat pouring off him as he leant into Eric. Whatever was wrong with the soldier it didn't look good.

Jack turned in a slow circle, keeping his rifle at the ready. He patted his vest, checking to see how much ammo he had left; a couple hundred rounds, he estimated. Dee reached out and squeezed his hand, her eyes finding his. They didn't need to say anything. The Variants had them surrounded like the Russians had surrounded the Sixth German Army during the battle of Stalingrad.

What movie is going to save you now, Jack?

Ben turned, looking first at Jack and Dee. His lips were drawn tight over his teeth.

"Renegades, I want you to concentrate all your fire on the south bridge. We need to move upstream. Take them out. We need to break through their ranks."

Jack checked his rifle and peered through the scope.

"Fire!" Ben yelled.

The Renegades let loose with a barrage of leaded death. Jack aimed, fired, aimed and repeated, looking for head shots. They eased their way upstream, careful to keep in the middle as they fired. Dozens of Variants started jumping into the river at the Alpha's bellow. Jack adjusted his aim, taking out as many as he could, but more poured in from the sides. So many noises assaulted Jack that he was having trouble picking out individual sounds. Screeches, howls, gunfire. Screams. Suddenly a deeper, foreign sound broke through. A sound he had heard only at Pacifica festivals. A conch shell being blown. He paused to reload, pulling out a magazine and slamming it home. *Booooorrnt.* Jack saw Dee's head turn towards the sound, her brow furrowed. She'd gone with him to the same festivals.

A commotion was breaking out on the campsite side of the river. The Variants gathered there were turning, howling and shrieking. War cries were screaming out and Jack stared, mouth agape. Dozens of men charged out of the bush and into the Variants. Jack shot another beast on the bridge and pivoted towards the charging men. His heart soared. He could see them more clearly now. He shook his head at the crazy sight. The men looked to be Maori. Most had traditional tattoos, ta moko, adorning their bare chests and arms. Some had the full-face tattoo. They raised their taiaha high, bringing them down hard on the skulls of the stunned creatures. Some of the Maori had mere and quickly brought them up, smashing them into the heads of the Variants, caving in their skulls.

"Renegades! Retreat to the campsite! Jack and Dee, take the north, Eric take the west!" Ben shouted.

Jack had thought that was it. He shook his head at

their luck. He wasn't a religious man, but after the events of the past few weeks, and now today, someone somewhere was definitely looking out for him. For Dee, too. He gritted his teeth and, with new determination, raised his rifle.

— 16 —

Maggie forced her breathing to calm as she jogged through the pines. She glanced over her shoulder, making sure Ian was following her deeper into the woods. As she ran, she kept a check on her location and peered up into the trees, looking for the knotted branch. On her frequent walks around the camp, she had looked for access roads. Maggie had seen the white van sitting out here numerous times. By chance, she had spotted the weird-shaped branch and decided to use it as a landmark to aid her escape.

Spying it, she slowed and turned, waiting for Ian to catch up. She strained to hear above the noise of the fire and the shouting coming from the camp. Her plan depended on the noise she waited for. Without it, she would have to fight Ian. She trusted her army training and thought she had a chance, but Ian deserved more than just a beating. Screeches rang out between the trees. Maggie smiled and put her hands on her hips.

Ian stopped a good body-length away, his ratty eyes glaring at her. He started swinging the police baton, its leather strap wrapped around his wrist. He twirled it around and up, catching it as it fell back down. It slapped into his hand with a thwack. He grinned at her, showing his crooked teeth.

"Nowhere to run, is there, Maggie?"

She gave him her best flirting smile and half closed her eyes. "No."

Maggie started to slowly unbutton her shirt, all the time keeping an eye on Ian. His thin lips broke to a grin as he watched her hand movements. Maggie stopped about three quarters of the way down. She took a step towards him and reached out, stroking his arm.

"What would it take to let me come back into the camp?"

"I always knew you would come around eventually." Ian licked his lips. "Let's put that pretty mouth to a better use."

He ran his hands roughly over her butt and pushed his mouth against her neck, licking her like a dog. A cold feeling enveloped her and she shuddered. His tongue reminded her of a slimy eel. Maggie could feel her muscles tensing as she did her best to remain calm and compliant.

Several howls echoed around the forest, louder. They sounded really close. Maggie couldn't help the smile that spread across her lips. She had been waiting for the beasts to arrive.

"You forgot something, you disgusting piece of shit!" Maggie said, putting as much venom into her tone as she could muster. Every time she had held her tongue, came out in that one sentence.

She pulled back and brought her knee up into his groin with everything she had, slamming her kneecap against one of his testicles, crushing it into his thigh.

Ian dropped to the ground, groaning, clutching his balls.

"Bitch!" he seethed through clenched teeth. "I'm going to let the monsters tear you apart."

Maggie smiled at him as she pulled off her pants, wriggling them over her boots. She quickly pulled off her shirt, revealing the red coveralls underneath. Ian stared up at Maggie, pure hatred boring into her. He squinted at her through thin slits before looking down at his open dressing gown. Maggie grinned at him. Ian had taunted her many times about how the Variants he worked for had instructed him and his guards to wear the coveralls. Do so and the Variants would leave them alone.

Maggie lashed out with her boot, kicking him in the face. She reached down and grabbed his baton, giving him a few whacks on the legs. Ian screamed obscenities at her.

A Variant shriek rang out behind her. Maggie turned. Half a dozen of the dark beasts bounded through the trees. Letting out a breath, she stepped to one side and pointed with the baton at Ian.

"Not me! Her!" he screamed as the creatures tore into him, ripping away muscle and tissue, blood and bone.

Maggie forced herself to calmly walk away. She had bet everything on these red coveralls.

So far, so good.

Maggie had formed her plan within a few days of arriving in the camp. She had noticed how the guards walked through the trees, their strides confident. Even when she heard the tell-tale screeches and caught whiffs of the rotting-fruit smell carried on the wind, the Variants had stayed out of sight of the camp. But she had seen their shadows. Maggie had deduced that the red coveralls told the Variants that the wearers worked for them, and so were protected. Ian's tormenting of her, and his boasting, had confirmed it. She had convinced Alice to get friendly with one of the guards, even selecting the quietest one, the thinker, the one who still had a conscience.

Ian had been right about one thing, Women talked. And Maggie had used this to her advantage, spreading false rumours about herself, knowing Ian and some of the guards would become curious. With their minds fixated on her, they didn't keep an eye on Alice, Jill or even little Becs. Becs had hidden the lighter and rag in the shed. After that, it had been a waiting game. When she'd first arrived, the LPG tanks had been half full. She'd had to wait another ten days for the scavengers to bring more.

Maggie just prayed that they could carry out the next step and, not for the first time, wished she had her rifle with her.

She caught a glimpse of the white van she was looking for and grinned. Alice stood by the passenger door waving an arm, motioning for her to hurry. She didn't need to be reminded of the excited howls of the Variants leaping through the forest, attracted by the noise, smoke and raging fire. She reached Alice and gave her a quick hug before hopping into the van. She reached for the steering wheel but grasped only air. She let out a laugh. *Of course. They drive on the left in New Zealand. The steering wheel's on the right.* Maggie crawled over and sat in the driver's seat. She glanced in the rearview mirror and smiled at the sight of the children in the back before pulling out onto the gravel forest road.

"We did it," Alice said, smiling. "I'm glad you found Becs and these kids."

"It's far from over yet," Maggie said. "Have you still got that package I gave you?"

"Yeah."

"There should be some caps in there. We need them for the next phase."

Alice reached down into the foot well and picked up the package. She pulled out the caps and handed one to Maggie.

"What's next?"

"If I remember correctly, there should be some sort of guardhouse coming up. Even though I was hooded when I was brought here, I remember the drivers talking to the guards. Just let me do the talking." She took her eyes off the road, quickly looking at Alice. "Tuck your hair under the cap. We need to trick the guards for a few moments."

Maggie peeked over her shoulder at the children.

"Okay, sweeties. I need you all to stay extra quiet for me, okay?"

She heard a few murmurs in response.

A white wooden shed appeared, tucked to one side of the road. The guards had fashioned a makeshift barrier out of 44-gallon drums and wooden poles. Maggie slowed down and wound her window down a few inches. She brought the van to a stop and surveyed the area. One guard sat in the small shed smoking, and another was standing a few yards in front of her, a rifle tucked over his shoulder. He was busy trying to light his cigarette and wasn't even looking at the van. The guard in the shed looked up and slowly got up from his seat. Maggie could see an AR-15 sitting behind him, leaning against the shed wall. *Sloppy, very sloppy.* She smiled and let out a breath. Taking her hand off the steering wheel, she gripped the door release and waited for the guard to get closer.

"What's going on back there?" the guard said, leaning in, bringing his head level with the door. Maggie shoved the door open, slamming the metal against his skull. The guard fell back with a grunt. Maggie pushed the accelerator down and the van lunged forwards, smacking into the other guard and throwing him back several feet. His body thudded into the ground and rolled a couple of times, coming to a stop against a tree, He didn't move. She turned her attention back to the first guard. He was sitting up, clutching his head. Maggie jumped out of the van, jogged a few steps and kicked him in the head like it was a soccer ball. His head snapped back, and he crumpled to the ground. Maggie reached into the guard shed and grabbed the rifle. Checking it was loaded, she flicked off the safety and put a bullet into the unconscious guard's head. She had a flutter of regret but brushed it aside. These bastard traitors deserved no less. She glanced over to the guard lying prone against the tree. He was grunting something.

Maggie looked down at him. He reminded her of the young men she had seen on reality programmes, all swagger but no brains. He clutched his side, nursing his ribs. His eyes squinted at her.

"You bitch," he groaned.

Maggie shook her head. Her finger hesitated on the trigger. "Where do they take the kids?"

The guard looked up at her, confusion etched on his face. "I don't know, and if I did, I wouldn't tell you," he grunted, his pain evident.

The guard kicked out at her, catching her on the shin. She let out a gasp and hopped back a step. "Wrong move, asshole."

Maggie put a round through his head and grabbed his rifle. Turning, she ran back to the shed and glanced around. Spotting the ammo she was looking for, she grabbed it and started to fill the small rucksack that sat beside the door. With one last look around, Maggie zipped up the rucksack and jumped back in the van.

Alice stared at her, eyes wide, her mouth turned slightly upwards. Maggie handed her the rifles.

"What?"

"You are badass. Bloody badass."

Maggie smiled back at her. "They deserved it."

Several Variants were scampering up the road as she gathered speed. The Variants sniffed at the two guards she had shot but thankfully ignored the van. Maggie pushed down harder on the accelerator, keen to put distance between themselves and the prison camp. Keen to leave that place behind and start her journey home.

She gripped the steering wheel tighter, thinking of the two guards. She had trained to both save lives and end lives, but it was the desire to help those in need that motivated her. It surprised her how easily she had executed the two men. Shaking the misgivings from her thoughts, she glanced out the window. The pine trees whipped by. Hundreds of them, stretching for miles.

"I hope you know the way, Alice, because I can't see the leaves through the trees."

Hearing no response, she looked over at Alice. She was holding one of the rifles, rubbing her hands over the barrel, testing the weight.

"Alice?"

Alice glanced up at her. "Sorry, what did you say?"

"Do you know the way to Towlewronga?"

Alice let out a giggle. "Yes, and it's Tauranga."

"Yeah, that place. Is it far. Will we make it in one day?"

Alice placed the rifle back down in the foot well, wedging it to one side. She nodded. "We should do. As long as the roads are clear, it should only take a couple of hours."

"I think they will be. If these traitors brought us in here for the Variants, they would have cleared the roads."

"I hope so. When we reach the highway, turn north. Once we reach the town of Tirau, I'll direct you."

"Thanks. You did good back there, kept a level head," Maggie said.

"I just followed your lead," Alice smiled. "What happened to Ian?"

Maggie took her hand off the steering wheel and rubbed her neck. She could still feel Ian's slimy tongue on her neck, his hands groping her. She shuddered. "I don't think Ian's going to bother us anymore. I'm more worried about who comes after us."

"He got what was coming to him, then?"

"You could say that. Yeah." Maggie tilted her head back towards the children. "I'll tell you about it later."

"All right. Should I load these guns?"

"That would be great. Thanks. Always good to be ready."

Maggie marvelled at Alice's resolve. She had been pulled from her bed in the early hours by Ian and forced away to do God knows what. After the explosion, she had run for the fence to help Maggie with the kids. Now she sat here, driving through Variant-infested forests with traitors gearing up to chase them. She took her hand off the wheel and squeezed Alice's hand, enjoying the comfort of her friend. As much as she portrayed the badass army woman, Maggie was terrified that she was leading herself, Alice and the kids to the slaughter.

— 17 —

The trees were beginning to thin out, and Maggie could see a sunlit clearing up ahead. She slowed the van down, bringing it to a stop before a dual carriageway. She looked left and right. There was no sign of life, not even an abandoned car. She wound down the window, enjoying the fresh pine scents that hung in the air. It made a nice change from the smells of the camp. Even though she was breathing the same air, this oxygen smelt like freedom.

Becs wriggled her way between the front seats and threw her arms around Maggie.

"Hey kiddo."

Becs nuzzled in closer. "Have the bad things gone?"

"Not yet, baby. But you go and sit back down and we'll keep going until they have, all right?"

"I wanna sit up here with you."

Maggie stroked Becs's head and pushed her hair behind her ear. "It's too dangerous, sweetie. Can you do me a favour, though?"

Becs nodded.

"Can you be a brave girl and look after the other kids?"

Becs looked at her, her lip quivering. She wiped her nose with her sleeve. "Okay."

Maggie turned around to get a better look at the other children. Most of them were staring out the windows at the trees. A couple stared straight ahead with vacant, shocked looks on their faces. She shook her head at the cruelty of the traitors, sending these kids off to such a horrible fate. Instinct told her they were being sent away to be eaten. Ian had called them tributes. Give the beasts what they desire and they'll let you live. A new world order. Ian had weaselled his way into survival to save his own skinny ass. Images of him being torn apart flashed through her mind.

You got what you deserved, traitor.

"Which way?" Maggie said.

Alice pointed right. Maggie took her foot off the brake and turned the wheel.

They drove through Tirau. Everywhere Maggie looked there were signs of violence and carnage. Cars overturned, broken glass. Fires had ravaged out of control through shop fronts, gutting buildings. The scent of burnt wood and plastic hung heavy in the air. But even amongst all this ruin, the weeds and plants were growing. With no one to maintain the gardens, the plants were reclaiming the land. She shook her head at the destruction. It had only been a few weeks, and already the extinction of the world of men was evident. *How are we going to recover from this? Can we?*

Alice nudged her shoulder and pointed to a road leading east, towards the bush-clad mountains. Several vehicles had been pushed aside in that direction, confirming they were on the right track.

Maggie gunned the engine and gathered speed. On they drove, following the road as it dipped and curved with the contours of the rolling countryside.

After a few miles, it started to look familiar to Maggie.

"Isn't the Hobbiton movie set around here?"

"Yeah it is, why?" Alice frowned.

"It's a pity those hobbit houses aren't real. Would've been a good place to hole up for the night."

"You really like those movies, don't you?"

"Just a bit. Don't you? I thought all Kiwis did."

Alice chortled and shook her head. "No, not everyone. I knew this guy once, he thought that anyone who didn't like them should have their passports revoked. Said they weren't Kiwi enough."

"He was joking though, right?"

"I think so, yeah. He was a bit of a joker."

Maggie glanced back at Alice. It was nice seeing her smile.

Alice tucked a stray strand of hair behind her ear and tilted her head to the sun. She looked over to Maggie. "This road should take us directly up over the Kaimais. Tauranga is just down the other side."

"Okay, thanks. We might need to feed these kids soon. Check that rucksack I took off the guards."

"Rucksack?"

Maggie pointed to the foot well. "That, the bag."

Alice grabbed the rucksack and started to rummage through it. She looked up from her search. "I've been meaning to ask you, how did you get captured? Watching how easily you handled those guards made me curious."

Maggie let out a sigh and pinched the bridge of her

nose. The events of the Variant purge and her capture flickered through her mind. Not for the first time, she berated her choices and her lack of caution. Perhaps it would be good to talk it out. The road stretched out, heading for the ridge of mountains; about ten miles away, she guessed. More vehicles lay on the side of the road, some in ditches, but most had been pushed aside, leaving the road clear. Maggie let out a long breath.

"I was in Wellington when news of the virus hit. I was a bit slow to learn of it, as I'd been enjoying the anonymity of staying offline. I was on a bus tour of the city when everyone's phones started beeping with the news. They cut the tour short and I went back to my hotel. I phoned Texas and talked to my family. They were being instructed to stay inside. I decided to head to the US embassy to try and get a flight home. It was chaos, hundreds of tourists were trying the same thing. A call went out asking for any military, active, veterans or retired, to report for duty, so I did…"

Maggie paused and looked in the rearview mirror. She thought she'd seen a flash of light, but could see nothing more.

"Everything okay?" Alice asked.

"I thought I saw something in the mirror."

Alice turned her head to look behind them. "I can't see anything."

"Have a look through that scope." Maggie gestured at the rifles in the foot well.

Her eyes flicked between the wing mirrors and the rearview, watching for the flash of light. She didn't want to admit anything to Alice, but she was surprised the traitors hadn't yet caught up to them, especially after what she'd done. Hopefully the explosion had caused enough chaos to give them the time they needed.

They came to a town and bumped over the railway tracks that dissected the main road. Movement to her right caught her attention. A couple of Variants jumped up onto the roof of a shop and watched them go by. One of the beasts raised its head and shrieked. Several shrieks from farther away answered. A couple of the kids cried out.

"It's all right, guys. They don't want us."

Must be the scouts.

"Can you see anything through that scope yet?"

"Not a thing. Just some of those Variant bastards."

"Good. Must have been sunlight reflecting off a car."

Maggie slowed the van down and made a right.

The road immediately started to incline steeply up the mountain. She gunned the engine, urging the van on. The road wound up the pass, revealing the countryside behind them. Maggie stopped the vehicle on the shoulder of the road at the top of the mountain and stared out at the view. It stretched for miles, a patchwork of farms, all in shades of green, with roads periodically cutting through. Smoke billowed out from the towns lying scattered across the plains. In another time, she would have spent hours here admiring the view, taking photos.

She shook her head in frustration at the destruction of this once-beautiful world full of life and people. Wonderful, creative, brilliant people. All gone. Turned back into some primal beasts with thoughts only of food. All that brilliance lost, and lost for what?

Maggie wound down the window, inhaling the cold mountain air. She blew out her frustrations and anger.

She needed to stay focused and get these kids to safety.

The sounds of an engine revving and tyres squealing reached her, carrying up the mountain. Maggie grabbed the other rifle. She unbuckled her seatbelt and jumped from the van. Bringing the rifle up to her shoulder, she searched for the source of the noise. She spotted two 4x4s tearing up the mountain road and caught a glimpse of red on the driver's side.

"Alice! You drive," Maggie shouted, warning her friend of the approaching danger.

She ran around to the passenger side and waited for Alice to shimmy over behind the wheel. Just as the 4x4s screeched around the corner, Alice launched the van into gear. It lurched forwards, its wheels spinning in the loose gravel before getting a grip on the tarmac.

"Maggie!" Becs cried out.

"Stay in your seat, sweetie."

As the van tore up the road, squealing around the sharp bends, Maggie checked that the rifle was fully loaded. She pulled some ammo out of the bag, shoving it into her pockets. Thoughts of her training focused her to the task ahead. She now understood the endless drills loading and unloading her rifle. It was during tense times like this when muscle memory was critical. You had to be able to do what was necessary when you needed it most.

She clicked on the safety and grabbed the other rifle, repeating the task. Ready, she spun her head around, searching for the 4x4s. The groaning of their engines sounded closer, but she couldn't see them anymore. Maggie felt the van crest the top of the pass and drop down with the road. She glanced forward. Rolling hills cascaded down, petering out to flatter land. A city hugged the small natural harbour. Turquoise water of the Pacific Ocean glittered, lapping up against the hundreds of boats moored in the bay. Maggie's heart leapt at the sight. *Maybe, just maybe, I can go home.*

The van swerved around a tight bend, its wheels screeching. Maggie manoeuvred herself around in her seat, watching for their pursuers. A black 4x4 squealed around the corner and bullets pinged off the van. The kids screamed.

She turned to Alice. "Keep going. Try to ignore what's going on. We have to reach that harbour."

Without waiting for an answer, Maggie wound down her window and steadied herself. Breathing out, she sighted the 4x4 and let loose with a barrage of lead, aiming for the tyres.

— 18 —

Boss peeked out from the flax bushes. He could see six of the beasts as they scampered back and forth along the edge of the crater lake, pausing and sniffing as they desperately searched for the humans.

He gently took off his pack and rummaged for more ammo, keeping one eye on the creatures as he filled his pockets and loaded his shotgun and Glock. Max and George were huddled against him. Their body heat and the sounds of their breathing calmed him somewhat.

Boss looked up through the twisted, gnarled branches of the pohutukawa tree. The darkness of the night was beginning to fade as the sun crept above the horizon.

Boss hoped he could hide out here for a while longer, knowing that the Variants didn't like the sun so much. It wasn't much of a plan, but it was all he had for now. Stay out of sight from the beasts long enough until they give up.

There is always a way out, eh Jack?

The waves lashed the rocks at the bottom of the cliff. Glancing once more at the tree, Boss wondered if the branches could take their weight. But then what? Swim out to sea? He tried to remember where the nearest boat was but came up blank.

Max broke free of George's grasp and ran to the entrance of their flax hidey-hole, growling a warning, his teeth bared. Boss looked up at the noise and scanned the lake shore. Two of the Variants stared back at him. They raised their heads and let out a blood-curdling shriek. A bellow answered, the awful sound bounced around the caldera walls and wrenched at Boss's soul.

The Alpha of his nightmares lumbered out of the cave. It looked out to the island and pointed its huge, meaty claw. The children's heads mounted on its shoulders jiggled as it bellowed again, ordering its Variant kin to attack.

The two beasts closest to the island leapt into the water and started thrashing their way over the lake. Several others scampered around the sides of the caldera, clinging to the cliff walls.

With their cover blown, it was time to flee.

"Climb over and hide," Boss said, lifting George into the pohutakawa.

"What about you?" George whimpered.

"I'll catch up. Go!"

He boosted George higher, watching his little hands and feet grasp the thick bark.

Boss pivoted and raised his shotgun, aiming for the beasts on the walls. He let loose with a blast. He hit a couple, but they didn't slow down. Cursing, he aimed a little in front of the lead Variant and squeezed the trigger. A section of its head painted the cliff wall, and its lifeless body splashed into the lake. A shriek and the thrashing of water shifted his attention to those swimming to the island. They were only a few metres away now.

Boss glanced up at the Alpha. He swore the monster grinned at him as it raised its left arm and howled. Dozens of Variants flooded out of the cave and started to climb and swim their way over to the island. Boss glanced to the island shore and quickly dispatched the two monsters climbing out. He risked a glance up the tree to see George had reached the top of the caldera wall.

"Go, George! Run. I'll hold them off."

George stared back at him, his red hair glowing angel-like in the early morning sun. He shook his head at Boss.

"Run! Please."

George's head dropped out of sight.

Boss squared his shoulders. He pumped the shotgun and twisted to his left, firing at the Variants. So many of the bastards. He managed to kill four. He aimed and fired until his shotgun clicked empty. With no time to reload, he reached down and pulled his Glock free. Several of the Variants had reached the island now and were standing on its obsidian-laden shore, oblivious to the sharp edges.

The Trophy King lumbered forwards and waded out into the lake, its bulk causing ripples as it strode towards the island, its towering frame easily staying above the surface. The Variants climbing around the caldera walls started to reach the island and were dropping down, landing with a thud, their yellow eyes watching Boss. Several pushed their sucker mouths towards him, tasting the air.

Boss slowly turned in a circle. He was surrounded. Sweat ran down his spine, soaking the waistband of his pants. He stared out at the Variant horde collected around the lake and island. He could feel his stump quivering, his nerves were starting to re-establish themselves, telling him that he hurt all over.

At least George got away.

Boss clicked a fresh magazine into his Glock. He looked down at Max, who was still growling and baring his teeth. Boss's heart thumped in his chest. *After all I've been through to survive, it's going to end like this? Surrounded by man-eating monsters. After all those hours playing video games, killing all manner of beasts, and I'm going to be torn apart by them. Ironic.*

Boss sighed, remembering his life. Home had been fine, and school was too, until he reached fourteen.

It wasn't his fault she liked him. Anya was her name. Beautiful blue eyes and long blonde hair. All the boys liked her, including Boss. Especially his best friend, Thomas. Thomas chased her for months. When Thomas finally asked her out, she declined. Boss was surprised when she texted him, asking him to the movies. Boss agonised over his decision, but in the end accepted. Thomas then turned on him and accused him of "swooping". He launched a vicious social media campaign, bullying Boss mercilessly.

Boss began to hate school, dreading each day. He spent his time hiding, away from the other boys and their taunts. He spent weekends online, immersed in WOW, joining guilds and raiding.

They were some of the worst days of his life and, weirdly, some of the best. His parents advised him to chalk it up to a life lesson and told him to remember that real friends stick by you no matter what.

Anya dumped him and moved on. Boss felt empty and without purpose. He struggled for the next couple of years. Now, with the Hemorrhage Virus, Boss had a motive. Survive!

With new determination, Boss stared into the yellow eyes of the approaching Alpha. As it got closer, Boss saw that the trophy heads were rotting. Bits of flesh and tissue had fallen off, and the whites of the skulls were gleaming through. He raised his gun, sighting the Alpha, though he doubted the bullet would penetrate its bark-like hide.

"You are one ugly bastard, aren't you?" Boss shouted at the beast as he squeezed the trigger a couple of times, the bullets harmlessly bounced off it.

He holstered the Glock and let his hands fall to his sides. Heat rose up through his body.

Strangely, he felt angry. Angry that it was going to end like this.

He bit his lower lip as the Alpha reached the island and hauled itself ashore. The clear lake water sloshed off it, making the green and black obsidian glisten in the morning sun. Boss shook his head. He hated to admit it, but he felt abandoned. Jack, Dee, and Ben had left him alone to look after George, and when he needed them most, they weren't here. Well, they had asked their friend Erin to stay with him, but Boss felt responsible for George. Dee had made him promise to always look out for him. Eager to please her, Boss had readily accepted. He'd never imagined this.

The Trophy King stopped a couple of metres away. It raised one of its claws and pointed above Boss. Boss turned around as screams reached him. Feminine screams. Beth's blonde hair appeared on the clifftop between two Variants as they man-handled her. The Alpha then pointed to its right. George appeared, firmly held by a large Variant, his blue eyes pleading.

Boss turned back to the Alpha. All his anger and frustration at the situation boiled up and over. He sprang forwards, pulling his knife. A blur of black and white followed. Max barked and leapt at the huge creature, managing to latch onto its ankle. Boss leapt, raising his hand, knife clasped tightly. He aimed for the Alpha's neck, hoping to penetrate the skin and cut the jugular. The Alpha bellowed and lunged forwards. It caught Boss in mid-air with one claw, holding him aloft. He reached down and, without taking his eyes off Boss, lifted Max off his ankle. The dog barked and howled in pain. The Trophy King grasped Max in his claw. With an evil glint in his eyes, he smashed the dog onto the ground. Max let out a whimper and fell silent.

Boss started to thrash and twist, desperate to escape. The Alpha lowered the squirming Boss to the ground. A Variant moved up in front of him and excreted a hot liquid into his face. Boss spat some of it out as his vision started to fade. He struggled to keep awake, but, thinking quickly, he reached down and untied his prosthetic. The sound of it clinking off the stones brought a smile to his lips. He twisted his heavy head, catching a final glimpse of George as his world went dark.

— 19 —

Dee scanned left and right, letting off short bursts at any Variant she saw. With the arrival of the Maori warriors, they had focused their efforts on the Variants crowding on the campsite. With Ben directing them, they were breaking through after some ferocious fighting. Dee shook her head, amazed at the ferocity with which the Maori fought. They didn't have any guns either. Just traditional weapons.

The Renegades and the Maori warriors entered the tree line and started to climb the surrounding mountains, screams and howls following them. Skirmishes broke out on all sides. Dee caught a glimpse of Jack running ahead, following one of the Maori. He was pointing farther up the mountain, beckoning them to follow.

Dee pushed Katherine's back, urging her forwards. The scientist was struggling. First, they had run through the lab, then flown across the zip-lines, and here they were running again. Even amongst the scents of mud and gunpowder, Dee could smell the rotten fruit smell the beasts expunged.

Katherine stumbled. Dee reached down and hauled her to her feet. "C'mon, don't stop."

The scientist mumbled something that Dee didn't catch.

On they ran, the lactic acid building in Dee's legs. The exhaustion of the last few days was beginning to take hold. If it wasn't for the imminent threat of being torn apart, she would stop right here and sleep, nestled against a rock.

But she hurried on up the winding path, ducking between slabs of limestone and jumping over gnarled roots. Several of the Maori jogged alongside her and Katherine, weapons in their hands. The distinct tang of blood hung in the air, adding to the gruesome cocktail of body odour and cordite. Sweat was pouring off her forehead, stinging her eyes. Dee turned, looking for Ben's comforting figure. He was bringing up the rear with a knot of Maori warriors, taking down pursuing Variants. He caught Dee watching and waved her on. She turned and hauled herself and Katherine up a steep rock shelf, straining at the effort.

Dee looked up to find Jack holding out his hand. She grasped it, enjoying his touch. For a fleeting moment, she let her mind enjoy the familiarity.

"Hey, you."

He smiled and kissed her cheek. "Hey."

A blur of movement on both sides rushed from the trees. Dee pulled away from Jack and raised her rifle back up. The fleeing humans had run straight into an ambush. Variants poured out from the bushes on both sides. There were dozens. Intense fighting broke out. Jack moved to Katherine's other side, sweeping his AR-15, taking out any beast he could. Motion buzzed all around, making it difficult for Dee to use her carbine without hitting someone friendly.

She slung her rifle and pulled out her Glock. She unloaded her magazine, dropping several monsters. Jack, standing beside her, had adopted the same idea. Katherine, crouched between her and Jack, screamed.

Three Variants broke through and barrelled into them. Dee twisted to one side, firing as she tumbled to the ground. Her bullet sailed true, smashing through the beast's throat before exploding out the back. The Variant slumped to the ground. Dee risked a peek at Jack; he had rolled out of the way and shot a Variant in the head.

The third Variant had straddled Katherine. It slashed at her torso with its claws, cutting deep and exposing her intestines. Dee screamed and ran forwards, reaching back to pull out her katana. She brought the blade down in a slashing arc, relieving the beast of its head. She watched, satisfied, as the head bounced along the forest floor. One of the struggling warriors kicked it and it ricocheted off a rock and dropped out of sight.

Yelling for Jack to cover them, Dee bent down and clasped Katherine's hand. "Lie still. I'll bandage you up."

Katherine looked into her eyes and squeezed her hand back. "Dee, I can feel how bad it is."

"Regardless, I'm not leaving you behind."

Katherine shook her head at Dee. All around them, the battle went on. Gunshots and war cries. The whacks of mere hitting skulls. Grunts of effort as the Renegades and their saviours fought for their lives. Jack reached down and grabbed Dee's katana, standing guard as she pulled out her first-aid kit and field dressed the wound. Blood immediately soaked the bandage, coating her hands. She quickly tied it off and signalled to Jack to help her. They lifted Katherine. She cried out and at the same time handed Jack the metal case she'd carried all the way from the lab, often hugging it close. "Get this to Colonel Mahana."

Jack nodded. "You're going to make it, Doc. You have to."

"Just take it. Please." She looked at Dee. "Everything is in there, all my research. I hope... I hope I've done enough to save everyone."

"Let's just concentrate on getting out of here first." Dee said.

She wrapped her arm around Katherine and held her up. She looked over at the warriors; they were dispatching the last of the Variants. Several were coated in blood and black gore. Dee couldn't tell if it was theirs or the beasts'.

Ben jogged up clicking a fresh magazine into his rifle. He looked Katherine up and down. "Bad?"

Dee looked into his brown eyes and gave him a slight shake of her head. "Not too bad."

"Okay. Let's keep moving. That attack was just a taster." He turned to the hulking tattooed warrior next to him. "How close are we to your Pa?"

The warrior pointed with his taiaha. "Top of the mountain. If we hurry, about ten minutes."

Ben nodded. "Let's go. I want this bloody day to be over."

Dee pushed on, holding Katherine up as they struggled up the mountain. One of the Maori dropped back and held Katherine on the other side. Dee smiled at him, thankful for his help.

As they climbed higher, she caught whiffs of decay. The morning sun broke through the clouds, illuminating the mist swirling around the trees and rocks. The muscles in Dee's arm and shoulder were straining under Katherine's weight. Not only was she straining with the physical task, but she was also struggling to grasp the fact that Katherine knew her mother. And that her mother was apparently alive.

The stench of decay became stronger as the steep path plateaued out. Dee glanced to her left, seeking the source of the putrid smell. The swirling mist dissipated, revealing several Variant corpses tied to trees, all in different stages of putrefaction. The nearest one's insides were spilling out, liquified, dripping to the ground in a black, oozy mess.

"Why do you do that?" Dee asked, gesturing with her head.

"The rewera don't like their own dead. It keeps them away." The Maori helping her grinned, showing his teeth.

Dee frowned. "Rewera?"

"Ummm…demon. What do you white fellas call them?"

Dee paused and looked down at her feet, watching where she put them as she stepped over some gnarled roots. "We call them Variants, sometimes beasts."

"Variants? Who came up with that?"

"Some American, I think. That's what we've been calling them since near the beginning. I'm Dee, by the way."

He nodded at her. "Tama."

Dee held his gaze, smiling.

Katherine whimpered something inaudible. They stopped and shifted their grips, trying to make it more comfortable for the ailing scientist.

Tama looked at her. "Not far now."

Dee gazed in awe at the intricate carvings surrounding the gateway to the Pa as the exhausted and bloodied Renegades passed under it. She could see the figures called tekoteko and other shapes with names she couldn't recall. She made a mental note to ask Tama.

Several women and men stood on either side, letting them pass. Two older women ran forwards and lifted Katherine away. They carefully helped the injured scientist towards a building to their right.

With Katherine's weight gone, Dee took in her surroundings. Immediately in front of her stood a large wooden building, the meeting house. Surrounding the whole facade were more intricate carvings. To either side were four smaller buildings, with a large rectangular building directly behind the carved meeting house. Dee could see gardens with a raised kumara store perched on a pole above them. She glanced back, happy to see the other Renegades enter.

The gates slammed shut with a thud and several of the inhabitants pushed thick, heavy logs into place. Jack handed back her katana and she slid it into its saya, savouring the swoosh as it slid home.

"That was too close," Dee whispered, pulling Jack into a hug.

"So much for a simple pick up." He pulled away slightly, grinning.

"I can't believe the Colonel sent us. I don't think I'm ready for this, Jack. I mean, we're not soldiers. We barely survived that."

"I know, right? I guess we were all they had. I

would've rather gone to Mayor and checked on the boys. Now we're stuck here, and Katherine is injured."

"I guess so. I suppose I should go and check on her." Dee paused. "I wonder if what she said about my mother is true." Saying the word "mother" felt hollow to Dee. She was so used to not having one.

Jack brushed some of Dee's hair behind her ear. "Do you really think she is alive?"

"I don't know why Katherine would lie. She'd gain nothing from it."

"True."

"I don't recognise her, but then I was young when Mum died. Well, when I thought she had."

Question after question flashed through her mind as she glanced around the Pa. Why had her mother abandoned her? Why had her father lied? A gnawing feeling ate away at her stomach as she tried to grasp the reasons. Since her father was no longer here, she vowed to ask Katherine what she knew.

Dee shook her head. She turned at footsteps and saw Ben approaching, the big warrior striding beside him.

"Jack, Dee, this is Hone."

Jack reached out his hand to shake Hone's. Hone pulled him closer and gave him a hongi — the Maori greeting, touching noses.

A fleeting memory of a school class flitted into Dee's mind. She recalled the hongi was so you could feel the breath of life. Dee watched, smiling to herself, knowing Jack would struggle with that. She reached out her hand to Hone in turn. Grasping it, she went in for the hongi, but Hone moved his head and kissed her cheek.

"A real kiss for the lady," he said, grinning.

149

Dee couldn't help but smile. "Thanks for saving us back there."

Hone grasped her shoulder. "You're welcome. Couldn't leave you to the rewera. Even you white fellas. You guys certainly made a lot of noise. If we hadn't been on a supply run, we'd never have found you. It's always nice to save the pretty ones."

He was grinning at her, his eyes glistening in the morning sun.

"Well, thank you." Dee blushed.

"What is this place?" Jack said, gesturing around the Pa.

"Always with the questions, you white fellas." Hone laughed. "First we eat, then we talk." He pointed to the rectangular structure behind the building with the carvings. "Kai is in there."

"Thank you, we'll meet you there. I want to check on Katherine first." Dee said.

Hone strode away. Dee couldn't help but admire his muscles and tattoos. Jack nudged her side. She squeezed his hand, smirking at him.

The Renegades moved into the shade provided by one of the buildings. Dee shivered despite the sun, the autumn mornings were chilly. She knelt beside Tony. He was shaking violently, obviously in shock.

"We'll take care of him. You go be with Yokoyama," Ben said, patting her shoulder.

"Look after this smart-arse for me," said Dee.

As Dee headed for the small wooden building where the elderly women had taken the scientist, she glanced back a few times at her injured teammate. As much as she and Tony butted heads, they had a mutual respect for each other. It pained her to see him in distress.

With each step she took, her trepidation grew. The questions that had nagged her on their flight up the mountain bubbled back to the surface.

Jack seemed to pick up on her feelings and wrapped an arm around her, drawing her in close. "I love you."

She pushed her body in closer, not minding that he stank of sweat, blood and gore. "I know."

Dee paused at the door, not sure whether to knock or just enter. She was clueless about Maori etiquette.

The door swung open, saving her. An elderly woman stood inside. Pulling the door open wider, she waved them inside. "She's asking for you, hun."

The room held six single beds lined up in two rows. Katherine was lying on the middle one in the far row, her head propped up on several pillows.

The other elderly woman sat next to her, holding her hand and wiping her brow. Dee caught the pungent stench of herbs as she moved alongside Katherine and sat in the empty chair.

The women had redressed her quick field dressing. She could see a dark green poultice oozing out the sides; that must be the source of the strong scent of herbs. But blood was beginning to soak through the new bandage.

Dee grasped Katherine's hand and her eyes fluttered open. She smiled up at her. "Dee."

Dee shifted closer on the chair. "Hey."

"She was sorry, Diana. Sorry for leaving you."

Dee searched Katherine's face, looking for any signs of deceit. "Why are you telling me this?"

"She would want me to."

"Before all this madness started, where was she?"

"She was working in a lab near Christchurch. But listen, I need to tell you this. All the labs are listed on a memory stick in that case."

Dee held her tongue. She wanted to hear what Katherine had to say.

"Your mother got obsessed with her work. She became so caught up in her pursuit of scientific greatness, she ignored her motherly instincts. Ignored the fact that she had a daughter. She talked about you often over the years, trying to think of a way to repair the damage she had done. Reconcile, if you will. But the longer she left it, the harder it became. She loved you, Diana, and I know she is sorry for abandoning you and your father. It was easier for her to work than to bring you up. Seeing you now, I can see she missed it all. Missed watching you grow into a wonderful woman." She squeezed Dee's hand and lifted her free hand out towards Jack. Jack moved forwards and tentatively grasped it.

Katherine looked between them. "Don't waste what time you have left. Enjoy each moment with each other. Another's love, and your love for others, is what is important. Not silly things like Bovine genetics." She coughed. Bubbles of saliva and blood escaped her mouth and dribbled down her chin.

Dee glanced up at Jack, pain and sorrow washing through her. She knew he would be processing everything Katherine had said too, mulling it over.

"I'll let you have some private time with Dee so you can tell her more. Can I ask you a question, though?" Jack asked once the scientist had finished coughing.

Katherine opened her eyes. "Sure, sure. Go ahead."

"What do you know about this Hemorrhage Virus?

For some reason, the army won't tell us much."

Katherine wiped her mouth and looked between Jack and Dee. "I'll tell you what little I know. I got this information from my ex, an American scientist. They asked those of us left in the science community to help figure out a way to fix this. Early on, I was working with a facility in the Blue Mountains before it went dark." She took a breath. "It started life during the Vietnam War as a drug called VX-99. Scientists at USAMRIID created a bioweapon by combining it with the Zaire strain of Ebola. They called the result X9H9, or Hemorrhage Virus."

Katherine coughed again, a racking, wet cough. Dee's mind reeled. Katherine had confirmed all she had suspected and knew already. Hearing it from a scientist left a hollow feeling in her stomach. All this death, all this horror and loss. Man-made. Dee rubbed a hand through her dirty, sweaty hair. She glanced up at the man she loved, finding some comfort in his eyes. He looked just as shocked and mad as she felt.

"So why was your lab built under the mountain?" Jack questioned further.

"We were doing some cutting-edge procedures. Some might call them questionable. Best to keep out of sight. I'm surprised we lasted so long. So many of my contemporaries went dark."

Dee's mind swam with this new information as she watched Katherine struggling, coughing up blood. The gnawing she felt in the pit of the stomach returned. "Hang in there. We're going to call in the chopper and get you to Mayor Island. Get you stitched up. We have a good doctor and excellent nurses to help."

Katherine shook her head. "It's too late for me, Dee. I'm bleeding internally. I don't have long to live. A few minutes at best."

Dee glanced down at the bandaged wound. It continued to seep blood, confirming Katherine's diagnosis. "I'll stay with you. I'm not going to abandon you like my mother did me."

Katherine chuckled. "She deserves that. Thank you. I was there at your beginning, it's poetic that you are here at my end."

Dee had no response to that, so she rested her hand in the dying scientist's. Katherine squeezed her hand weakly, her breathing becoming shallow and laboured.

Jack and Dee sat with Katherine as the sun crept higher, casting its beams through the window. The sun had just reached Katherine's face when she gasped a couple of times and let out a whistling breath. Her eyes opened, fluttered, then closed.

Dee leant forwards, pushing her head against Katherine's chest. She waited, listening for her heart. Hearing nothing, she rose up and wiped the tears from her eyes.

"She's gone."

Jack didn't reply. He embraced Dee and kissed her cheek.

One of the elderly women covered Katherine with the sheet and said something in te reo Maori. "She's with the spirits now," she said.

Dee nodded her thanks and let Jack take her from the room, leading her outside. The exhaustion of the last few days was eating away at her. Add in the emotion of the last few hours, and she had never felt so utterly spent. Jack stayed silent, walking beside her. He gently led her towards the central building with the carvings and guided her to sit on the steps.

"You okay?"

"I just feel numb, and confused."

"Just something else for us to work through."

"Yeah."

"You hungry?" Jack nudged her ribs.

"Starving."

They followed the smell of food to a smaller building beside the carved meeting house. Piles of shoes were cast to either side of the entrance. She followed Jack into the building, the cooking smells making her stomach rumble. Dee realised that she hadn't eaten anything wholesome for several days, and the thought of food cast aside her emotions. She breathed in, enjoying the smell of bread and the tell-tale whiff of frying bacon.

— 20 —

The swell of the waves rolled under the fibreglass hull of the boat. James watched the Indonesian Sigma-class corvette draw closer. A smaller RHIB — rigid-hulled inflatable boat — broke away from the grey hull of the ship and moved out to meet them.

James planted his feet wider and tried to move in sequence with the sea, assessing the boat as it approached. A figure stood apart from the other men, back straight, head held high. James guessed that this was Captain Arif Koto.

As the boats drew together, he was pleased to see them unarmed, as he had requested. The boats bumped, the contact vibrating under his feet.

James's soldiers helped the Indonesians into the boat. Once they were aboard, the pilot gunned the engine, the bow lifting slightly at the extra power. James clasped Koto's hand in greeting and indicated for him to sit in one of the boat's three spare seats. The accompanying soldiers remained standing. He swivelled to face Koto, getting a better look at him. He had jet black hair and mocha skin. His limbs were thin, but he had a large paunch.

Koto, seeing where James directed his gaze, patted his stomach. "Too much curry, Colonel."

James let out a bark of laughter. Despite his displeasure at the arrival of the Indonesian refugees, he admired Koto for his tenacity at finding a new home for his people. They had spent the last few weeks sailing the Pacific, looking for that home. Who was he to deny them that? Hadn't everyone on Earth been a refugee at some stage? His own ancestors had fled slavery on Hawaiki and sought new lands, spending months and years searching before finding a virgin land tucked away in the deep Pacific. Some believed the land had been populated before the Maori, by a people called the Moriori. James smiled to himself, remembering the oral history of his Iwi. It told stories of a people to the south and the outlying islands, a peaceful people of great songs. People now lost to the mists of time.

He looked back at Koto, who was assessing him in turn, by the way his eyes flicked back and forth. He watched over Koto's shoulder as Great Barrier Island drew closer. James had stationed a platoon of soldiers on the small dock. They saluted as the boat nudged against the wooden piles. James stood and indicated with his hand for Koto and his men to disembark first. James's men stood at attention as he led Koto to an awaiting vehicle.

The jeep turned away from the dock, past a small fisheries' building and into the village hugging the shore. The civilian population stood in doorways and stared out their windows, trying to catch a glimpse as the jeep sped past, heading to the FOB.

Badminton stood at the open door, saluting as James

led Koto into the head room. Happy to see the refreshments had been laid out, James waited until Koto had seated himself.

Taking his seat at the head of the table, he indicated for Badminton to shut the door. Hearing it snap shut, he placed his hands on the table and looked at Koto.

"I must admit, Captain, this is a very unusual way for two officers to meet. But these are trying times. With so few of us remaining, my superiors have ordered me to reach an agreement with you. For the record, I don't agree with them. In my opinion, people of different religions and moral beliefs always end up killing each other. History, if anything, has taught us this time and again. But I'm an officer of the New Zealand Army, so I will abide by my orders. But that doesn't mean I have to like them."

Koto shifted in his chair, holding James's gaze. He cleared his throat. "Thank you, Colonel. I thank God that he blessed us, that we will not be turned away again. We want nothing but peace. As you can see, we are unarmed and have shown no sign of anger…anger? Is this the right word? Please my English is rusty." James nodded, so Koto continued. "I know you must be asking yourself, why didn't we stay in Indonesia, we have thousands of islands? But I assure you, Colonel, we tried. We lost so many people to those Jinn, time and again we just escaped with our lives. But praises to God we survived. Island after island we tried. The ones with no Jinn, we couldn't live on. So I decided, Colonel, to try out here in the Pacific."

James steepled his fingers together. "Why not Australia? Big country, lots of room."

Koto smiled and leant back in his chair. "Yes, Australia. In truth be told, Colonel, the Aussies…they don't like us. Think all of Indonesia is to blame for Bali bombing, for all the boat people over the years. They have bigger navy. Too risky, we come here. Kiwis friendly. I think I was right."

James nodded in agreement. As much as he loved Australia and he honoured the ANZAC spirit, they did tend to be aggressive. Koto had made the right decision in choosing to avoid Australia. He glanced out the window at the bush-clad mountains. He never would've thought he'd be negotiating with refugees during the Variant apocalypse. He pushed his personal feelings aside and looked back at Koto.

"We have some islands not far from here. A group called the Mercury Islands. The Brigadier is offering your people the biggest one. In exchange, he asks that you sign accords to farm the land and trade with us in the future. He also asks that you provide whatever military assistance we require now, and in the future, to help defeat the Variants, or Jinn as you call them, infecting our mainland. Captain, I don't think you will get a better deal. A treaty is being drawn up as we speak. I hope you honour this treaty better than the last lot did."

Koto raised an eyebrow at James. "The last lot?"

James let out a sigh. "Yes, the last lot. You're going to have to learn some New Zealand history if you want to live here, Captain. The British signed a treaty with the Maori in 1840, at a place called Waitangi. They promptly ignored it and destroyed our way of life."

Koto nodded. "We will honour our agreement, Colonel. In this new world, we must if we are to survive."

"Yes, I agree with you, Captain. Let's hope so. Please join me for some food. Looks like the men caught some nice crayfish this morning."

James reached out for a plate and started to fill it. There was a knock at the door. Badminton entered. Saluting, he said, "Sorry to interrupt, Sir, but I thought you would like to know. Captain Johns just radioed. He's asking for immediate evac. They're alive, Sir."

"Very good, Lieutenant. What do we have available? Let's get our troops home."

"That's the thing, Sir. It's all on Mayor, dealing with that."

James clenched his fist under the table.

"Ahh…Colonel?"

James looked over at Koto. "Yes?"

"Perhaps we can be of assistance. In honour of our agreement, I mean. We have a helicopter that you can use."

James looked at Badminton, then back at Koto. "How soon can it be in the air?"

"Fifteen minutes, twenty at the most."

"Make it so, Captain. And thank you."

James stood and walked over to Koto. He reached out, offering his hand. "Let this be the start of a real treaty, Captain."

Koto grasped his hand in a two-handed shake. "Let's get your men home."

— 21 —

Maggie leant out the window and fired at the pursuing 4x4, aiming for the tyres. She squeezed the trigger, shifting her aim higher. Annoyingly, it clicked empty. She cursed at the small magazine of the New Zealand AR-15s and quickly jammed another into the rifle.

The countryside flew past. Maggie didn't have time to take anything in. She shifted her attention from the tyres and aimed for the windshield. Remembering the driver was on the other side to what she was used to, she estimated where the driver's head was and let loose with a barrage of bullets. The rounds tore into the windshield, shattering it. She watched, satisfied, as the 4x4 swerved, fishtailed across the road and smashed into the bank, flinging debris onto the road behind like a NASCAR car hitting the wall. It careened over the bank and out of sight.

One down, one to go.

The second 4x4 managed to avoid the carnage. One of the men leant out the window and fired a volley at the van, hitting the back windshield and showering the cowering children in tiny shards of glass. Leela screamed and ran towards the front of the van. Becs reached out and pulled her into a hug, crouching between the front seats.

"Try losing them in the suburbs!" Maggie cried out, firing again at their pursuants.

"I'm trying. I think we're nearly there!" Alice shouted back.

Maggie squinted through her sights and aimed again for the windshield, but this driver wasn't as ignorant, and swerved from side to side. She felt the van slow down as Alice squealed around a corner. From the corners of her eyes, Maggie could see houses flying past now, lawns overgrown, the sections littered with rubbish. Several Variants leapt over fences, chasing them, shrieking loudly.

Alice steered the van left and right. Maggie was pretty impressed. To her chagrin, though, the 4x4 matched them with every turn.

Gritting her teeth, Maggie turned to get her bearings. "If you have any ideas, now's the time." she said to no one in particular.

Alice glanced at her, then grimaced as she took another turn, wrenching the steering wheel down hard. The van squealed as two wheels lifted off the road. The screaming of the children went up a few octaves, piercing through Maggie's brain.

Alice managed to regain control of the van. "I'm trying to reach the city centre. Lots of narrow roads."

"Good idea. Then we can ambush the bastards."

Maggie turned and, dropping back into her seat, busied herself loading their weapons. She looked up from her task and over at Becs, holding a crying Leela. She squeezed the girl's arm, hoping she could reassure her with this small sign of affection. The van screeched again as it took another turn, and Maggie felt it bump and judder as the road surface changed. She looked up through the windshield. Alice had piloted them in amongst the tall buildings of the city centre.

Maggie looked left to right, searching for a good spot. Up ahead she could see a large fountain. Metal sculptures made to look like plants sprang up from the pool at the bottom. The water had turned green and murky with algae.

Howls and shrieks bounced around the narrow spaces, alerting her to the Variants. Then she heard the squeal of the chasing 4x4's tyres as it tore down the road.

Maggie pointed to the fountain up ahead. "Quickly! Smash the van into there." Turning to the kids, she yelled, "Hold onto something!"

Maggie reached over and hugged Becs and Leela, protecting them. The van smashed into the fountain. The back wheels lifted up off the ground before thumping back with a thud. Maggie slammed into the door pillar with the impact. Pain lanced down her right side.

"Keep down out of sight. Don't move. Please. Whatever you do, don't move," Maggie whispered, glancing at Becs.

Maggie flung open the door and threw Alice a rifle. "Jump into the water but keep the gun up, and fire when I do."

Alice nodded and jumped in. Maggie eased into the slimy water, submerging herself. She lifted the very top of her head above the water and rested the rifle on the concrete lip.

The 4x4 came to a stop a few metres from the van. Three men in red coveralls emerged. One held up his rifle, scanning the buildings to his left. He stayed behind the van door.

Smart. I'll kill you last.

The other one, on Maggie's side, moved away from the van and looked around. She watched as he looked back at the man behind the door, shrugging his shoulders.

The man behind the door shook his head. "Go check the van, Terry," he said, waving his hand.

Terry moved forwards, his shotgun pointing at the ground.

Silly boy.

Maggie waited for him to get a few feet from her. Then she adjusted her aim and shot between the door and the 4x4.

The man behind the door's head snapped back as an arc of brain and skull flew out, his lifeless body crumpling to the floor.

I lied, asshole.

She quickly fired at the one called Terry, a couple of quick bursts into his chest. Terry looked down, shock etched on his face. Maggie didn't have time to feel sorry for him. There was still another occupant to worry about. She heard Alice fire, and waited for any return fire. Hearing nothing, Maggie swivelled around, her carbine raised, and glanced towards Alice. The remaining traitor was shuffling along the ground, holding his leg and screaming.

Maggie jumped out of the fountain, green water sloshing after her. She ran up to the front of the 4x4, using the grill as protection. Glancing under the vehicle, Maggie could see that the injured man had moved back a few feet.

"Wait! Don't shoot."

Maggie paused, her finger hovering over the trigger, planning her next move. She knew that he was trying to stall her. "Why shouldn't I?"

"I'm unarmed."

"Tell you what. You answer me a question, and I'll let you live."

"Anything. Just don't shoot."

"Where do they take the children?"

Maggie heard him cough, a wet, fluid-filled cough. Alice must have hit him somewhere else as well.

"I'm waiting."

"Fine. It will do you no good. There's hundreds of them. They're in the dam."

A high-pitched shriek reminded Maggie of the Variants. She risked a peek around, searching for them. The concrete road exploded next to her foot, bits of concrete and tile stinging her face moments before she heard the crack of a rifle.

Stupid, Maggie. Real stupid.

She lowered her aim and fired at the traitor, hitting him in the torso. He grunted and slumped to the ground, blood and saliva dribbling from his mouth.

Bastard. What did he mean by dam?

She waved at Alice and ran around to the man. Grabbing his gun, she slung it over her shoulder, searching for any danger. The Variants would be close. With all the noise and spilt blood, she couldn't rely on these disguises.

As if on cue, howls and shrieks echoed around the buildings, announcing the Variants' arrival.

"Quick, let's grab the kids and find a boat." She

pointed past the fountain to where several masts bobbed around in the distance. Drawing a deep breath, the hint of salt surprised her. The familiar scent refocused her attention. She was within reach of going home. With new determination, Maggie ran to the smashed-up van. She helped Becs and Leela out, grabbed each by a hand, and led them towards the harbour. Alice jogged after them with the other four kids.

The sight of all the boats in the harbour made Maggie's heart pound in her chest. There was an abundance of yachts and motorised launches of different sizes. Her eyes scanned the edges of the wharf, stopping on a couple of sturdy-looking fishing vessels. Maggie nodded to herself; that was what she was looking for. Fishing boats were built tough. Her eyes flicked farther out, to where the yachts were moored. One or two looked suitable for a long sea voyage. Was she finally going to head home? She'd never thought she would be stuck in a foreign country in a time of such crisis. She'd always assumed, like everyone, that she would be at home. Home, to protect her family. But instead she was here, herding a bunch of kids to what she hoped was safety.

Maggie glanced at the last few shops as they went past, looking for Variants. The generic shops you would find in most western countries. Bakeries, telco, clothing. They all stood silent and untouched. No one had the time or desire to loot when flesh-eating monsters were lurking in the shadows.

She caught their reflections as they walked past the walls of glass. Her dark hair poked out in wispy strands from under the cap. The children between her and Alice reminded her of a bunch of street kids from a Dickens novel. Sighing, Maggie hoped that the red coveralls she and Alice were wearing would fool the local creatures too.

Maggie followed Alice out from the relative cover of the shopping street and onto the wooden jetty that jutted about three hundred feet into the harbour. At the far end sat a small green building, facing the harbour entrance and the open ocean beyond. As they drew closer, the large sign nailed to the side became legible. Bay of Plenty Game Fishing Club.

Despite the danger, the children ran to the edge of the wharf and peered over, looking into the water, laughing. Maggie considered telling them to be quiet, but with no signs of any Variants, she let them have their fun.

Alice turned towards her. "What do you think? One of these boats?"

"Yeah. I guess we just try and get one of them started. How far is it to this Mayor Island?"

Alice shrugged and gestured towards the open ocean. "I'm not sure. It's just out past the Mount there."

Maggie looked to where she was pointing, but all she could see was a big hill at the end of a long, low stretch of land. Dotted along the coast were tall apartment blocks and flash-looking houses.

"Mount?"

Alice pointed to the big hill. "Yeah, sorry. The Mount, as in Mount Maunganui."

"Oh right. Any idea on how long it would take?"

"I've never actually been to the island, but I think about three to four hours?"

Maggie tried to do the math in her head for how much fuel they needed, but with no idea on the tank size or range of the available boats, she gave up. She looked out at the multi-coloured yachts moored in the harbour. "You don't know how to sail, do you?"

Alice followed her gaze. "Not really, no. I know the principles."

"Boat it is, then. You keep an eye on the kids, I'll find us a ride."

Alice nodded and turned, walking over to the kids.

Leela looked up as she approached. Spotting Maggie, she ran over. "I'm hungry."

Maggie crouched down and hugged the little blonde-haired girl. "Tell you what. You play with the other kids and Alice. I'm going to get us a boat. Then we can eat. What do you think?"

Leela twirled her fingers together before reluctantly walking back to the other kids.

Maggie watched her go, more driven than ever to get her, Becs and the others to safety. She couldn't help her daughter Izzy when she was sick, but she could help these kids. Maggie felt her cheeks flush. Not for the last time, she cursed those responsible for the situation she found herself in.

She turned and headed for the nearest fishing boat. Wafts of its working life assaulted her nose as she jumped on. Diesel, oil and fish; the pungency surprised her.

Maggie opened the pilot house door, taking in the cabin. It was a simple room with a large, comfortable-looking seat and a tiny steering wheel. A small curved window faced out to the water, and below it, a wood-veneer dashboard ran the width of the cabin. Dotted near the wheel was an array of radios and instruments. Maggie's heart soared at the sight of the radio. She reached out and clicked it on. Nothing. No lights, nothing. She looked at the ignition, hoping for keys. The slot lay empty. A quick search of the cabin proved fruitless, and Maggie moved on to search through the other moored boats. None had keys, and she couldn't get any of the radios to work.

She finally stood on the last fishing boat, holding her hand over her mouth trying not to not gag on the stench of rotting fish coming from the hold. A large motor launch bobbed up and down with the swell at the end of the jetty. She could just make out its name, *Sea You Later*, painted in bright blue on its white hull.

She made her way over to it, smiling at the children, who all lay on their stomachs watching the fish swimming under and around the jetty poles. Alice sat with them, rifle clutched in her hands. Her head swivelled back and forth, watching for any movement. Maggie grinned. She admired Alice's resolve. She had never told Maggie what had happened to her, but here she was, focused on protecting everyone.

Maggie jumped over the gunwale of the boat, landing softly on the deck. She quickly brought her rifle up and headed into the covered area. Flinging open the door, she could see it had been well lived in, and recently too. In the wheelhouse, Maggie spotted the keys, tied to a yellow plastic float, dangling from the ignition. She pumped her fist. Finally, some luck. Tentative, she reached out and turned the key. An orange light next to the ignition came on, splashing light over the gauges. The fuel gauge read nearly empty. Maggie clicked off the ignition. She didn't want to drain the battery for nothing. She headed back onto the deck and scanned the jetty, looking for a fuel tank. Spotting a grey tank with rusty streaks nestled against the green building, Maggie jumped out of the boat and jogged over to Alice and the kids.

"Found us a ride, but it needs fuel," she said, pointing to the boat and tank.

"You get the kids on board. I'll see if we can get some fuel," Alice said.

The children had lost interest in the fish and were beginning to mill around. Maggie crouched down and looked at them. "All right. Who wants to go for a ride in the boat?"

The kids all turned to where she was pointing, their cheeks flushed from their fish-watching activities.

"We do," they answered in unison.

Maggie took Leela's hand and walked her over to the white and blue boat. She jumped over the small gap and lifted Leela in after her.

"Take them in there. Thanks, Becs."

Becs nodded, leading Leela and the other kids into the cabin.

Maggie turned, searching for Alice. She had unhooked a hose and gas pump, and was bringing it over to the boat. "Look what I found."

"Thanks Alice."

"You put it in the tank, I'll pump. There's a manual hand pump on the side."

"Sounds good. Really, thank you." Maggie held Alice's gaze for a moment. As much as she thought and knew herself to be strong and independent, she was thankful for Alice's company. She wouldn't have kept her sanity or her anger in check if it hadn't been for her. The last few hours together had proven how determined Alice was to survive and help those in need.

Maggie watched the fuel rise to the top of the tank. It just needed a few more minutes. A shriek bounced over the water. She turned her head, seeking the source. The creature was perched on the roof of the building across the road from the jetty. Several more Variant heads popped up and howled. They were looking out to sea, raising their heads as if sniffing the breeze. The thumping of feet on the boat deck caused her to turn. Becs was running towards her.

"Maggie, there…there's boats coming!"

Maggie frowned and grabbed her hand. "Show me."

She signalled to Alice to stop pumping and ran with Becs into the cabin.

Her mouth dropped open at the sight. Half a dozen boats were making their way between the Mount and the long flat island on the other side, and several men with guns were dotted on the decks. Maggie raised her carbine so she could get a better view through her scope. Standing on the deck of the lead boat stood the biggest Variant she had ever seen. It was at least seven foot tall. It had bark-like skin, and spiky bones protruded from its shoulders. With the aid of her scope, she could see children's heads mounted on those spikes.

Maggie let the rifle drop. Bile rose from her liver and travelled up her oesophagus, burning the lining as it went, as if her body was rejecting what she'd just seen. *Horrific!* She had heard rumours of bigger Variants, but until now had not seen any. She shook her head. This one was not only big but seemed to have command over the Variants and the human helpers. Maybe that was what Ian had meant when he'd been boasting?

Thinking quickly, she spun around, raced outside and waved for Alice to come over.

Alice raced up and looked over Maggie's shoulder. "Oh, shit."

"Shit is right. We have to hide. Now!"

They ran the few steps into the cabin. Maggie was struggling to keep her fear for the children from bubbling over and making her do something rash, something stupid that would nullify everything they had done to escape.

Alice started flinging the cushions off the seats, revealing storage cells. "Kids, I'm sorry, but the bad creatures are coming. We have to hide."

"Just pretend it's the world championship of hide 'n seek," Maggie said, helping Leela in, admiring how they didn't question why. They just did. She guessed they were used to this sort of thing by now, hiding from the monsters. After they'd placed the cushions back on the seats, Maggie went to the engine cover and lifted it off. She peered down into the semi darkness. It would be a tight fit, but it would have to do. She turned to Alice. She had her rifle up, watching the boats through the small window. A pained look crossed her face.

"What is it?"

"I know that kid," Alice murmured.

Maggie looked through her scope. The boats had moored at the next jetty down. A couple of gunmen had driven vans down and were herding children into them. Dozens of Variants flanked one side of the jetty, watching. Maggie swore she could see them salivating. The giant Variant lumbered onto the jetty, a figure under each arm. A teenager with one leg under the right, and a small red-haired kid in the left.

"Which one?"

"The bigger one the ugly bastard's holding… What is that on his shoulders…? Oh God…"

Maggie glanced at Alice. She'd dropped her rifle and slid to the floor. Maggie sat down next to her and took her hand. "I'm sorry, Alice."

Alice wiped a tear from her eye and looked at Maggie. "He was whole, when I knew him. Back in the beginning. He hid in the basement with Dee and the others. We, we decided to go our own way. He's just a kid."

Maggie stood up and moved to one side, careful to keep out of sight. She watched as the demons and their human captives moved up the jetty. A small truck with a flatbed backed up to the jetty and the giant Variant bounded onto it, causing the suspension to buckle with its weight. Then it bent down and wrapped its two captives in chains. It leant back and bellowed. The deep baritone sound reverberated around the harbour, sending shivers up Maggie's spine. Everything about the Variants disgusted her. Their smell, their look. That horrible popping sound their joints made when they moved. Their howls. And now this giant Variant's bellow. Sounds that she could add to the sounds of war. Something else to keep her awake at night.

The warmth of the carbine in her hands penetrated and, remembering her oath as a nurse and the promise she'd made to her daughter, she decided to act. To fight. To make a stand.

Maggie checked her rifle and reached down to grab the bag she had stolen from the camp guards. She grasped Alice's shoulder. "I'm going after those children."

Alice met her eyes and nodded. "Okay. What about these kids?"

"You take them to Mayor Island. Hopefully you have enough fuel. If you run out, drop the anchor." Maggie looked up at the radio. "Radio for help, but only once you're out in open water. Otherwise you don't know who's listening. I'm sorry to do this, Alice, but I can't bear the thought of leaving those kids to such a horrible fate. I'm going to track them to wherever they take them. It's unfinished business."

Alice drew Maggie into a hug. "Please come back. I like you."

"I'll do my best. I like you too, hun." The seats behind them thumped. "I'm going to go. Tell Becs and Leela to behave for me."

With a last look back, Maggie smiled and jumped over the gap onto the jetty. Glancing towards the new arrivals and seeing no activity, she ran for the cover of the shops.

— 22 —

Jack sat back and rubbed his full stomach. It was the first decent meal he'd eaten for a number of days. He reached forwards and started to fill another plate when Dee elbowed him in the ribs. "You pig, how much are you going to eat?"

Jack smiled at her. "Oi. This is for Eric."

"Oh yeah, sorry." She giggled.

Jack let a grin spread across his face. After all she had been through, she still had the knack of lifting his spirits. Maybe her mirth was a cover. Hone and his whanau had scheduled to cremate Katherine and the other casualties at noon. Ben had secured them a lift back to Mayor Island. Jack was happy that they would finally be on their way. He was eager to see how Boss and George were. Eager for a shower and a change of clothes. Jack sniffed at his shirt. *Definitely need a shower.*

He glanced down at the silver case Katherine had given him. He couldn't help thinking it was cursed. All this over the contents of that rectangle of metal. He looked up into the adjoining room, taking in its beauty. There were expertly woven flax mats covering the floor.

The building was made from strong native timber, its high-raking ceiling soaring to a good six metres. Adorning the walls behind him, and in front, were huge carved pieces. He knew each carving told a story of Hone's Iwi. He made a mental note to ask him another time; the history buff in him was piqued.

Jack nudged Dee and stood, grabbed the food-laden plate and, with a nod to Ben, headed outside.

Eric was sitting next to Tony who was lying on the ground, wiping his brow with a cloth. As Jack drew closer he could see Tony's skin had become all blotchy with bruise-like patches. He offered the plate to Eric. "Here, eat. We'll take over."

"Thanks, guys." Eric started shovelling the food into his mouth.

Jack knelt down next to Tony. He wasn't quite sure, but he thought he detected a faint fruity smell.

Dee sat down next to him and took one of Tony's hands.

"His nails have grown really long."

Jack looked at Tony's other hand. The skin had become stretched and thin, giving it a translucent look. He picked it up and looked at the nails. On closer inspection, Jack could see that the nails had fallen off, exposing the bone underneath. The bone had hardened and yellowed, and the tips of the bony digits were now sharp claws. Jack dropped Tony's hand and leapt up, backing away.

"Dee, let it go, now!"

Dee scampered back from Tony, a confused look on her face. Her eyes questioned Jack, but she didn't voice her concerns.

Eric looked up from shovelling his food. "What?"

Jack glanced between Tony and Eric, trying to decide the best way to voice what he suspected. He knew they were close friends. "I...think he's infected by the virus. He's turning into one of them. Look!"

Eric leant over his mate, searching. "He's just sick, that's all. You guys have been wounded by the Variants. You're okay."

Jack rubbed at his scar, feeling the ridge of hardened tissue. Maybe Eric was right. He had been clawed, Ben had been speared and Boss'd had his lower leg ripped off. All of them were still human. He looked back down at Tony who was trembling like it was freezing cold, yet sweat was dripping off him.

Jack rubbed the stubble on his chin. "He was bitten, right?"

Eric nodded.

"So maybe, if these beasts bite you, they transfer the virus."

"They're not bloody zombies!"

"We know, Eric. Jack's trying to figure it out. We really don't know..." Dee said.

Dee pointed towards the far corner of the Pa. Twelve bodies lay next to a pyre of wood, wrapped in sheets. The casualties from their battle with the Variants that morning. Katherine lay amongst eleven brave warriors. Warriors who had saved them. Warriors who would never see their loved ones again. The thought of their sacrifices saddened Jack. Hone had insisted that they be burnt to limit the possibility of infection.

"The person who had the best knowledge is lying there."

Eric raised his hands, palms out and lowered his voice. "I know, Dee. I'm sorry. I'm just saying, we don't know enough to jump to conclusions. Let's get him back to Mayor and get some drugs into him."

Dee nodded and looked at Jack.

He shrugged. "I don't know, guys. What if he turns back on Mayor and kills people? Hell, we don't even know what's going on over there. Everything's a mess." Jack flung his hand towards the mountains. "We've got a bloody cabin just over there. I still don't know what's happened to my family."

"I know, guys. Can we just give him time?" Eric said. "That's all I ask."

"Okay. Sure."

Jack grimaced before nodding in agreement. Who was he to deny Eric? He walked away, glancing back at Dee. She caught up to him.

"Do you think he is turning?"

"I'm not sure, but his hands sure looked like claws. Did you see his skin? It was weird and blotchy."

Dee shook her head.

Jack said nothing further, using the time to calm down. It wouldn't last. He knew he had a quick temper. He glanced around at the thick wooden logs surrounding the Pa. The shrieks of the Variants sounded in the distance, but so far nothing closer. The Variant corpses rotting on the trees must be doing their job. He admired the craftsmanship of the Maori. They had built a strong, defendable complex. They had lasted six weeks and looked to be well-organised.

Jack stopped near the pyre. "Are you ready for the cremation?"

"I think so, yeah. I just feel hollow and angry. Why would Dad lie about Mum?"

"I don't know, baby. The only thing that I can think of was he wanted to protect you. Maybe the lie just got away from him."

Dee nodded and wrapped an arm around him. "We should get the chopper to do a fly-by of the cabin, just to be sure."

"That's why I love you, always looking out for me."

Dee nudged him gently in his side. "Only one reason? Harsh."

"Yeah, I know. I'm working on more, but lust overpowers me every time." Jack wrapped his other arm around Dee and lifted her off the ground, kissing her deeply. He held on to her, enjoying the familiar feel of her bones, her curves, her passion.

"I know I've said it before, Dee, but thanks for coming for me. If I had to choose someone to experience the apocalypse with, I would always choose you."

"And I you, Jack, without a doubt," she said. "You were so obsessed with the apocalypse, it was like you were guarding it."

Jack grinned and eased her down. "Yeah. And now we are living the bloody thing."

Shadows fell across the ground to one side of them, and Jack turned his head. Hone and Ben were leading a group of Maori over to them. Three elderly ladies dressed in black and wearing crowns of kawakawa came up alongside them. They lifted their heads, and a haunting song filled the air. A powhiri, if Jack remembered the name correctly. Though he could not understand the words, their meaning was clear from their tone. It spoke of sadness about those who had fallen, sadness at what had become of the world, sadness for those left to pick up the pieces and who must try to carry on. It thanked those who had given the ultimate sacrifice so they, the survivors, could have more time.

The tone of the song shifted as those gathered behind the kaumatua joined in. It now spoke of the lives of those fallen, of how every life was a blessing, something to be treasured and remembered with song and story. And so each life was honoured. Jack recalled a visit to a marae where the carver had explained that the great people, their stories, are carved into the history of their whanau.

Jack lost himself to the haunting song. He too remembered friends, family, pets and travels. He remembered peaceful days reading. Days exploring and going on adventures.

The emotional song finished, several men moved forwards and lifted the fallen onto the top of the pyre. Jack's eyes glistened. He felt Dee hug him tighter as they watched Katherine's body join the fallen warriors. Hone signalled to a couple of torch bearers, and they moved forwards to touch the timber with their flames.

Jack watched, entranced, as the flames grew in intensity, wrapping their fiery fingers around the wood. The air filled with heat as the pyre came alight. He took a step back. There was something morbidly beautiful about a funeral pyre, and thoughts of the final scenes of *Return of the Jedi* flashed through his mind.

As the smoke thickened, it billowed around those gathered, as if the spirits of the dead kissed the mourning goodbye before departing on their next journey. He gave Dee a squeeze and turned, looking for Ben. He was anxious to get going and find out what had happened on Mayor Island. He could feel his stomach twisting as he thought of George. He hoped their evacuation drills in the bunker had done their job. George was a smart kid and Boss treated him like a little brother. So Jack had hopes, but doubts crept in, threatening to cripple his demeanour.

He looked up as Ben stepped closer, his brown eyes twinkling with friendliness. He reached them and drew them into a quick hug. Pulling back, he grasped each of them by the shoulder. "Great send-off for the fallen. I've seen a lot of funerals in my time, but the Maori tangi is one of my favourites. This one wasn't traditional, but Hone and his people have adapted it."

Jack and Dee nodded in agreement.

"The chopper is due in ten minutes. Gather your things. Let's get home." Ben held Jack's gaze for a moment. "Have you got that cursed case?"

Jack pointed to their gear. "Yeah. It's over there."

"Good. Let's get ready. Hone said the far end of the Pa, by the gardens, should be sufficient for an LZ."

"I meant to tell you. I think Tony is turning...well, I suspect...he's different to others who've been injured," Jack said as he rubbed the back of his neck, waiting for Ben to answer. He wasn't sure if he should have said anything, but something about Tony's condition nagged at him.

Ben looked over to the Joneses. "You sure? Okay. Let's be safe and strap him down to a stretcher. We don't know what the hell we're dealing with."

Jack followed Dee over to their gear and started to assemble it. He lifted his pack over his shoulders, smiling at the bright green fabric. If this pack could tell stories it would keep people entertained for weeks. He checked his rifle and slung it over his shoulder.

Dee wiped the black gore off the blade of her katana and slipped it back into the webbing of her pack. Jack paused, admiring her for a moment. She had certainly adapted well to this new world order and wielded that blade with the ruthless efficiency of a samurai.

"You guys ready?" Hone said, striding over.

"Just about, thanks. Thanks for your hospitality, Hone."

"You're welcome, Jack. Look after your little Eowyn."

Jack grinned at his reference. "So what is this place you have here?"

Hone glanced between Dee and Jack. He had a proud look to his posture.

"A couple of years ago, I decided to search out a lost Pa. Songs in our history told of a lost, abandoned Pa on top of a mountain. A few of us wanted to try to live by the old ways. We were tired of the way we were losing our children to lives of crime and seeing them waste away in prison. We searched for a few months, and after a few flights over, we found it. I then advertised for like-minded people to join me, and here we are. We call ourselves 'Tamariki o kohu Te Maunga'. Simply put, 'Children of the Misty Mountains'."

Jack grinned at him. "Like in *The Hobbit*?"

Hone laughed, a deep bass laugh, and clapped him on the shoulder. "Yes, just like in *The Hobbit*." He turned, looking Dee up and down. "Look after yourselves, you hear. Don't be strangers."

"Thanks, Hone. I love what you've done here."

"Keep up the fight. We'll take back our land."

Hone turned and walked back over to the burning funeral pyre, greeting some of the men shovelling the ashes back into the fire. The acrid smell of burning wood and flesh stung Jack's nostrils. He turned and adjusted his pack.

The distant thump of the incoming chopper reminded Jack of home. He associated the sound with rescue. With hope. Now he hoped it would take them to the boys. He moved over to help Eric with Tony, using duct tape to secure him to the makeshift stretcher. The thumping grew louder as Jack picked up one end of the stretcher, straining his tired muscles to lift the worsening Tony.

The wash of the rotating blades blew soil and leaves into Jack's face as he struggled with the load. Moving into position, he waited for the chopper to descend.

The Maori warriors who had saved them gathered to wave them off. A couple ran over and helped load Tony into the chopper. Jack looked into the cockpit and was surprised to see the pilot had Asian features. He stood back, looking at the chopper. Come to think of it, he wasn't familiar with the model. He shrugged and leapt in, taking a vacant seat. Dee jumped in and went to the cockpit; Jack watched her speaking to the pilot and pointing towards their cabin. The pilot nodded, and Dee moved back to join Jack. Ben shook Hone's hand and jumped in beside his Renegades.

— 23 —

The engines whined as the chopper lifted, throwing more debris into the air. Jack looked down with pride as they flew away. He'd thought that all was lost on the mainland, but here, on top of this mountain, a determined group of people were holding out. They had refused to surrender to the Variant horde. So far, they were succeeding. Jack vowed to come back and fight with them. From what he'd seen, the love and empathy of the people there deserved everything he had. They had opened their homes to the Renegades. He wanted to stand with them and fight. Jack turned his head and looked east towards Mayor Island. His home. First, he had to secure his family.

Fourth phase: We fight back.

Jack looked down, searching for the red corrugated iron roof of his cabin. He spotted it nestled in the bush, tapped the pilot on his shoulder and pointed. He cupped his hand over the small microphone. "Can we land? I want to check it out."

The pilot shook his head. "Sorry. I can't spare the fuel. I can circle a couple more times."

Jack nodded and kept looking down, waiting. After a

couple more circles, the chopper banked away, heading south-east. Jack shook his head and looked down at the metal floor of the helicopter. Dee slid her hand into his.

Ben patted his shoulder. "Sorry, Jack."

Jack held his gaze for a while before turning to watch the bush-clad Kaimai mountains whizz by. Far below, small towns lay still and silent. Nothing moved on the roads. It was like someone had clicked the off-switch on a giant Scalextric set. The bush gave way to fields of grass and orchards. Jack watched as the chopper buzzed over the land then swept out over the Pacific Ocean where whitecaps broke on the surface as far as the eye could see.

A primal howl echoed around the cabin, jolting Jack out from his reflection. He turned his head. Tony arched his back, straining against his duct tape bonds. His eyes were yellow and reptile-looking. His mouth still looked human, but his teeth were now deformed and yellow. He howled again. Eric jumped onto him, holding his arms down. Tony spat and hissed. The smell of rotten fruit filled the cabin.

"Hold him down!" yelled Ben, joining Eric in sitting on Tony's legs.

Tony howled again and arched his back violently, throwing Eric and Ben off with ease. The duct tape snapped.

Jack pulled out his Glock, aiming for Tony, but Tony had spun into a crouch, his back to the door. The creature that was once Tony tilted his head, looking at the Renegades, assessing them. His yellow reptile eyes flickered, and his mouth deformed into a snarl.

"What the hell is going on back there?" shouted the pilot.

Ben reached up for the door handle. "Just keep flying. We'll sort this out."

He pulled on the door and air rushed in. The creature dug its claws into the frame and, with a snarl, leapt at Eric.

Eric rolled back and held it off with his feet. "Get him off me!"

Jack held out his Glock, trying to get a clear shot. There was a glint of metal and Dee lunged forwards, spearing the creature through the throat with her katana. Blackish blood gushed out, coating the floor.

Eric shoved the creature off him with a kick. It reached up, trying to stem the flow of blood pouring out of the wound. Eric backpedalled against the seats.

Jack watched, amazed, as Dee kicked the creature out the open door. It sailed through the air, tumbling and thrashing wildly, before it splashed into the waves below.

Ben slammed the door shut and the air in the cabin stilled.

Jack reached over and patted Eric's shoulder. Eric shoved his hand away. Jack left him to his grief and looked out to see the distinctive volcano shape of Mayor Island.

Smoke poured from the small settlement, and Jack's heart sank. He couldn't see much from this distance, but seeing the smoke rising from the island confirmed all Jack's fears. He glanced at the pilot, urging the flying tin can to go faster. He was eager to fight the bastards that had attacked their sanctuary.

Dee nudged his shoulder and pointed west towards Tauranga. A number of boats were making their way into the harbour. He felt the hairs on his neck bristle. This day was getting weirder. Jack reached down and laced his fingers in Dee's. He needed something loving and familiar to help settle his shattered nerves.

Jack turned his attention back to the island as the chopper flew closer. Sunlight pierced through the swirling smoke and mist, giving it a surreal, mystical look. Jack shook his head, trying to shake away his fears. He squeezed Dee's hand. He knew he had to persevere. They hadn't come this far, fighting the darkness, to fail now. He rubbed a hand over his carbine, eager to dish out punishment on the Variants.

— 24 —

Thick smoke hung in the air, swirling around like fog on a winter's day. Dee stared at the scene unfolding before her as the chopper jolted onto the ground.

The husk of a large boat, still burning, was moored to the jetty. Dozens of Variant bodies lay scattered around, their rotten fruit smell overpowering the stench of death that hung in the air.

Dee looked skyward and prayed that Boss and George had made it to the bunker and were safe. Crouching low, she crab-crawled away from the wash of the blades. Once the Renegades had exited, the engines hummed and the chopper lifted off, banking away out over the bay.

"Let's go find the boys," Jack said, nudging her arm.

She scanned the far side of the bay as they walked, looking for the villa they had made their home. She could see its white paint gleaming in the early afternoon sun, like a lighthouse guiding ships to safe passage. Dee hoped that this day would end well.

A man dressed in army fatigues walked briskly over and saluted Ben. Ben saluted back, and Dee heard them exchange some words. She wasn't listening though, as she could see bodies lying in rows on the boardwalk near the old hotel. She gasped and her hand flew to her mouth. Jack had spotted them too and stood with her, his head lowered. She estimated at least fifty to seventy bodies. Army personnel were picking their way between them, making notes on clipboards. Dee adjusted her rifle on her shoulder and made to walk over to them.

Ben saw her moving off and held up his hand. "Dee, Jack. Wait."

She turned and waited for him.

Ben looked grim. "They haven't found Boss and George amongst the dead. At this point they are MIA. Szabo here counts seventy-eight dead so far, many more wounded. Doc is attending now. Thankfully, most of the kids made it to the bunker. It looks like Haere and his men died protecting it."

Dee glanced over to the bodies. "Beth? Six? What about Max? Has anyone seen him?"

"Beth is MIA too. Six is wounded. He's in the hospital now. No one has seen Max either."

Ben looked over at Jack. "You guys go search the villa for the boys. I have to attend to things here, and sort Eric out. Stay frosty. We don't know how many Variants, if any, are still on the island. Keep me updated via two-way, especially if you see any of the bastards. Don't be heroes. We've already lost too many."

Dee pulled him into a hug. His long beard tickled her face.

"Be back by 1800 hours," he said.

She nodded and turned. Grabbing Jack's arm, she pulled him over towards the hospital.

They walked along the boardwalk, passing the bodies. Some had sheets covering them, others were lying open.

She recognised a few faces. Erin, whom she'd had dinner with a few times. Henry, who had a boy around George's age. She turned her head towards the sea, not wanting to see any more. The guilt threatened to overwhelm her. It gnawed at her, taunting, whispering. *You should've been here, you should've been protecting the children.*

The stench of blood mixed with disinfectant made Dee retch as she entered the hospital. Doc was furiously trying to save someone in one corner, with a couple of nurses handing him instruments. Bloody rags lay scattered around. All ten of the beds held someone. More people lay on the floor, blankets and pillows trying to keep them comfortable.

Dee spotted Six lying on the far bed, A woman with brown hair and wearing army fatigues was wiping his brow. She smiled as Dee and Jack approached.

"How's he doing?" asked Dee.

"It's touch and go. Doc stitched him up as best he could and pumped him full of antibiotics. It's a waiting game now."

"Can he talk?"

Six's eyes fluttered open and smiled. "Yeah, I can talk."

Dee sat down opposite the army woman, the bed creaking with her added weight. "Hey, Six. Still trying it with the ladies, eh?"

Six gave a weak laugh. He tried to raise himself, wincing with the effort. "Don't make me laugh. You'll pop my stitches." He pulled back the covers, revealing his heavily-bandaged side.

"What happened?" Jack said, helping him with the blankets.

"I got a call on the radio around 1830 hours. Flotilla approaching. Said they saw our lights. I reported it to the Sarg, and he okayed it. I watched out the window as they cruised in, this huge luxury boat leading. It had just tied up at the jetty when those Variant bastards swarmed out. It was chaos. They caught us totally by surprise." Six stopped and looked away, looking out the small window. He turned back, searching out Jack's eyes. Six lowered his voice. "I saw it…th…the big one."

Jack exchanged a look with Dee. "The big one?"

"The one you guys talk about, the Alpha. With three heads."

Dee scrunched the blanket in her hand. Could it be? She'd thought they'd left that horror behind.

"Are you sure, Six?" she queried.

"I think so, yeah. I couldn't see too many details, but I saw the heads. It was so chaotic, and there was this huge Variant leading them. Bullets just bounced off him."

Dee felt Jack's soothing touch on her hand. She looked up, meeting his gaze. Tears filled his eyes. Her worry for the boys amped up, and her heart pounded. She forced herself to take some deep breaths. She needed to remain strong and clear-headed. Nothing was achieved angry and foggy-brained.

Letting out a breath, Dee grasped Six's hand. "Boss? George? Beth?"

Six smiled, looking at Dee. "Boss, he's a hero, Dee. Both him and Beth were leading a bunch of kids to the bunker but they got cut off by a group of Variants. I'm sorry Dee. The last I saw of them, they were running up the hill towards your place."

"They could still be alive out there, hiding somewhere," Jack said, his voice rising.

"Thanks, Six. You get better, okay?" Dee pushed off the bed and stood next to Jack.

"When you find Boss, tell him he owes me a game?" Six grinned.

"All right, but I think you should tell him yourself," Dee said.

The shell-strewn path crunched under their feet as they strode up to the villa. The Walsh Villa, as Jack called it. Jack and his movies. She smiled at him, catching his eye. He would have likened the scene that confronted them as they approached the village to something out of *Saving Private Ryan*. All that smoke, bodies and chaos. The smell of burning flesh and cordite hanging in the air would stay with her for a long time, if not forever. In truth, the events of the last few weeks would be on a continual loop in her mind. She doubted if they would ever find peace, some sort of normal. It was only going to get worse as the Variants grew stronger and more desperate. She feared that this attack was the first of many.

Dee bounded up the steps and onto the verandah of the house they shared with their new family. A Variant body lay slumped on the deck, its brains blown out. She glanced to her right. Two more bodies lay on the bank. *Boss?*

She turned to Jack. "Looks like they put up a fight."

"He did well. Let's check in the house. You ready?"

Dee sighed. "Yeah."

Dee and Jack moved inside. The first thing she saw was the open gun cage, with a rifle and shotgun missing.

Half a dozen boxes of ammo were missing too. She glanced over to the coat rack where they kept their go-bags. She was thankful to see the pegs empty.

She ran into their rooms, calling, searching. Her calls became desperate.

"They're not here," Jack said. "Boss must have fled into the bush with George."

Dee slumped onto the bed and held her head in her hands. She took a couple of deep breaths, trying to control her growing anxiety. She felt the bed depress as Jack sat next to her.

"Shall we go?"

Dee sniffed and poked out her tongue. "God, I need a shower first. We reek."

Jack looked at her, confused. "A shower, now? Shouldn't we go look for the boys?"

"I want to go find them too, but I need to get some of this stench off me. We've been on the go for days, with little to no sleep. I just need this to centre myself."

"But what if we're too late? Wasting precious time on showers?"

"I'll be quick, I need this. I know it's weird. I want to find them as much as you."

She could see Jack searching her face, looking for a reason to deny her. He wouldn't come up with one. Dee knew she was right; they needed a breather. Showers had a bizarre way of washing away bad feelings as well as dirt.

"Okay, you win."

"Don't I always?" Dee punched him on the arm. "Go use the downstairs shower, I bag this one. Ten minutes?"

"Okay, see you in ten."

Dee watched him leave. Sighing, she started stripping

off her sweat and gore-soaked clothes. Just taking them off felt heavenly. She stepped under the warm water and washed away the sludge coating her hair and skin.

Dee met Jack in the kitchen. He handed her a protein bar before tearing the wrapping off his own. He raised an eyebrow at her. "Better?"

"So much. Let's go find the boys."

Jack nodded and shuffled into his pack. Dee held the door open for him. He was still looking for something.

"What are you doing?"

"My machete. I can't find it."

"The rusty one?"

"Yeah."

"Leave it. Let's go." She watched him look around one last time. "C'mon!"

"All right."

Dee looked up the bank into the bush behind the house. If she were Boss, where would she go? Did he flee in panic, or did he have a plan? There were a few broken branches directly to their left. She pointed. "It has to be them. C'mon."

Dee followed Jack as he bashed his way through the bush. Branches scratched at her face and tangled in her hair, but she didn't care. She could see indicators that Boss and George had fled this way: scuffs in the soil here, a broken branch there. Dislodged rocks everywhere.

Up and up they climbed. Dee grunted with every step and the sweat trickled down her back. Only her desire to see the boys again fuelled her exhausted body to climb farther up the hill. After forty minutes of exertion they broke out of the bush and stepped onto one of the tracks that circumnavigated the island. Dee glanced left and right, searching for more signs. She looked down at the path in front of her. Seeing footprints, Dee frowned. There was a different print, human-like, but not quite human. Variants, she realised.

"Jack, look!"

"Yeah. And look." Jack showed her some other impressions in the dirt.

Pawprints! Max! Her heart soared, and a new batch of adrenaline surged through her veins. Dee looked out to sea. It shone back turquoise, sunlight dancing off the breaking waves. She looked back up the mountain.

"What about those caves George found?"

"It's worth a try," Jack said. "Do you remember where they are?"

"What? Mister-I-never-get-lost can't remember?"

"I know. Shocking news." Jack laughed.

"This way, Doofus."

Dee pushed past him and broke into a run. She could hear Jack's boots thudding on the ground as he caught up and fell in step beside her. Dee rounded a corner and saw the cave opening ahead. She ran up to it and ducked inside.

"Look! Good old Boss." Jack stood in the entrance holding up his rusty red-handled machete.

Dee couldn't help but smile. Good old Boss indeed. Smart kid, leaving them a huge clue as to his path. She reached into her bag, grabbed her torch and clicked it on, illuminating the lava tube cave twisting away. She was just about to head into the cave when she caught a whiff of rotten fruit.

Jack stopped, clearly smelling it too. He raised his rifle

and lowered his voice. "You smell that, right?"

"We should radio Ben," Dee cautioned.

"Let's check out that lake first. Carefully." Jack smiled. "Give him some good news."

After twenty minutes of navigating their way through the many caves, Dee stared across the crater lake to the small island on the far side, a lone pohutakawa tree standing sentry over it. She would have admired the scene if it wasn't for her growing fear for the boys' safety. A screech sounded moments before movement to her left flicked into her peripheral vision. Half a dozen Variants scampered down the crater walls, howling as they ran.

We should have radioed Ben.

Dee let out an angry scream and, bringing up her rifle, let loose with a barrage of hot-leaded death. She quickly dropped two. Jack shot another one. Their bodies splashed into the lake. The other three dropped onto the sandy beach in front of them and charged in a sudden burst of speed. Dee squeezed off another burst, hitting one in the neck. Black gunk sprayed out. It stumbled and rolled before lying still. Jack hit the other one in the head with a quick burst from his AR-15.

The last Variant leapt off the ground, claws extended, howling as it flew through the air. Dee yelled a warning to Jack. He pivoted, bringing his rifle up in front of him, which saved him from the gnashing mouth of the Variant. It dug its claws into his legs instead and Jack screamed in agony.

Dee dropped her rifle onto the sand and drew her Katana. All the pent-up anger she had about what the world had become, and these man-made abominations,

196

coursed through her veins. Screaming, she ran forwards and swung her blade like a skilled assassin. Bringing it up in an arc, she sliced the creature's head off with one clean cut. It spun away and landed with a thump on the obsidian-laced beach, a snarl forever etched on its face.

She stared at the decapitated head. These creatures disgusted her. The thought of what they could have done to the boys pained her. She wanted to make a statement. Memories of the Variants tied up and decomposing on the trees flashed through her mind. Yes. A statement. Dee glanced around the lake and smiled.

She stalked over to the head and speared it with tip of her katana. Then she walked over to an old fence post and slammed it down on top, spiking it.

There's your statement!

Dee returned to Jack and helped him to his feet. "You okay, baby?"

"Bloody Variants. Thank you."

Dee nodded and looked out to the island. "I'm going to check the island. Wait here."

"Okay, be careful. I'll radio Ben. Let him know we found Variants."

Dee swam the last few strokes to the island and pulled herself up, pricking herself on the sharp obsidian as she did so. There were a couple of Variant bodies, but no sign of the boys. Then a glint caught her eye. She knelt down on the ground and found a makeshift prosthetic leg. She smiled. *Boss! Clever boy.*

"Jack! Look!" She held up the leg.

Jack waved and beckoned her to come back. Within moments she was back and drying herself off with a small hiking towel from her pack.

"What are you thinking?" Jack asked, rolling the prosthetic over in his hand.

"I think they've been taken. It's the only logical answer." Dee said.

"You don't think the Trophy King took them, do you?" Jack said, swallowing a sob.

Dee nestled her head into his shoulder and let the tears flow. Her head swam at the thought of Boss and George being taken away to be consumed, or worse. She had seen inside one of those nests. Seen what they did to people. Once was enough.

Composing herself, Dee pulled away. She stared at the island. A barely audible whimper reached her ears. She pricked her ears, straining. There! Another whimper, clearer this time. She scanned the island, looking for the source. There was a small patch of black and white fur amongst the flax bushes. Max! *How did I miss him?*

Dee ran back into the water and once again was splashing to the island.

— 25 —

Where are the bodies? Maggie scanned the area around the 4x4. Three of its doors stood open, dark pools of blood stained the cobblestones and empty shell casings lay scattered around. But no bodies. Maggie paused and breathed, searching for the tell-tale rotten fruit smell. She could detect faint decomposing garbage and the salty air of the ocean, but no Variants. She flicked her eyes up to the rooftops. The creatures loved to jump down from above. She had learnt that the hard way.

Maggie, like any veteran, reported for duty to the US Embassy in Wellington after they were recalled. She helped ferry American citizens to chartered planes flying home. The Commander promised that all personnel would be evacuated by the end of the week. She was then ordered to accompany a Marine platoon to rescue an official who had injured himself on a hike. Chopper extraction was out due to poor weather, so she and the Marines hiked into the Tongariro National Park. Into the mist, and back into hell. Variants swarmed over them in the car park, and they barely made it out with their lives.

Entering the town of Turangi, their rescue mission went south. Hordes of Variants harried them, attacking the APV. Running low on fuel, they pulled into a gas station. It all looked clear. Then a lone Variant jumped down onto the Staff Sergeant, tearing out his throat. It severely injured two others before they managed to kill it.

Maggie took over the driving from then. After the weather cleared, she radioed for extraction. Variants attacked them constantly, so to avoid the towns, Maggie started to take back roads, hoping to avoid any further entanglements. The chopper called in the new LZ.

Ten miles out, the injured soldiers succumbed to the virus, turning into Variants, they attacked the remaining platoon. In the confusion Maggie slid off the road, damaging the APV. Now three remained of the original twelve. Maggie, the official, and some fresh-faced kid from Nebraska. On they ran, through the thick tussock grass of the volcanic plateau. With five miles to go, Maggie's legs were burning: carrying the injured official was taking its toll. She sent the kid up ahead to scout since, from the looks of his skinny frame, he wouldn't be able to take the load. Gritting her teeth, Maggie shifted the official and trudged on.

They saw the army base in the distance, with choppers buzzing in and out. She tried the radio again, but only received static. She was relieved when the guardhouse came into view and she sent the kid up ahead for help.

She heard screams and she watched, horrified, as the kid turned and ran. Two Variants chased him down and tore him apart. She was frozen with indecision. Should she run? She was exhausted, and the official was useless. The Variants charged them. Maggie brought up her M4, letting off a burst. She hit one in the torso, causing it to tumble, knocking the other one down. She flicked the selector to auto and unleashed a barrage of metal death, unloading a full magazine into the still-advancing beasts. Even with their chests full of holes, black flesh torn off, they still crawled at her. Maggie *clicked a new magazine and, flicking her selector back to semi, she shot both of them in the head. Finally, they lay still.*

Maggie left the official in the guardhouse and went looking for either a radio or a vehicle to get them the hell out of Dodge. Bloodcurdling shrieks filled the air as Variants leapt off the rooftops, swarming the remaining soldiers on the base. Maggie fired, taking as many of the monsters down as she could. Soldier after soldier fell. A jeep picked her and the official up, and they fled into the wilderness surrounding the base. Maggie looked west to the mountains, filled with guilt at their escape. She scanned the skies, looking for the chopper that never arrived.

After that, the Variants hunted her relentlessly. Maggie survived by sheer determination. Variants ambushed them on a bridge. Maggie killed as many as she could, but there were simply too many. The injured official was no use. Variants swarmed over them. In desperation, Maggie launched herself and the official off the bridge. They managed to cling to a floating log, shivering in the freezing water. Surprise turned to hope when the Variants stayed out of the water. The injured official died during the night from what Maggie suspected was hypothermia. Wary that she would follow the same fate, Maggie left the relative safety of the river and fled into the chaos. Alone, and far from home.

Maggie pivoted a full 360, searching the rooftops, wishing for the hundredth time she still had that M4. Nothing was wrong with the AR-15 she held, apart from the fact that the magazine only held seven bullets. Alice had explained it was to do with the firearm laws of New Zealand. Maggie had adapted a few magazines to take more, but not enough.

With no sign of Variants, she quickly shut the vehicle doors and turned the ignition. She said a silent prayer as the engine roared to life. Doing a three-point turn away from the fountain, she glanced back at the disappearing harbour with its boats — boats that could take her home. Home on the range, to the big open skies of Texas. Home to family. Sighing, she concentrated on navigating her way through the inner-city streets of Tauranga. Earlier, she'd been too busy firing at their attackers to take notice of their route. She quickly worked out that, like most cities, the streets were laid out in a grid. After a few turns, she found the main road and gunned the engine, urging more speed out of the 4x4. Sunlight reflected off several windshields a mile or so up the road. Hurrying to catch up, she slid into the back position of the convoy, taking up the tail-end Charlie spot. A radio squawked to life.

Maggie shuddered involuntarily.

"Who the hell is that at the back?"

She scrambled around, one hand on the wheel, the other searching for the radio.

"Answer me, back vehicle."

Lifting up the centre console, she found the black radio. *What the hell was that guy's name?* Thinking quickly, she pressed the talk button. Coughing and hacking, Maggie made her voice as deep as possible. "It's Terry."

"Terry? From the farm?"

Keeping up her coughing, Maggie prayed it would disguise her American accent. "Yeah."

"Terry, you sound awful. Where the hell have you been?"

"I stopped for a piss, then I got lost. Saw you guys drive past."

"Okay. Did you catch the escapees?"

"Yup, shot the bitch. Kids are en route back to the farm."

"About bloody time. I still don't know how you idiots let some women escape with a bunch of kids. Follow us to the highway. I'm coming down to the farm tomorrow to sort your mess out. Over."

"Okay. Copy."

Maggie let out a breath and, tucking the radio beside her, turned the volume up so she could keep up with any chatter.

She followed the convoy as the road wound up the river valley and climbed its way up into the foothills, heading back to the Kaimai mountains. Maggie counted twelve vehicles, mainly 4x4s like hers and a couple of white cargo vans. The flatbed truck on which the huge Variant with his grotesque trophy heads rode followed two lead vehicles. It reminded Maggie of a documentary she'd once seen on wolves. A couple of strong wolves led the pack through the snow, with the rest of them following.

The Alpha Variant had positioned himself behind two 4x4s, each with five of the creatures clinging to the roof racks. Even from this distance, she could see that they were bigger than most Variants. Maggie caught glimpses of red and the shadows of human collaborators through the windows.

As they climbed higher up into the clouds enveloping the bush-clad peaks, Maggie stole a few glances at the scenery. It was so green and lush. Tall forests of beech and podocarps hugged the rugged hills. She could understand why they had chosen to film *Lord of the Rings* here. It was perfect. Sweeping fields of grass curved away, and farm buildings dotted the landscape. Farms that had once held sheep and cattle, farms that had once hummed with life. Maggie thanked God that Izzy was safe with Him and not living through this nightmare. She missed her princess every day. Thoughts of her daughter motivated her to continue fighting. Maggie could feel her looking down from heaven, protecting her. She smiled. She really did have a guardian angel watching her.

Good. I need all the help I can get for this crazy mission.

Doubts nagged at her with every mile. Was she doing the right thing? Would Alice get Becs, Leela and the other kids to the safety of Mayor Island? Maggie knew she couldn't leave that boy Alice knew to the horrible fate that awaited him. What was his name? Bruce? Brian? Something like that. She knew she had to find out where these kids were being taken. If she died saving them, then at least she would know she had died trying. She could be at peace, and finally be with Izzy and God.

Maggie brushed away her doubts and thoughts as the road finally breached the crest of the peak and began its descent. She gasped at the view. A patchwork of fields lay spread out like a giant quilt, stretching away to the west, to the spine of the green mountains that ringed the plains. She grinned at the sight. Even during the apocalypse, nature had a way of taking hold of her and capturing the moment. It forced its beauty into her memory, to be thought of and appreciated at some future time. She drove on, her trepidation growing.

The convoy slowed, edging its way between a knot of cars that had tangled with a truck. The truck had jack-knifed and snagged itself on a fence. Burned out husks of cars had been pushed aside, allowing enough room for the convoy to pass. The truck carrying the Alpha passed through the gap, scraping against the crashed lorry. The shriek of metal on metal rang in Maggie's ears, making her shudder. Another higher-pitched shriek echoed out and Maggie watched, mesmerised, as a black wave of Variants poured out from behind the abandoned cars, attacking the convoy.

Maggie slammed on the brakes, bringing her 4x4 to a skidding stop. She glanced in the rear-view mirror, checking her six for an escape. More Variants poured out from the fields to attack the convoy, cutting off that option.

Her radio blared to life. "Stay down!"

Chaos erupted as the Alpha bellowed, a terrifying deep howl that shook her bones as it reverberated up through the metal floor of her vehicle. The Alpha jumped off the truck. The Variants from the two lead 4x4s sprang into action. Five of them jumped up onto the flatbed truck, forming a semicircle around the two kids slumped against the cab. The other five grouped around the Alpha, shrieking and howling.

Maggie locked her doors and grabbed her rifle. The attacking Variants ignored her and the others in red coveralls. Instead, they attacked the convoy Variants. Claws drawn and sucker mouths smacking, the two rival groups smashed into each other. They tore hunks out of flesh and snapped limbs. Maggie watched, horrified, as the huge Alpha waded through the melee, plucking Variants off the ground and snapping their necks with flicks of its huge claws. It speared one creature with a claw and bit off its head with a single snap of its mighty jaws. New howls joined the racket. She turned her head and watched as a new horde joined the battle to fight alongside the Alpha and its Variants. Tearing, snapping, clawing. As the Variants continued to fight each other, there was no mercy given, no quarter. This was a fight to the death. A no-prisoners massacre.

The Alpha and the new arrivals made short work of the attackers. Maggie watched as some of the attacking Variants were chased down and disposed of. With a final huge bellow, the convoy Variants jumped back onto their rides and the convoy started to move again, heading west. Maggie shook her head. It was as if nothing had happened. She pulled her cap down tighter over her head and prayed her disguise would last a while longer. As she crept her 4x4 through the gap, she could see the victorious Variants picking up the bodies of the dead and lumbering away across the fields.

Maggie held up a shaking hand. She had faced the Taliban in Afghanistan and insurgents in Iraq, but seeing the Variants battle each other had shaken her to the core. She gripped the steering wheel, willing herself to stay strong. She had some kids to rescue.

She glanced up to heaven. *Look out for me, Princess. Mom has to fight a demon.*

— 26 —

Jack helped Dee from the lake. Pain from his fresh wounds shot up his spine. He took the whimpering Max from Dee and laid him on sand. Max's eyes met his. He managed a small wag of his tail and licked Jack's hand. Gently, he checked over their adopted dog. He had no cuts or tears on his skin. When Jack pressed his hand against Max's ribs, the dog let out an anguished howl. Jack couldn't help his tears. As an animal-lover, seeing any injured animal pained him. Especially a loved pet. He leant down and kissed the dog on his head.

"All right buddy, we'll get you home. Hang in there."

He looked up at Dee. She was rubbing herself dry again. She paused, smiling at him, watching. He always admired how she found the time to smile at him despite everything that was going on. He knew she was just as concerned about the boys as he was. Six had told them about the Trophy King being on the island, and with what he and Dee had discovered, he was in no doubt now: this attack had been planned.

Could they even think like that?

Like the others, he'd thought they'd had left that beast

behind on top of that mountain. With this attack, it seemed to Jack that this Alpha not only had retained its human intelligence, but used it to collaborate with humans, and had come for them to settle a score. Memories of the nest he and George had escaped from and the horrors that lay within came flooding back. Jack swallowed down the lump forming in his throat. Not only did he feel guilty for not being on the island to help defend against the attack, he also felt some responsibility for it. His escape and his actions had caused the Alpha to purposely track them down to mete out his revenge.

Dee reached out, grabbing his arm. "Hey, come back to me, babe."

"Sorry, I just feel guilty. What if this is our fault? What if the Trophy King came here for us?"

"I know. I feel it too." Dee knelt with him beside Max and kissed the dog's cheek. "We're going after him, right?"

"Remember in *Fellowship of the Ring* when Aragorn, Gimli and Legolas went after Merry and Pippin?"

"Of course. We've watched that movie so many times!" she said, punching his arm.

"Dee, we're going after them, because the thought of the boys being in that place cuts into my soul. I know what's there. I couldn't go on knowing that and not doing anything about it."

Dee shouldered her pack and checked her rifle before holding it ready.

"Well, come on then. Pack light, for we travel far and swift."

Jack grinned at her. Standing, he cradled Max into his arms. With a last look at the crater lake, he followed his wife's striding figure back into the caves.

***

Jack's arms burned with the exertion of holding the injured Max. He paused and shifted the weight of his load, attempting to relieve some of the pressure. Dee was scanning ahead, looking for other Variants.

Where there is one, there are many.

He had radioed Ben with the news of what they had discovered. Ben had relayed the information that patrols had encountered several groups of the beasts, and warned them to stay vigilant. They stopped several times to rest, the last few days of madness finally catching up with them. After forty-five minutes, they made it back to the village. The sun was beginning to sink lower in the sky, bathing the small settlement in an orange glow. Activity buzzed all around them as they made their way to the old hotel. Several soldiers wearing chemical suits and masks were stacking dead Variants into piles, ready to be incinerated.

Entering the FOB, he gently laid Max on his bed near the door. Jack scooped out a few biscuits and scratched the dog's ears. He licked Jack's hand and wagged his tail in appreciation.

Jack scanned the room. Ben was standing at the main table, deep in discussion with a couple of sergeants. Spotting Jack and Dee, he waved them over.

As Jack approached, he could see a large map of the island spread out on the table. Red circles were drawn over it, one of which circled the lake. It was going to take them a while to flush out the remaining Variants, and with so many caves on the island, perhaps never. Ben gave one of the sergeants an order to set up a perimeter with rotating patrols before looking over Jack and Dee, shaking his head.

"You two have to be the luckiest sons of bitches I've ever met."

Jack glanced at Dee. "Why?"

"How many Variants were in that crater?"

"Five or six?"

"Five or six. Yet here you are, still living and breathing."

Ben glanced down at Jack's wounds, which were seeping blood. "Jack, go and see Doc after we've finished here. I'm going to be tied up here most of the night. I want you two to get some sleep." He paused, looking at them in turn. His voice softened. "Look, I know you're worried about the boys, and you have every right to be. If what you say about the Alpha is true, I know you want to go charging off after them. But you guys need rest. You look like shit. Get some sleep. We'll plan a search and rescue in the morning. I'm posting a couple of guards at the villa."

Jack rubbed the back of his neck, feeling the wispy hair with the tips of his fingers. "We think he's taken them back to the dam."

"You don't know that for sure, Jack. He could've moved his nest somewhere else."

"Maybe Ben, maybe. I just know he has. Like that friggin' dam has some weird cosmic meaning."

"Get some food and some rest. We'll sort it out in the morning."

Dee gave Ben a squeeze. "Thanks, Ben. See you in the morning."

Jack smiled as she hugged the grizzled old soldier.

A private Jack didn't know ran out of the radio room. "Sir, I received a radio call. We have a boat coming. She says she has children on board."

"Thank you, Private. Radio back to approach slowly to the south dock."

Ben turned to one of the sergeants. "Tell your men to lock and load. We don't want to get caught out again."

The man turned and left.

"Jack, go and get patched up. That's an order. Dee, if they do have kids on board, they will respond better to a friendly face. I need you with me," Ben said.

Jack embraced Dee and headed to the infirmary, stopping only to scratch Max behind the ears. He was pleased to see the dog had eaten all his food.

Dee walked along the boardwalk, struggling to match Ben's long strides as they made their way down to the smaller of the two jetties. A white and blue boat was slowly chugging its way towards them. Armed soldiers lined the jetty; Dee heard the synchronised sound as they clicked their rifles off safety.

The boat nudged the jetty. One of the soldiers jumped on board and tied the painter to the bollard. He lashed it tight before standing back, rifle raised and ready. Dee caught a glimpse of blonde hair in the wheelhouse. The door to the cabin creaked open. The soldiers on that side of the boat tracked it opening. A blonde-haired figure emerged from the cabin.

Dee's heart leapt in her chest as she recognised the

woman. "Don't shoot! I know her."

The woman turned towards Dee. Her mouth dropped open. "Dee?"

"Alice!" Dee leapt onto the boat and wrapped Alice in a hug. "I can't believe it! You're alive. What about Matt? Austin?"

Alice shook her head, tears falling freely down her cheeks. "Dee, I saw Boss. Some big ugly Variant had him."

"What? Really? Where?"

"Back in Tauranga. Maggie…she…she went after them."

"Maggie? Who's Maggie?"

"She helped us escape the camp. Rescued the kids." Alice paused and pointed to the cabin. "Becs, Leela. Kids, you can come out now."

A red-haired girl exited the cabin first with a small blonde girl in tow. More children followed them out one by one. Dee counted six all together. The kids' eyes went wide at the sight of the soldiers and their guns.

Ben turned and waved them away. He shook Alice's hand. "I'm Captain Johns."

"Alice Quinn."

"Ben, she has intel on Boss. She saw them in Tauranga. The Trophy King had him. I suspect George too," Dee said. "Alice, was there a red-haired boy?"

"Yeah, there was."

Dee looked down at her feet, thinking, trying to gather in her racing mind. Alice had just confirmed her and Jack's worst fears. That was it. Tomorrow she was going to end this.

"We have to go after them, Ben. I'm not taking no for

an answer. I'll take this bloody boat and do it myself if I have to."

"Okay, Dee. I believe you and I agree. Get this lot up to the villa. I'll tie up some things down here then join you. It sounds like we have a lot to plan."

"Thanks, Ben."

Dee hugged Alice again. She couldn't believe it. Alice here, on this island? Somehow, against all the odds, she was seeing her friend again. She had hoped they'd made it to Alice's family's sheep station, but with the horrors she, Alice and her friends had faced, barely escaping with their lives both times, her hopes had faded.

Alice grasped the little blonde girl's hand and helped her off the boat and onto the jetty.

Dee turned and helped the red-haired girl. "I'm Dee, what's your name?"

"Rebecca. But everyone calls me Becs."

"Well, Becs, it's nice to meet you. You hungry?"

"You have food?"

"We sure do. C'mon."

Dee led them off the jetty and up the path towards the villa. The kids followed, with Alice bringing up the rear. The children looked wide-eyed at all the soldiers walking around, guns slung over their shoulders.

Reaching the old house, she ushered them into the kitchen and pointed to the table. A few of the kids asked for the toilet. After Dee showed them where it was, she returned to the kitchen. She never would've thought she'd be preparing a meal for six hungry children. It was only after the end of the world and meeting Boss and George that she'd started to warm to kids. Seeing the children sitting at the table gave her a motherly glow. She subconsciously rubbed her belly. Maybe she and Jack still had time for children.

The kitchen door banged open and Jack walked in, legs bandaged around his thighs. Dee smiled at him as he took in the scene. Max padded in behind him and gingerly sat down on his bed next to the fire. Alice stood up from the table as Jack walked over.

Dee kissed him on the cheek, searching out his blue eyes. "You good?"

"Yeah. Just a flesh wound."

Dee elbowed him in the ribs. "'Tis but a scratch," she replied.

Smiling, Jack glanced over her shoulder at the dining room. "What's all this?"

She turned away from the stove. "Alice. Jack. Jack. Alice."

Alice pushed back her chair and moved around the kitchen to meet him. She reached out and hugged him. "*The* Jack?"

"Yes. *The* Jack."

He looked between the two women. "Okay? What's going on?"

Dee turned to him. "Alice hid with me down in the basement back in the beginning with the others and Boss. Jack, she saw Boss, George and the Trophy King in Tauranga."

"When?"

"Earlier today."

Jack pursed his lips. He rubbed a hand through his hair and let out a sigh. "That must have been those boats we saw from the chopper. We're definitely going after them tomorrow. I don't care what Ben says."

"He's already agreed. Ben's coming up later to talk it through."

"Okay, that's good. What's for dinner?"

"Come and help and you'll find out."

Dee turned back to her cooking, busying herself with the task. Thoughts of what that abomination was doing to her boys frightened the hell out of her. Jack started cutting up some vegetables and she smiled at him, grateful for his silent encouragement. She knew that he was just as keen to get them back. Dee was wrung out. In the last twenty-four hours she had found out her mother was probably alive and an animal geneticist, she had hiked up a mountain to escape a Variant horde, and to top it all off, the Alpha they called the Trophy King had attacked their haven and captured her boys.

She stared down at the bubbling cheese sauce. It was time to end this.

— 27 —

The star cluster known as Pleiades hung low in the early morning sky. James smiled at the sight. The festival of Matariki, the Maori New Year, was tonight, his favourite time of the year. It was an occasion to remember those lost in the past year, among other things. The civilian population on the island had insisted they celebrate it. He was happy to oblige, and thought it would be a good way to welcome the new arrivals from Indonesia.

He turned, looking over the campground he had sequestered for the refugees. The medical staff were bustling around in preparation. He had insisted that everyone be tested for the Hemorrhage Virus and other common diseases, as well as malnutrition, before being placed in the temporary housing. His gaze drifted out to the bay. HMNZS *Te Mana* had arrived last night to assist. Seeing the ship settled his nerves somewhat. So far, Captain Koto had kept his word that they were merely seeking refuge. James was a cautious man, so he had ordered his men to stay alert and vigilant. Satisfied with the preparations, he jumped in the waiting jeep and headed back to the FOB. He had a helicopter pilot to discipline.

James looked over the man standing to attention in front of him. He kept his face clear of emotion and stared into the man's eyes. He was struggling to keep his seething anger in check. The pilot had dark hair and brown eyes. He carried a little weight around his middle, as though all the sitting down in the cockpit had forced his fat to one central location.

"You know what, Evans? I don't even want you to explain to me why you abandoned Team Renegade. Because of you, the one scientist left alive in New Zealand who had any chance of finding a cure to this mess is dead. Gunner Tony Jones is dead. Captain Johns and the rest of his team are lucky to be alive, no thanks to you. I'm stripping you of your wings. You have six months of sentry duty. I look forward to Captain Johns catching up with you."

James waved him away, dismissing him. He was still seething at the pilot's cowardice when there was a knock at his door. Badminton entered.

"Morning, Sir. The Indonesian pilot's report," he said, handing James a manila folder.

"Thank you, Badminton," James said, dismissing him.

James flicked through the pages in front of him. Nothing stood out in particular, and everything confirmed what Johns had reported. He rubbed the back of his neck, trying to knead out the stiff muscles. His eyes glanced at the Vodka bottle tucked away on his bookshelf, whispering to him to take a sip. But he looked back down at the report, reading about the fortified mountain top. Johns had reported it too. He couldn't help but smile to himself at the thought of an old-fashioned Pa holding out against the Variant hordes. Pride surged in his heart for the resilience of his people. Against all the odds, there were still people alive out there. New hope for his family in the East Cape rose to the forefront of his mind. The Renegades had proven themselves out in the field.

He contemplated sending them on a reconnaissance mission to search for more survivors holding out like Hone and his people after Mayor Island was sorted. Perhaps he could send them to search for Major Hinds. Thinking of the attack, he sighed and swivelled around to the old typewriter. The Brigadier wanted his report.

When he had finished writing, James walked down to the rugby ground in the town. He was keen to see the Matariki preparations for himself. The civilians had been cautious at first after being informed of the refugees. Heated arguments had broken out about whether they should let them in. Half wanted to welcome the refugees, the other half wanted to send them on their way. James had informed them of his orders. Thankfully, humanity won the day.

He reached the rugby ground and glanced around. Several marquees had been set up with long tables. Lights had been strung up, linking the tents and winding their way up the trees at both ends. Diesel generators sat at the far end. People were gathered around a huge burning open pit, where a hangi was being prepared. Piles of food wrapped in aluminium foil sat waiting for the fire to die down. Once the fire had heated the rocks enough, the rocks would be extracted and all the wood removed. The rocks would then be placed back in the hole and hit with wet sacks to create steam. Then the food would be placed in old shopping trolleys and lowered into the pits, the heated rocks piled around them, and the wet sacks added before the earth was piled back on top, forming a mound. Three hours later, the feast would be ready.

James looked up to the sky, hoping the gathering clouds stayed away.

"Colonel!"

James turned to the source of the voice. Captain Koto strode towards him, smiling as he looked around. The two men shook hands. "Ah Captain. Thank you for helping us out with your helicopter."

"You're the most welcome, Colonel. Thank you for all this." Koto gestured with an arm, waving at all the activity. "It's like Thanksgiving, yes? I'm happy to try the hangi."

James smiled at him. "Thanksgiving? Close. We call it Matariki, Captain."

"Please, call me Arif. Matariki?"

"Yes Arif, Matariki. Our new year." James pointed to the north east. "Matariki means 'Eyes of God'. When the stars rise, we come together to remember those who we lost in the past year. So many this year. Crops have been harvested and seafood collected. Tonight we will enjoy the feast and welcome you to New Zealand. Some people will sing and dance."

Arif turned back to James. "We've lost so many people. It seems strange to have a feast. But we must carry on, must we not? So thank you, Colonel." Arif smiled. "I'm just glad it's not Ramadan yet, so my people can enjoy your hospitality."

James didn't reply; he was lost in thought. Thinking of his time in Iraq. Thinking of all the mates he had lost, both now and before the Variant scourge. Matariki had arrived at a perfect time. Everyone needed a night off. But they had to stay vigilant. You never knew what was lurking in the shadows these days.

The two men stood side by side for some time, lost in their separate thoughts as the preparations continued. James couldn't help but wonder if they were doing the right thing. Should they be enjoying festivities while others suffered at the claws of the Variants? He had yet to think of a way to defeat these monsters. He hoped that whatever Dr Katherine Yokoyama had discovered would help turn the tide. The Americans and the British were busy fighting all manner of horrors, if the reports filtering in were to be believed. New Zealand, like before, had escaped those monstrosities. Sitting out here in the deep South Pacific, New Zealand had developed unique and strange fauna. But the Variants haunting the land were no different. Reports had told him that most Variants had broken off into packs with an Alpha leading, that they continuously fought amongst themselves, fighting over the last scraps of food. How long before they turned their attention to the islands which the last dregs of Kiwis now called home?

He shivered, thinking of Mayor Island. The Alpha Captain Johns called the Trophy King had attacked the island with a band of human collaborators. James reached out and clasped Captain Koto's hand, shaking it. "Please excuse me, Arif. I have duties to attend to."

"Thank you, Colonel. I'll see you tonight."

James nodded and turned. He signalled to his driver to

bring the jeep around. As he made his way across the rugby ground, he murmured his greetings to those working. He was happy for the boost in morale the festivities would provide, but he had a war to plan.

— 28 —

Dawn broke over Mayor Island, bathing it in pinks and purples. Jack lay snuggled against Dee, the covers pulled tight against his chin as he battled to keep out the early morning chill. He stared out the window, watching as the sunlight changed the colour of the ocean.

He loved the early morning, that half an hour before the world really woke up. He used the time to reflect, meditate in a sense, to get his thoughts in order and prepare for the day. Most of the time Jack had movies buzzing around in his head on a loop. Scenes played themselves out, sometimes mashed up like some crossover movie.

He concentrated on his breathing; he inhaled deeply and let each breath out slowly. It was a way to centre himself. After leaving school, he had gone straight into an electrician's apprenticeship. He had worked long hours, six, sometimes seven, days a week, eventually running his own business. At thirty, Jack had felt burnt out. On a whim, he had decided on a trip to Thailand. When he got there, he'd read a pamphlet in a backpacker's advertising a week-long retreat at a Thai Buddhist monastery. Sceptical at first, Jack had been pleasantly surprised. There he had learnt to calm his racing mind using different techniques. Something he was thankful for now, because today his mind was racing like an F1 car. Serious doubts ate away at him. He wasn't a soldier, so how were he and the others going to rescue the boys? He knew the horrors of the meat locker they were most likely in. Tears welled up, threatening to spill over. He wriggled closer to Dee, enjoying the feel of her skin on his, her warmth. He breathed deep, catching the sweet scent of her shampoo.

Dee stirred against him and opened her eyes. "Hey."

"Hey."

"How long have you been awake?"

"Not long. An hour or so."

"Okay." Dee searched for his hand under the covers. Finding it, she squeezed it tight in hers. Jack squeezed back and kissed her, savouring the feel of her lips. He couldn't get the feeling out of his head that today was going to be his last. He wanted to go and bring the boys back home, but a part of him wanted to stay under the covers with Dee. Make love to Dee. Forget the world for a while. Just be them again.

"Can I ask you something, Dee?"

"Yeah."

"When you came after me, how did you cope with the hopelessness of it?"

Dee poked him in the ribs. "You've been thinking, haven't you?"

"Yeah, I know. I'm just worried that whatever we do won't be enough. We're not soldiers. Up until a couple of weeks ago, we'd hardly fired a weapon. What if we're too late?"

Dee brought her arms up and cradled his head in her hands. "When there was a chance you were in Karapiro, I had to find out. I honestly didn't think I'd make it out of there, but I had to know. The thought of you being eaten by those monsters chilled me to my core. I figured that if I found you dead, then at least I could die knowing. Whatever the outcome, we would be at peace together. I feel the same now. I'm not letting that Trophy King add the boys to his collection. Alice said the prison camp she was in gave children to the Variants. I'm going to help the children too, even if it means dying in the process."

"I'm so glad you did come. I want you to know that I bless the day that I met you. Up on top of that waterfall. I fell in love with you that day. You saved me, Dee, saved me from a life of loneliness and gave me hope."

"You too. I was lost to the crazy world and then you come along. Yes, you gave me hope too. A new hope." She grinned as she said the last part.

Jack let out laugh. "You are now officially part of the tribe. The movie geek tribe." He snuggled back into her, holding her tight. The doubts in his mind lingered, but Dee's words had given him the courage to rise. She had given him the courage to take up arms and fight the monsters that had infected the beautiful land that was his home.

We're coming for you, Trophy King. Enjoy your rest, for today will be your last.

Jack spent a couple of hours preparing his gear for the battle. He packed his green hiking pack, stuffing in extra food and ammo. He cleaned his AR-15 and Glock like Ben had taught him. He sharpened his rusty red-handled machete before securing it to the side of his pack.

Alice had the rescued children up and fed. The kids raced around outside on the small lawn. Jack marvelled at how quickly the kids had adapted and accepted the new situation. Twenty-four hours ago, they had been held captive, awaiting a horrific fate.

Jack changed the batteries on his and Dee's two-ways, checking they had full power. He glanced at the clock. Ben wanted them in the war room at 08:00. He walked over to the kitchen and flicked on the kettle. He wanted to enjoy a cup of tea with Dee before heading out into the unknown. His mind drifted, thinking of his grandfather fighting on D-Day in 1944. Had he drunk his tea, thinking that it could be his last? He and all those thousands of men had risen that day knowing full well that it could be their last. They went off to war so others could live on in peace, free of fascism and tyranny.

Jack let out a breath, calming himself. *Today is our D-Day.*

The village was well awake as Jack and Dee walked down the path, heading for the FOB. Signs of the battle were still evident, but everyone had pitched in, trying to get the town back to normal. He nodded a greeting to the two guards posted at the old hotel entrance.

They stopped outside the war room and knocked. Jack paused to look around the harbour. At the far end of the bay, three helicopters sat idle on the concrete. Army personnel were loading supplies and refuelling them.

"Enter," came Ben's muffled voice.

Ben and two sergeants stood at the large table, a couple of maps spread out in front of them. "Ah. Jack, Dee. Good morning."

Jack hesitated, unsure whether to salute or not. Dee walked over and hugged Ben, saving him from his indecision. "Morning, Captain."

"Jack. Dee. This is sergeants Hollis and Bryant. They're going to assist us on this mission."

Jack shook their hands, noting their strong grips. They looked serious army. He was glad for their help. They were going to need all the support they could get today.

Ben looked each of them in the eye. He pointed down at the map in front of him.

"All right. This is what we have. We have three choppers and thirteen soldiers. Including us. We need to come up with a distraction so we can enter that hell-hole and extract the boys and any other civvies alive. I'm going to plant explosives and, once we are clear, blow that meat locker to hell."

Jack grinned. Yes. A big kaboom would do the trick. Smash that cursed place apart and flood the land, returning it to the river valley it once was, drowning the demons from hell with it. Images of war movies played through his mind, men screaming and explosions ripping them limb from limb. He glanced up at Dee, smiling at her. He looked back to the map, tracing the Waikato River with his finger back to the other hydroelectric dams farther upstream. A spark of an idea formed in his mind.

"Captain, how much explosive do you have?"

"Enough. What are you thinking, Jack?"

"Well, okay, this is crazy, but what if we set off a small explosion here at Arapuni?" Jack pointed to the map. "It's what, twenty kilometres upstream? As far as we know, the Trophy King reigns over them as well if there are Variants in there too. So we head south in one chopper while the other two head north. At a set time, we set off the explosion, hopefully pulling enough Variants out of Karapiro. We skirt around the mountain and then drop in, landing on the roof."

Ben stroked his long beard, he smiled at Jack, a twinkle in his brown eyes.

"I like it, Jack. We don't want to cause too much damage and cause the dam to fail. We also don't have the means or time to work out how long we'd have before any wall of watery death would reach Karapiro if there was one. Okay. Here's what we'll do. Hollis, Bryant, you each take two men in a chopper. Fly north to Hamilton and swoop upriver. I'm thinking the collaborators are housed at the town next to the lake. It's the only logical location. It's close enough for them to protect the Variants, but far enough away for them to feel normal. I want you guys to attack them after you see some of their forces leaving. Once we arrive and land, Hollis, I want you to fall back as backup for extraction." Ben let the plan sink in.

Jack nodded. It was crazy, but it was all they had.

"Jack. When we get inside, you lead us. You know the layout better than anyone. Dee, you go with him. Kill as many of those bastards as possible. Then get out. If I order you out, you go. Understand?"

Dee glanced at Jack with a grim expression on her face. He knew what she was thinking. Ben was telling them to save themselves. Jack looked over at the sergeants, meeting their gazes. They stared back at him, determined. He felt inspired by their inclusion.

"What if we play some crazy music out of the loudspeakers for added distraction?"

"Such as?" Ben raised an eyebrow.

"Well, I was thinking *For Whom The Bell Tolls* by Metallica."

Dee barked a laugh and shook her head at him.

"If whatever that music is distracts those bastards, then play it! It worked for us in Vietnam on occasion," Ben said with a grin.

Both the sergeants chuckled, and Jack couldn't help but laugh with them. It was a nervous laugh, but it felt good to release it and share it with the others.

The meeting drew to a close as Ben outlined the rest of the plan, going over the timing with them. He handed each of them a digital watch and they synced them.

Jack moved over to Dee and hugged her. "Let's go get the boys."

"Yeah, let's end this."

Jack turned to the sound of knocking. Eric pushed the door open. "Don't forget about me!"

"You made it."

Eric nodded at the gathered Renegades. "Let's do this for Tony, for all those we lost."

Ben stepped around the table and grasped his shoulder. "Yes. Let's do it for Tony. You're in charge of the explosives. I want ten small bundles made up, six with five-minute timers and four with two-minute timers." He paused, looking around the room. "Just so you all know, I haven't okayed this with Command. I'm giving you all the chance to back out now. Those who want to come, we leave at 1100."

Jack smiled at his words. So what was new? His and George's rescue had been off the books too.

Dee grasped Ben's arm. "We're Renegades, right?"

Looking at each of them, she carried on. "So let's Renegade!"

Dee's words were answered with a cheer and an "Oo rah!" as the council broke apart. Each Renegade moving off to prepare.

Jack felt strangely calm as he headed for the armoury. *Hold on, boys. I'm coming.*

— 29 —

It was the smell that woke Boss from his coma; the putrid stench of decay and death. It surrounded him, seeping into his pores and assaulting his nose. He tried breathing in through his mouth, but that made him gag. The thick air tasted like rotten meat. Bile rose in his throat and he vomited. He gasped for air, but breathing in the polluted air made him gag again. He forced himself to calm his breathing, to focus.

His breathing under control, his other senses kicked in. Excruciating pain lanced through his arms and legs, threatening to return him to his coma. Turning his head, he could see a sharp bone, like a nail, protruding through his left hand. He struggled against the fastening as panic set in, his heart thumping in his chest. Boss turned to look at his right hand; that too was held with bone. And he could feel another one through his foot. Waves of pain cascaded over him and he clenched his teeth together, riding it out.

What was it Dee had said to him? There is always a way out?

He peered through the dim light. He could see another figure strung out on a rack of bones across from him.

Boss shuddered, realising what had happened; he had been crucified on a cross of bones. He could make out Beth's blonde hair a few metres to his right. She was motionless, eyes closed. Boss prayed she was alive. He glanced around the room. It was a large open area, as far as he could see through all the bones and entrails. The walls, floor and ceiling were concrete. A steel set of stairs rose up from the floor to a small metal landing. Turning his head, he could see another set of stairs at the other end of the room.

In the centre of the room, bones had been piled up into a throne. The Alpha they called the Trophy King sat on top. A small cage made from bones lay to one side. Inside it, a small figure was curled up.

The Trophy King was watching Boss, his yellow eyes glaring at him. He leant his head back and bellowed. The bellow shook the bones beneath him. Boss screamed, and desperately tried to wrench himself free. He had tried to remain strong for George, for Beth. He had tried to protect them from the beasts. But he had failed. Now the Alpha was to have his revenge. An avid gamer, Boss had spent hundreds of hours facing monsters; but when the monsters had become reality, he'd run and hidden. It was Dee who had inspired him to fight and survive, to live on.

He looked around again as despair washed over him, pulling him into its dark embrace. Hundreds of skulls on spikes lined the walls. Skulls of all different sizes. The Trophy King bellowed again, rising from his throne. Variants poured into the chamber, surrounding him. He reached down and pulled the figure from the cage, then pointed at Boss and howled. The gathered Variants joined in. The howls grew in intensity, rattling his teeth and hurting his eardrums. Boss gasped as he recognised George's red hair. Tears flowed freely as he contemplated their fate.

The Alpha lifted George up, grasping the boy around the neck with one of his huge claws. He picked up a shard of bone with his free claw and, with another look at the crucified Boss, stabbed George in the eye. George's scream tore Boss apart, shattering his soul.

"Leave him alone! Kill me! Just please, leave him alone." Boss screamed at the Trophy King.

The Alpha shoved the still-screaming George back into the cage and, with an astounding jump, leapt in front of Boss. His sucker mouth pulled back, revealing rows and rows of sharp teeth. His rancid breath fumed out. With a snarl, the Alpha jabbed the shard of bone into Boss's leg, twisting it. Boss screamed and fought to free himself. He didn't care if he died trying, but he just wanted to kill this monster from hell. He managed to lift his left hand off the bone, and feebly hit the Alpha on the shoulder. The Trophy King hissed at Boss and clenched the boy's wrist in its claw, cutting into the skin. Then he slammed Boss's hand back onto the bone nail. Boss screamed again, his voice going hoarse. The Alpha bounded over to the crucified Beth. She was now awake, the horror evident on her face. Her gaze met Boss's as tears streamed down her cheeks. The Trophy King turned to Boss again and bellowed. Turning back to Beth, he stabbed her in the right eye with the shard. Beth let out an agonised scream, squeezing her remaining eye shut as blood poured from her now-ruined one. Boss cried with her, trying to comfort her with his empathy.

A Variant leapt in front of Boss, and he felt crushing

pain on the side of his head as his vision dimmed and faded to black.

— 30 —

Maggie crept along the highway in the 4x4. The late afternoon sun was quickly descending, casting long shadows on the road in front of her. She had left the main group a few hours back and now followed the trail, looking for the Alpha and his human traitors. Radio chatter told her she was close, and vehicles pushed to the side of the road indicated that she was on the right path. She could see a green and white road sign ahead, and as she drew closer, she read that it said Karapiro. She slowed the 4x4 to walking speed and crawled along the road.

Maggie spotted a long driveway just after the Karapiro turnoff. She pulled in and made her way up the tree-lined drive. At the end, a large grey house sat amongst landscaped gardens. Once-manicured lawns were now overgrown and neglected. Maggie recognised azaleas and rhododendrons flowering, and a few camellias lined the garage to her right. She manoeuvred the 4x4 between the house and garage, tucking it out of sight. Moving her rifle to within easy reach, she scanned the property, looking for any Variants or red suits. Seeing nothing, she wound down the window, sniffing the air. She couldn't detect the Variant's smell. Satisfied that she was alone, she carefully and silently exited the vehicle.

After a quick walk of the perimeter, Maggie tried the back door of the house. Thankfully it gave, and she quickly entered, closing the door behind her. A quick search of the kitchen turned up nothing of use. Making herself comfortable on the sofa, Maggie rummaged through her small rucksack, searching for what little food she had. Chewing on beef jerky, she contemplated her next move. The red coveralls had proven their worth against the Variants, but she knew it would only take one human to spot her for a fraud and she would become dinner. She needed to wait for morning to do some recon. She had considered sneaking into the collaborators' camp and killing a few of them, but she wasn't sure how the red suits operated at night. Were they just a day thing? Did they even leave guards out? Did the Variants roam the night, leaving the red suits to stay within their camp?

Maggie moved upstairs, searching for a room she could secure. In the master bedroom she found what she was looking for. A large walk-in wardrobe lay off to one side. She piled blankets and pillows inside it and pushed a chest of drawers across the doorway. It wasn't perfect, but it was all she could do. She lay down, snuggling into the warmth of the blankets. She strained her ears, listening for any sounds. She was greeted by silence. Checking her rifle was close by, Maggie let out a sigh and closed her eyes. The exhaustion of the last couple of days washed over her, dragging her down to sleep.

Maggie spent the morning sneaking around the small village, watching the routine of the collaborators. Satisfied she had it memorised, she now found herself crawling through the scrub that lined the eastern side of the river so that she overlooked the buildings nestled at the bottom and top of the hydroelectric dam. This must be the dam the traitor had spoken of. Water gushed from the spillway and thundered into the river. Limestone cliffs soared up from the river bed, creating a gorge.

She checked her watch: 11:15. She glanced up again. The sun was straining to peek through the overcast sky. The town of Karapiro was nestled on the eastern shore of a lake — of the same name, apparently. So far, she had counted twenty-seven men in red coveralls, many of them milling around with rifles. A few had walked out onto the concrete walls of the dam and stood looking over the lake.

Some others, clearly guards, were posted at various doorways around the dam, their red coveralls standing out. Maggie peered through her scope, sighting each one in turn. She reached back and moved away the branch digging into her side, then rubbed her sweaty palms on her pants. She looked through her scope again. Like all new recruits, she had gone through rifle training, shooting at targets from different distances. She had surprised herself, accurately shooting targets at 300 yards from a prone position.

The scope on her stolen rifle told her the distance to the nearest guard was 82 metres. Maggie knew there was 0.9 metres to a yard, so was confident she could take care of the guards from this range.

Turning slightly, she could make out a metal ladder attached to the near side of the dam. It ran from top to bottom, with metal safety loops every few feet.

Importantly, it was unguarded. Maggie checked her watch again: 11:25. The patrol she was waiting for would be coming soon. She needed intel before she dared enter the buildings. She needed to know how many Variants there were, where the children were being held, and if there were any human guards on the inside.

She wriggled back from the cliff top and pushed her way backwards through the bush. Then, raising her rifle, she crept along the path, heel to toe, swivelling her head from side to side. She could smell the beasts' faint rotten fruit stench but, so far, hadn't seen any Variants in the village. She found the fallen tree stump and nestled behind it.

She didn't have to wait long before she heard voices carrying through the silence. That was the thing about the apocalypse; all the ambient noise had disappeared. That background hum that had been a day-to-day occurrence had been snuffed out. Traffic noise, electricity humming through high-powered lines, lawnmowers, chainsaws... Gone. Sound travelled far these days.

Maggie took a few deep breaths, calming herself. She tensed her muscles, ready to spring her trap. As the voices drew nearer, she caught the tail end of their conversation.

"...lost a lot of men on that island. Jim said they were well-armed; they even blew up that fancy boat I was telling you about."

"Really? Why did they want to go there?"

"I don't know, dude? I just follow orders. I don't want to get eaten."

"Shit yeah."

Maggie burst out of her hiding spot like a 100-metre sprinter out of the starting blocks. The two guards' eyes went wide with shock. Maggie slammed her rifle stock into the nearest one's head, knocking him unconscious. The other guard took a step back and went to raise the shotgun he was carrying.

"Don't even try it. I'll shoot you where you stand."

Maggie took a better look at the guard. He had sandy blond hair. Hazel eyes stared at her from behind thick glasses. He looked to be about twenty.

Glasses smartly dropped his shotgun onto the ground and held up his hands. "You're American."

"Five points for Mr Obvious."

Glasses stayed silent, watching Maggie warily.

"This can go one of two ways. One. You tell me what I want to know, and you live. Two. You don't. I knock you out like your friend here, I strip those red coveralls off you, and leave you to the Variants."

"Variants?"

"Beasts, monsters, whatever you call them." Maggie nodded her head towards the dam.

Glasses held his hands up higher. "All right, whatever."

"First thing. How many of you are there?"

Glasses flicked his eyes towards Karapiro village. "I'm not sure, exactly, because a lot died yesterday on the island. Maybe thirty of us now?"

Island? Maggie kept her face devoid of any emotion. She hoped he didn't mean the island she had sent Alice and the kids to.

"How many of the creatures are in that dam?"

Glasses shrugged his shoulders. "I don't know, really, I don't. A lot, maybe two hundred?"

"What about the kids? What do they do with them?"

Glasses looked down at the ground, and blood rose in his cheeks. When he looked back at Maggie, tears were in his eyes. Hoarsely he replied, "I'm sorry, but I don't know. They never come out. Sometimes, on still nights, you can hear screams."

Maggie tightened her grip on the rifle. "Last question, asshole. How many guards are inside?"

"None that I know of. I'm always on perimeter patrol though, so it may have changed."

Maggie mulled over this new information. She was confident about taking out guards on the outside, sneaking down that ladder and into the building. The Variants were another issue. She had no idea how long her disguise would hold out, if at all. She contemplated leaving, getting back to the island and coming back with an army. The thought of children being eaten spurred her on.

She stood watching Glasses, deciding what to do. As they stood, a distant thumping sound echoed up the river, bouncing off the limestone cliffs. She watched as Glasses frowned, confusion on his young face. Maggie knew that sound. She would never forget it. Hours spent inside the flying tubs of metal, skimming over the hot sandy wastelands of Iraq and Afghanistan, insurgents taking pot-shots as they landed, dispersing them into hell... What *she* was confused by was, why was a chopper heading this way? But then again, as her favourite quote from *Art of War* told her, *"In the midst of chaos, there is opportunity."*

She would strike while she could. She spun her rifle around and slammed it into Glasses' temple. His lanky body slumped to the ground next to his mate's. She reached down and grabbed his shotgun. Then she searched the pair for extra shells and shoved it all into her pack. Spotting the other guard's shotgun wedged under him, she reached down and yanked it free. With a last look around, Maggie jogged back to the clifftop. The thumping of the chopper was growing louder. Adrenalin surged into her bloodstream at the promise of a battle.

I'm doing this for Izzy, to save the kids from this hell.

She reached the clifftop and looked north, searching for the chopper. Above the thumping came a distant booming sound. She pivoted, looking south. *Explosives. These guys mean business!* This was a full-on assault. A cacophony of screeches echoed as dozens of Variants poured out of the dam. They scampered up the walls and disappeared, heading south.

These guys are smart! Classic divide and conquer. We just might have a chance after all.

— 31 —

The three NH-90 helicopters sat waiting on the concrete pad. Dee walked towards them, holding Jack's hand. For a moment she thought about the other soldiers smirking at the public display of affection, but quickly cast that thought aside. She glanced up at the split windscreen, grinning to herself. They always reminded her of bug eyes staring at their prey. She could feel the weight of her combat vest, stuffed full of extra magazines, pushing down on her small frame.

Ben stood with Sergeant Hollis next to the nearest NH-90 chopper. He smiled as she and Jack approached, waving them over.

Jack lifted up the metal case Katherine had given to him. "This is for Mahana. I didn't want to give it to the Indonesian pilot. In all the confusion yesterday, I forgot about it."

Ben took it from Jack and shook his head, looking down at it. "All that madness, for what's in here. It better be bloody worth it." He turned, handing it to Sergeant Hollis. "Secure this in the bunker."

"Yes, sir."

Dee watched him jog off. "Do you think we have a chance today, Ben?" she asked smiling.

He glanced between her and Jack. "We've survived, guys. Against all the odds, we've survived this far. All we can do now is try. Try to save the boys, and with the new intel Alice provided about the camp, save them too. We'll always have a chance." He paused and grasped Jack's shoulder. "What was it that Gimli said? 'Certainty of death. What are we waiting for?'"

Jack grinned at Ben. "Yeah, something like that."

"We fight on, guys. We survived the lab. Dee, we rescued Jack. Let's go get the boys and bring them home."

Dee adjusted the straps on her pack. "Whatever the outcome, if we lie dying and drawing our last breath, promise me something, Ben."

"Okay. What?"

"That we'll blow that bastard Alpha back to hell."

Ben tilted his head back, letting out a deep chuckle. "That I can promise!" and he thumped the side of the chopper. "Let's go!"

Eric jogged over and jumped into the hold, slamming the door shut after them.

The whine of the engines increased as the blades started to wind up, thumping through the air. Some of the civilians had gathered on the boardwalk to watch them leave. As the chopper lifted off, Dee scanned the hold. Jack sat next to her, still holding her hand. Ben had moved forwards and was in the co-pilot's seat. Eric sat opposite them, alongside a soldier Dee didn't know. He glanced up at her and gave her a nervous smile before shifting his attention back to the rifle cradled in his arms.

Dee looked down at the villa they called home. Alice and the kids had gathered on the verandah and waved as the chopper rose and banked away over the ocean, back towards the hell the mainland had become. Back to free Boss and George. She had hugged Alice goodbye earlier, both women holding tight. Alice had pulled away, telling Dee to come back. Dee had avoided a movie reference; she'd just wanted to savour the moment with her friend. Even with all of Ben's confidence, she was scared. Scared of what she would find. Scared of dying.

Dee didn't know what happened when you died. Did you really go to heaven? Was it just blackness? If she did die and go to heaven, would her father be waiting for her? Dee reached down inside herself, brushed away her doubts and questions and drew on the strength that she knew lay within. She had drawn on it, waiting in the basement for Jack. Now she needed it once more. She squeezed Jack's hand, eager for his touch. She and Jack had had many late-night discussions on topics such as death. She had always admired his measured and considered responses. Jack acted all fun and joked around, but when he dropped the wall that surrounded him, he could get very serious, and had an intelligent outlook on life. Dee let out a sigh. Yes, she was scared. Scared of losing it all.

She watched the view out the small window in the door as the chopper flew over the grey ocean. It stayed low as it swept over the beaches of Papamoa and continued inland, reaching the thick bush of the Mamaku ranges that surrounded the twin lakes of Rotorua. The blue lakes stood out, gleaming, surrounded by the city. Parts of the city were smoking. Dee didn't know if it was from fires or from the geothermal vents dotting the land. She grabbed her seat as the chopper rose sharply, rising over the hills. Dee checked her watch: 11:20. She looked around for the Waikato River; it should have been snaking its way below them. They rounded another pine-clad hill and the chopper dropped down the other side, keeping close to the ground. Jack squeezed her hand. The chopper banked again, sweeping down and they skimmed over the deep, dark waters of the Waikato.

Ben's voice crackled over the headset. "ETA five minutes. Eric, get the explosives ready. Jack. Alan. Man the guns. Give them hell, people."

Dee looked over at the soldier she didn't know. Alan, apparently. He secured his rifle next to him and moved over to one of the .50 cal. guns at the door.

Well, you're not wearing a red shirt.

Eric handed her a couple of green brick shapes. Timers stuck into them read 2.00 minutes. Eric reached down and plugged two wires hanging loose into the tops of the bricks. "Press the red button before you chuck it out. That starts the timer."

She nodded. Turning, she watched as Arapuni Dam came into view.

Ben's voice crackled over the headset. "Drop the explosives on the roof of the turbine building. Jack, Alan, when the Variants come out, kill as many as you can."

Dee looked up at Jack, meeting his gaze. It was time; time to end this.

The pilot banked around the dam, and the chopper descended the concrete face. Steep limestone cliffs, with bushes clinging to every available nook, plunged down into the swirling river. Dee waited until the flat roof of the largest building came into view. She pushed down the red button and, checking to see the timer had started, hurled the explosive out, watching as it tumbled through the air and bounced along the roof, stopping against a large vent.

Variants started to pour out of the building, their shrieks just audible above the thumping of the chopper. Dee hated that sound. She pressed the button on her second explosive and tossed it out. It too flipped through the air and bounced off the lip of the vent, falling inside. She grinned, satisfied.

The chopper lifted and banked away from the dam. Jack and Alan started firing the .50 cals, peppering the emerging Variants with leaded death. Dee watched, mesmerised, as the rounds tore into them, shredding their diseased flesh from their bones. They may be tough, but not enough for these guns. The *brrooottt* of the guns echoed around the cabin as the pilot pulled back, raising the chopper higher above the dam and the screeching Variants. Jack stopped firing his .50 cal. and held on. The chopper hovered 100 metres above the river, downstream from the dam. A succession of explosions thundered out, first two close together, then two more quickly followed. The chopper rocked wildly as concrete, wood, steel, glass and hunks of Variants flew out in a huge kaboom! Dee smiled as a blue metal shape flew out of the destroyed building, splashing down into the river.

Jack sat back down next to her. Touching her shoulder, he was grinning from ear to ear. "Did you see that? That blue thing was one of the turbines!"

"Is that what it was?"

"Yeah, it looked like it."

"Your friend in Ohio would have loved that explosion."

Jack cast his eyes downwards before looking back at her. "Yeah, he would have. I hope he made it out."

Dee took Jack's hand in hers. "I'm sure he has. Let's hope the world gets back to normal and we can go visit all our friends one day."

"I never thought I would live to see such times."

"Me neither. I guess no one did. Do you remember that guy we met, who had spent his childhood in bomb shelters?"

"Yeah. He loved movies as much as I do."

Dee kissed Jack on the cheek. "That's right. I remember you two talking for hours, ignoring us girls. His girlfriend was so boring."

Jack laughed, his laughter sounding weird as it echoed off the metal walls.

"I remember him telling us about that. He said he hoped he would never see such times again."

Jack nodded, suddenly lost in thought.

Dee turned away and looked back out the window.

The chopper whined as it banked around Maungatautari Mountain. Dee's thoughts drifted back a few weeks to that terrifying flight up the mountain, away from the Trophy King. She reached for her rifle and checked it again out of habit. She drew her katana from her pack, admiring how it felt in her hands. She slid it back into the webbing and watched as Lake Karapiro stretched out, long and thin. She could just make out the rowing club and the dam in the distance.

Ben's voice came over her headset. "Lock and load, Renegades. ETA two minutes. Whatever happens today, thank you for making this old soldier proud. Proud to call you fellow soldiers. Proud to call you friends. Let's go kill these bastards!"

Dee glanced up at Ben. His long grey beard hung over his combat vest. She nodded.

Let's kill these bastards!

— 32 —

The thumping of the approaching choppers thundered up the river as Maggie pressed herself into the ground. Quickly she positioned herself and sighted one of the guards through her scope. She glanced downriver as two grey military choppers swung around the bend of the river, making directly for the hydroelectric station. Using the distraction, Maggie breathed out and gently squeezed the trigger. The guard's head snapped back, and blood and brains coated the concrete wall behind him. She swung her rifle to the right, and dropped two more guards as they stared, stunned, as the choppers buzzed over the dam and attacked the village behind her.

Maggie's stolen radio sprang to life and desperate cries rang out. She ignored the radio and shot two more of the guards, wounding one and killing the other. That left two more, higher up. Maggie panned the rifle, searching for the last two guards. One had begun to climb the ladder on the opposite side of the dam. Maggie shot him in the torso, then watched as his body tumbled down the ladder, bouncing off the metal rungs before smacking onto the roof. She searched around for the last guard. Seeing no one, she jumped up and headed for the ladder closest to her.

The two choppers buzzed around the village, spraying it with .50 cal. rounds. The rounds tore into wood, metal and flesh. To Maggie's surprise, music pumped out from the buzzing choppers. She recognised the song and allowed herself to smile for an instant. She dared to have hope again.

These guys are my kind of crazy.

Screams rang out, and panicked voices continued to chatter on the radio. To Maggie, it seemed the guards had no idea what to do. One chopper broke away and positioned itself over the narrow, single-lane road that stretched across the dam. Dozens of Variants poured out of the dam and into the bush on the western side. Maggie shook her head at the sight of them sprinting away from the battle. She deduced that the Variants were splitting their forces. Some would engage the choppers while the others searched for the source of the earlier explosions.

The chopper was too low. As if the pilot read her mind, the chopper lifted just as several Variants leapt off the ground. Some clung to the wheel arches, while others clambered over them and sprang into the chopper. As the chopper rose higher, Maggie saw muzzle flashes as the soldiers inside desperately tried to kill the Variants. The chopper swung round and its tail rotor caught in the power lines. Maggie reached the ladder and grabbed the safety rail. Looking back, she watched, horrified, as the chopper spun out of control. The whine of its engines went up several octaves as the pilot tried to bring it back under control. But to no avail. It slammed onto the roadway, exploding in a fireball of glass and metal.

The main rotor blades broke free and spun out over the dam, slicing through dozens of Variants as they tried to fling themselves clear. Hunks of Variant muck spat out in a sickening arc. Acrid smoke from the burning chopper caused Maggie to cough. Mixed with the sickly rotten fruit smell of the Variants, it made her stomach turn. She gritted her teeth and descended the ladder.

"In the midst of chaos" all right, she thought as she ran for the nearest door.

***

Boss snapped his eyes open. That sounded like a chopper. He had fallen into a melancholy as he lay crucified. He had failed to keep George safe, failed himself and failed all those on the island. He had also failed his mother when he'd run away, leaving her to be eaten by his once-father. Glancing down at his missing lower leg, he grimaced. Yes. I even failed my body.

All around the nest, the resting Variants were waking up. A muffled boom rang out, shaking the bones he was crucified to. He looked over at Beth. Her head was rolled to one side and her eyes were squeezed shut. But as he watched, confusion spread across her face.

Boss turned his head, searching out George in the cage. He didn't get a chance. The Trophy King sat up and bellowed, pointing a claw towards one of the exits. Boss stared, repulsed, as dozens of Variants emerged from under piles of bones and entrails — he couldn't tell if the offal was human or animal — and headed for the exit. He gagged against the stench, freshly roused by the Variants' movements. It invaded his nostrils and ticked the back of his throat as he tried to breathe without being sick.

He started to wriggle his right hand free. The pain from his efforts threatened to overcome him. Boss risked a peek at George, gathering strength at the sight of him lying curled up in the cage. The thumping of the choppers grew louder and, with a final surge of determination, Boss ripped his hand free. Pain shot up his arm, stabbing into his brain. He gasped for breath, ignoring the putrid taste that rode on the air. All around him Variants were scrambling for the exits, shrieking as they scampered up the walls, squelching over the remains of their meals. Boss craned his neck and peered at the Trophy King. Its back was turned towards Boss as it watched its beasts leaving the nest. Several of the larger Variants stayed behind with it.

The bone rack that Boss was crucified on was angled back, allowing him to get some leverage. He reached up and tugged at his left hand still nailed to the bone cross. As he tried to pry it loose, he searched for a weapon of some sort. He couldn't see his pack anywhere. That would have been too lucky. But he could see several discarded bones, some snapped in two with jagged edges. Knowing he had limited time to escape, Boss gritted his teeth and yanked hard on his hand. It jolted off the bone nail with a sickening, sucking sound. He couldn't help the scream of agony that escaped his lips. He glanced towards the Trophy King, fearful of being discovered. The Trophy King still had its back to him.

Boss could feel his heart hammering hard in his chest. With the arrival of the choppers, and the nest emptying of Variants, he dared to have the will to survive again. He didn't know if that was Jack and Dee up above, but he knew that this was his only chance of getting himself, George and Beth out of this hellhole. He could hear Dee's voice in his head telling him to focus his energy, look for a way out. *If the answer appears, act on it.*

With his hands now free, Boss worked on freeing his foot. The bone through it was grating against his own bones, a most unpleasant sensation. Strangely, the wounds were not bleeding. He tried squatting so he could leverage his foot off, but pain coursed up his body in ever-increasing waves. He paused and risked another glance at the remaining Variants.

The thumping grew louder, drowning out the howls of the Variants. Then the rattling sound of rapid-fire machine guns rang out. Boss was thankful for the distraction, as the Trophy King remained close to its throne and kept its back turned. Boss pushed his backside against the bone rack and finally, gritting his teeth, yanked his left foot free, slipping off the rack with a thud. He raised his head, looking at the Variants.

One had turned and was watching him. It shrieked and sprang through the air, claws curled, sucker mouth pulled back in a snarl. Frantic, Boss willed his good leg to move. He managed to bring it under him, then pushed off the ground and leapt for the broken shards of bones. Grasping one, he turned, holding it out before him. He felt like a Neanderthal facing down a sabre tooth tiger. The Variant landed beside him and pinned his leg to the concrete floor. Boss stabbed out at it, but the Variant knocked his hand away and clenched its claw around his neck. Lifting him up, the Variant scurried over to the Trophy King, holding out Boss like he was a radioactive doll.

The Alpha glared at him with its cold yellow eyes. It bellowed at him, spittle flying onto Boss's face, coating it with rancid slobber. Taking Boss from the Variant, it opened the cage next to its throne and crammed him inside.

Boss's lanky frame scraped against the bone bars. George scrambled up and huddled in the corner, cowering from him. Boss used his remaining strength to reach out and pull him into a hug. George sobbed into his chest as Boss peered out, praying for the Renegades to hurry. "They're coming for us, G-man. We have to be ready."

He smiled, looking down at the bone spear he had managed to hold on to. *I'd rather have my gun, but a spear is better than nothing.*

— 33 —

The NH-90 helicopter banked around Maungatautari Mountain, then swooped down the bush line and out over the grey-green waters of Lake Karapiro. Jack grasped the hold bar, his knuckles white with the effort. He peered out the small window at the black smoke pouring from the roadway on the dam. A horde of Variants was running south towards Arapuni and the explosions they had set off there. He grinned. A few lifted their heads, watching the chopper fly overhead. He glanced over at Dee. She had a determined look on her face. Her eyes met his and she smiled at him. He leant over and kissed her neck.

Dee brushed his cheek. "Are you ready?"

"Yeah, I guess."

"Promise me something."

"What?"

"When this is all over, can we watch *The Goonies* and eat hot dogs?"

"I thought you hated that movie?"

"I don't hate it. You just watch it so much. But all that stuff seems irrelevant now. We need to enjoy and appreciate what time we have."

Jack smiled and kissed her again. "If we survive this and get back to Mayor Island, you can watch whatever movie you want."

"Even *Dirty Dancing*?"

"Yes, even that one." Jack laughed and poked her in the ribs.

"It's funny. It all began here at Karapiro. Now let's end it here."

Jack nodded. Lifting his eyes, he watched Ben squeeze out of the cockpit and face them.

"All right, Renegades. Time to rock and roll. Kill any Variant bastard you see. Eric, you're with me. We're going in the top entrance by the road. Jack, Dee, descend the stairs and enter through the turbine room."

He reached into his backpack, extracting the remaining explosives. He adjusted the timers and handed five to Jack.

"Plant these on the back wall, closest to the lake. Press the red button to arm them."

Then he held up a small device Jack wasn't familiar with. It looked like a bicycle handgrip with a red button on top. On its side was a metal switch. Ben flicked a guard over the button. "This is the detonating trigger. I've taken them off timer. It's too risky. We go in, find the boys, and once we are clear, we'll blow this bastard place to hell!"

"Hell yeah!" the Renegades answered.

Jack put the explosives in his pack and checked that his rifle was ready. He knew it was, but Ben had drummed the habit into him. And besides, it helped take his mind off the horrors that awaited them. Looking out, he could see the source of the black smoke. Flames had engulfed the village end of the dam. It was the burning wreckage of a chopper. As he stared, Variants scrambled around the flames, trying to reach the other chopper that hovered above the village, spraying them with .50 cal. rounds. His heart sank at the sight. The men in that chopper had risked their lives for the rescue of the boys. They had paid the ultimate sacrifice.

Feeling the loss, Jack channelled his anger and frustration to steel himself with new determination. Gazing around the cockpit, he could see the same grim expressions on the other Renegades' faces.

The chopper thumped to the ground. Eric flung the door open and Jack pushed off his seat. Crouching low, he waited for Dee to join him. He felt the touch on his shoulder and moved left and around the building. In his peripheral sight, he saw Ben and Eric head directly for the building, their destination visible over the sight of his rifle. He took up a covering position and watched Dee descend the ladder. Dozens of Variants were on the far side of the dam, but for now the Renegades' way was clear. Jack heard his two-way click with the signal that the coast was clear.

He took a calming breath and climbed down the ladder. With every step he took closer to the inside of the meat locker, his trepidation grew. He had reached deep down inside himself to escape this place, to find an inner strength and a will to survive. Then, thoughts of Dee alone and worried had spurred him on. He paused at the door.

Dee glanced up at him as if reading his concerns. She grasped his hand. "It's all right, Jack. We do it together this time, okay?"

"Okay." He breathed deep, trying to calm himself. "Let's do it."

Dee flung open the door and moved through it with the grace of a cat. Jack followed and looked around the cavernous room beyond. Four giant turbines sat in a row, silent. Metal walkways ringed each turbine and huge metal pipes disappeared from each one into the walls of the dam.

Jack remembered a school trip many years ago. The sound of the spinning turbines had been deafening. His young ears had rung for days after. Like after a rock concert. Dee moved out into the room, signalling for him to keep an eye on the walkways as she swivelled around, searching for the foul beasts. He couldn't detect the rotten fruit smell in here, but the stench of death wafted from the far end. Jack clicked his two-way to get Dee's attention. She glanced at him. He held up one of the explosives. She nodded. Glancing around the room, he decided that the intake pipes were the best place to set the charges.

Jack jogged behind the turbines and placed the four charges. Meeting Dee at the far end, he gave her a quick smile. He thumbed his radio. "Charges primed and ready. Over."

There was a short pause before Ben answered. "Received. We are heading for the main room. Move it."

"Wilco. Over." Jack glanced at Dee and nodded.

She cracked the door open and peered out before moving into the corridor beyond. Glancing left and right, Jack recognised the corridor he had woken in all those weeks ago. They were farther along, but it was the same corridor. Evidence of the strange membrane that had trapped him, George and the others to the walls was still there. Screeches echoed down the hall, forcing Jack to pay attention. The strong, rotten fruit smell reached him before the sounds of their scampering did. He moved his selector off semi-automatic onto full. A hideous howl sounded from around the corner. Jack nestled the rifle into his shoulder. A black blur of movement careened towards them. Jack squeezed the trigger, aiming for the torso. He watched, satisfied, as he filled it full of holes. It tumbled to the ground and lay still. He quickly moved forwards, taking down a few more with controlled bursts. Dee's rifle spat, but with more Variants joining the battle, Jack had no time to admire her kills. Another wave joined the first group. Jack and Dee fired at anything that moved. Firing. Loading. Firing. Sporadic gunfire echoed down the hallway from the far end. Jack assumed it was Ben and Eric.

He yelled above the din. "There's too many, we have to go back!"

Dee shook her head. "It's better here in the hall. We can trap the bastards in a bottleneck!"

Jack nodded and moved to one side, taking down another Variant. The stench of death mixed with gunsmoke made his eyes water. Casings from his ammunition clinked off the concrete walls. Jack centred himself and fought on. He fought for the boys, he fought for all those moments he wanted to still share with Dee. He fought for all the sunsets they had yet to see. He fought for the children he wanted to have with his beautiful wife. He fought for humanity.

Shrieks rang out above the gunfire, and another wave of Variants scampered around the corner. They stopped, hissing at Jack and Dee, watching them with their cold reptile eyes. Jack squeezed his trigger. His rifle clicked empty.

"Changing!" He reached into his vest and grabbed a fresh magazine.

Dee let loose with a burst, hitting one in the head and another in the leg. The remaining four howled and lurched towards them. Jack looked up and sighted one of them. With a sudden burst of speed, it bounced off the wall and leapt at him. He pivoted and flung himself to one side, hoping to avoid its outstretched claws. The Variant landed next to him with a shriek. He only just managed to bring up his rifle to protect his head. Jack glimpsed a flash of red down the corridor. Thinking he was having a flashback of the man he killed, Jack opened his eyes wide when the red figure ran towards them, firing at the Variants. But as surprised as he was, Jack had more pressing matters to be concerned with.

Jack reached down and grabbed his knife. Lunging, he buried it deep into the Variant's neck, killing it. He pushed the dead beast off him and scrambled up, looking for Dee. She stood over the body of a Variant, but had her carbine pointed at the red figure.

It was a dark-haired woman. She had tied the arms of her red coveralls around her waist. She held her rifle to one side and had a hand lifted up in surrender.

Jack looked at Dee, then back to the woman. "Who are you?"

"I could ask you the same thing?"

"American?"

"Yes."

Jack shook his head. *What the hell is an American doing here?* "We don't have time for this. Dee. Do it."

"Wait!" The woman held up her other hand. "I'm not one of them. I just killed those bastards. I'm here for the kids, all right?"

Jack watched as Dee lowered her rifle. "Maggie?"

"Yes. Wait. How did you know? Alice?"

Dee nodded. "She's safe, and the kids."

"Oh, thank God. I guess you're here for the kids too, right?"

Jack butted in. "Yes. Let's go. There's always more of those bastards."

Howls and shrieks reached them from farther down the corridor. Jack took a deep breath. It was time. Time to end this. Time for the final battle. He leant down and wiped the black gunk off his knife. Shouldering his rifle, he jogged down the corridor towards the horrors of the throne room.

— 34 —

Dee jogged a few paces behind Jack, with Maggie running alongside. The bodies that once lined these walls had gone, but the stench of their deaths still lingered. The last time Dee had run down this corridor, she had been searching for Jack. She had promised herself to come back and help these people, but the army had refused her request. Seeing the vacant spots fed her guilt. She was determined to make up for that failing and rescue the boys. Deep down, Dee wanted to kill the Trophy King too. It was the only way to end this properly. He had shown that he didn't forget by attacking the island, and by kidnapping Boss and George he had let them know that he was king. The apex predator. Thinking of the boys, she grimaced. *Not if I can help it.*

Dee could hear the rattle of Ben's rifle and the boom of Eric's shotgun coming from behind the green door. She clicked the talk button on her two-way. "Ben. We're in position."

"Get your arses in here. Now!"

Dee exchanged a look with Jack and Maggie. She saw their determination. *All right, Trophy King, I'm here.*

Jack reached the door and gripped its handle. Dee

swung her rifle up and nodded, meeting his gaze. In that brief second, she saw the love and admiration he had for her. It was all the encouragement she needed to carry on with the mission. Gritting her teeth, she moved through the open door, looking over the rifle's sight.

Dee gaped at the scene greeting her. A dozen Variants had grouped together under and around the metal stairs opposite her position. Ben and Eric stood on the metal landing above, firing down into the group of snarling beasts. Each blast of Eric's shotgun sent Variant gore spraying into the air. The Variants he was hitting merely shrugged off the rounds, rising and crawling over the bodies of their fallen kin. Their shrieks and howls filled the cavernous room.

Ben fired controlled, expert shots from his carbine, hitting the Variants in their heads. Gaping holes opened up in their deformed skulls as they crumpled to the ground. Dee stood transfixed, watching the old soldier kill the hideous beasts with ruthless efficiency.

The Trophy King stood in the middle of the room, surrounded by a guard of larger Variants. Against the far wall was the prone figure of Beth, slumped against a rack of bones. Dee prayed that she was alive. Frantic, she searched for the boys. Jack nudged her arm and nodded towards the cage at the Alpha's feet.

Adrenalin surged through Dee's veins as she recognised the figures of Boss and George, huddled together. Dee squeezed her eyes shut, wanting to block out the image. The stench of death was suffocating. Maggie brushed past her, firing into the mass of monsters. Dee snapped back to the battle and screamed at the Trophy King. All the motherly instincts buried deep down inside her, all her anger and frustration, came out in one long scream.

Dee raised her rifle and let loose at the Trophy King. The bullets bounced off its thick bark-like skin. It looked up at Dee and bellowed. She swore it was grinning at her. A few Variants scampered around the room, running towards the Renegades.

Dee reached into her vest and grabbed a couple of grenades. She waited until the Variants were beneath her before dropping them.

"Grenade!"

She yelled more for the boys' sake, hoping they heard. She pulled Jack and Maggie back through the door and slammed it shut. The exploding grenades shook the metal stairs. Variant screams mixed with the constant sound of gunfire. Smoke and concrete dust hung in the air, making her cough.

Dee grasped Jack's arm; he looked back at her. She didn't speak. He knew what she was thinking. She turned to Maggie. "I'm going for the boys and Beth. You two, cover me. If you can keep those big bastards off me, I think I can get them out."

"Gotcha. Give him hell," said Maggie.

Dee raised her rifle, flung the door open and ran down the stairs, firing at the Alpha as she went. Jack and Maggie added to her barrage. The Trophy King swatted at the bullets as if they were pesky mosquitos.

Dee skirted around the side of the room. She risked a quick glance to see Ben's progress. He was sweeping his rifle back and forth, mowing down any Variant that happened to be within range. Their numbers were dwindling. She estimated about twenty Variants remained, including the Alpha and its guard. Her radio squawked.

"Keep firing, Renegades. Jack, Dee, get the kids!" yelled Ben.

Dee quickened her pace, pumping her legs. She sighted a Variant over her AR-15 and squeezed the trigger. The bullet entered its neck, spraying her with black, putrid-smelling blood. The scent of rotten fruit almost overwhelmed her. The beast tumbled and fell at her feet. It looked up at her, pure hatred in its eyes, and clawed at her legs. Dee unsheathed her knife and rammed it into the Variant's deformed skull. The knife grated on bone before entering its brain, killing it. She scanned her immediate vicinity, looking for targets. Seeing no more, she ran the last few metres to Beth.

Dee checked the girl's pulse. Her heart leapt. Weak, but present. It was then that she realised: the poor girl had been crucified. The depravity of it sickened her. With a silent apology, she yanked Beth off the cross and flung her across her shoulders in a fireman's carry. Grunting with the effort, she struggled back to the stairs.

Jack had made it to the floor and continued to fire at the Alpha and its guards. He stopped firing to take Beth from Dee.

Dee pivoted and fired her penultimate magazine at the Alpha. It bellowed at the barrage of metal.

Her two-way squawked, and Ben's voice rang out. "Keep firing, I'm going for the boys."

She looked over, and watched as Ben and Eric descended, firing as they went.

Dee concentrated on covering them. The Alpha bounded towards her and, bellowing, swung a huge claw at her. She spun to one side, but its claw gouged her shoulder. Dee winced at the pain. She ducked from its follow up, slipped on some intestines, and skidded. As she slid, she fired up at the Trophy King, hitting it in the groin. She saw its eyes go wide, and realised that her bullets had hit a weak spot. She peered closer. She could see patches of pink skin on its inner thighs and at the bottom of its stomach.

The Trophy King bellowed a deep, angry roar and swung another huge claw. Dee rolled away, avoiding certain death. The Alpha caught her rifle and it slipped from her grasp.

"Dee!" Jack yelled.

She didn't look at him. The Trophy King turned towards her and snarled, flashing its sucker mouth filled with teeth. The grotesque heads mounted on its shoulders jiggled. Dee let out a breath. She reached back and drew her katana.

The Alpha was three metres away; its feet planted wide, arms and claws outstretched. It let out a ferocious screech.

"Dee! No!" Jack screamed again.

She smiled. She looked over at Boss and George, huddled in their cage of bones, watching her with tears in their eyes.

She let out a breath, and charged the Trophy King, katana held high. Screaming all her anger. All her hate. All her frustration. Everything she had.

As she reached the Alpha, she tucked into a roll, ducking underneath its swinging claws. Passing through its legs, she leapt up and slashed deep into its groin, continuing the slice up into its stomach. Then she reversed the blade and swung down, slicing through the backs of its ankles. The Trophy King stumbled, turned, and fell to one knee, eyes fixed on Dee. A wet sloshing sound made her smile as the Alpha looked down to see its intestines falling to the ground.

Dee leant back and shoved the katana through its eye. The Alpha grunted once and toppled sideways.

Dee dropped to the ground next to the Trophy King, relief overcoming her. She heard running feet and, looking up, saw Jack. He reached down and hauled her to her feet, pointing to the door above Ben and Eric where Variants were struggling to get back into the room. Jack handed her rifle back to her before turning. He aimed his carbine and shot the Trophy King twice in the head.

Rule #2. Double tap.

Dee clicked in her last magazine. She ran over to the cage, opened it, and grasped the boys in a hug.

George sobbed into her shoulder.

"I'm sorry we weren't there," she sobbed.

Boss struggled to stand on one leg, so Dee wrapped an arm around him, helping him steady himself. She watched as he glanced up at the Variants fighting through the barrage of bullets to get to the humans. "Thanks, Dee. Let's get out of here."

***

Jack reached down and picked up George. Then he ran for the stairs, taking them two at a time. Ben, Eric and Maggie fired into the knot of Variants swarming into the throne room. The Renegades backed out of the room of horror. Jack put George down next to Beth in the corridor and laid down covering fire as Ben and Eric ran up the stairs. Screeches filled the cavernous room, bouncing around like an aviary of parrots.

Jack fired at a beast to his left, taking a chunk out of its face. The Variant howled and leapt, landing on the stairs next to Eric.

Eric spun, bringing up his shotgun. The Variant speared him through the torso, tearing into his flesh. Eric screamed and smashed his fist into the Variant, trying to get it off. The monster held on and tore at his chest.

The Renegades looked on in horror. Jack met his gaze. Tears forming, he raised his AR-15.

Eric shook his head. Holding up one of the explosive bricks, he reached down for a grenade.

Ben pushed Jack back out into the hallway. "Go!"

Jack reached down and lifted George into his arms. He could see Dee a few metres farther down the hallway with the hopping Boss. Ben slammed the door behind them. Jack ran with George, away from that pit of despair. Away from the horrors that would be forever in his mind. Away from the Alpha and its disciples of death. He shook his head, remembering Dee's desperate move that ended the Trophy King. As he rounded the corner, a huge explosion tore through the air. He cradled George's head and dropped to the floor. The heat of the fireball washed over him. Jack said a silent prayer for Eric, rolled over, stood and ran for the exit.

— 35 —

Maggie was struggling with the weight of the unconscious girl she was carrying, so she concentrated on putting one foot in front of the other. Sweat poured off her forehead and onto the concrete floor. She had no idea where she was going; she just followed the figure in front of her.

She looked around at this motley group of soldiers, amazed at their tenacity. "Renegades", the older guy had called them. He reminded her of Gandalf with his long beard, leading by example, never wavering. Trusting his friends. The petite woman she had saved from that onslaught had just killed the biggest Variant Maggie had seen yet. She was certain it was the same one from yesterday. The woman had just sliced open the Variant's stomach, spilling its guts before stabbing it through the eye.

Maggie had hoped she would find such people. She still wanted to keep her promise and rescue those she had left behind in the camp. She looked up at the petite woman, who was standing in the open door, a faint smile on her lips. Maggie liked her already. She had a way about her. Something that put you at ease. She gave a friendly nod as they exited the dam. The jarring sounds of battle from outside made her tense her muscles. She peered across the dam. One chopper buzzed around, firing its .50 cal. ammo into the Variant horde. The wreckage of the other was still on fire, the smoke pouring out and swirling with the wash of the attacking helicopter. Maggie adjusted the girl, gritted her teeth, then pushed on up the metal stairs, eager to escape this hell.

The Renegades stopped at the top of the stairs. Maggie looked around. The petite woman and the tall guy were gasping for breath. The old guy pulled out his radio and yelled into it, "Seven ready for extraction. Over."

There was a pause, hissing and static crackling out. "Copy that, Renegades. LZ extremely hot. Can you reach the rowing tower? Over."

Maggie caught the old guy's eye. He frowned, and then looked out over the lake. She followed his gaze. Sitting two hundred feet off the shore was a small square building, raised up on metal stilts with thick concrete feet that extended below the waterline. Looking around desperately, Maggie spotted a small pontoon tied up to the dam, next to a large metal grate.

"Down there!" she yelled, pointing.

The old soldier spoke into his radio. "Yes, we can make it. Sergeant Hollis, cover us."

Maggie heard something else said, but it was garbled. She followed the others over the small wall that bordered the narrow road and headed for the boat.

***

Dee helped Boss onto the pontoon. All around, battle raged. Hollis continued to fly above them, carpeting the howling Variants with covering fire. So far, it was keeping them occupied. Dee looked over at the burning wreckage of the other chopper. It was wedged across the road, the intense heat palpable even from this distance. Variants on the far side were desperately trying to reach the fleeing Renegades. A number had managed to skirt the flames and were sprinting for them. She glanced around, looking for their ride out of this madness. She spotted it, hovering a few metres above the rowing commentary tower.

A black wave surging alongside the lake caught her attention. She turned quickly and rushed to help Maggie and Beth into the boat. She pointed towards the mass of Variants. "Hurry!"

Ben's head snapped around and he spun, firing into the mass.

Dee drew her katana and slashed the painter, releasing the rope. She searched for a paddle, or some other means at propulsion. Seeing nothing, she gave the boat a shove and plunged into the frigid water.

"Jack!"

Jack and Ben jumped into the water, and together the three of them managed to get the pontoon moving out into the lake. The tower was a good 80 metres away. Dee kicked hard, urging the boat to move faster. She was surprised that it didn't have an engine of some sort. Howling from the dam wall and lakeshore shifted her attention back to their pursuers.

Ben turned his head, water dripping off his long beard. "Dee, get on. Give us some covering fire."

She looked up. Maggie had heard, and moved over to haul her onto the boat. Gasping from the effort of moving the boat, Dee took a moment to catch her breath.

Maggie moved to one side and began firing into the mass of Variants. Several of the beasts had reached the water and were hurling themselves in. Dee started firing, trying to take down the lead monsters. They just scrambled over the fallen and plunged into the lake. Variant after Variant jumped in. She watched, fascinated, as they thrashed about, trying to swim. Most of them drowned, but a few bobbed around and managed to swim a few metres after them.

"Dee! Above us!" yelled Boss.

She looked up. Dozens of Variants had crawled along the powerlines above the dam. They started to swing like demonic monkeys. Their howling reached fever pitch and four let go, sailing out, claws outstretched.

"Maggie!"

Dee swung her rifle up. She breathed out, picturing her time at the shooting range with Jack, where they had spent a few weekends shooting clay pigeons. She shot a Variant through the neck before adjusting her aim and hitting a second in the side. Maggie shot one through the head, and another through the leg. The two injured Variants slammed onto the pontoon. Shrieking, they hissed, spittle flying from their sucker mouths. A shotgun boomed and the head of one of them exploded like a melon. Dee squeezed the trigger of her rifle. Nothing. She dropped it and pulled her katana out. The Variant howled and flung itself at Dee. She slashed at it but missed.

The Variant had twisted in mid-air to land behind her. With astonishing speed, it leapt onto Dee, knocking her to the deck. Time seemed to stop. The Variant sat on top of her, hissing and spitting. Boss looked in horror. As Dee struggled she saw George staring at her, squinting.

She frowned. What was with his eye? Rage exploded, adrenaline surged, and with her last ounce of strength, she screamed and shoved. The beast held tight, gouging its claws into her flesh. She cried out in pain. She brought up her knee and was able to nudge the katana towards Maggie. Maggie caught her meaning and grabbed it. She stabbed the beast through the head. Dee stared into its cold reptilian eyes and watched the light go out. She felt no sadness, no remorse. These beasts had taken so much from her. No, she had no sympathy. She shoved the beast off her and into the lake.

The pontoon bounced as at last it hit the concrete foot of the tower. Jack and Ben scrambled onto the boat. Dee looked at Jack before hugging him. She couldn't help the tears. He held her tight. She broke the embrace and helped Boss to his feet.

Jack picked George up.

She turned, looking for Maggie and Beth. Maggie was helping Beth to her feet. The blonde-haired girl had finally regained consciousness.

The Renegades and the children climbed up the ladder on the side of the tower. Dee looked back out to the still-burning wreckage of the helicopter. It was then that she glimpsed a blur of white sprinting out along the road. As it got nearer, she could see it was a man. He leapt onto the wall, dived into the lake and started swimming for the tower. Dee shook her head and hauled herself onto the roof of the building. The chopper had been hovering off to one side, and now moved over to them so the open door was within easy reach. It was a skilful bit of flying. Dee turned and helped Boss and George inside the chopper. She glanced back at the swimming figure. He was only twenty metres away now. Dee nudged Ben, pointing.

He shook his head. "Leave him. He chose his side."

"We can't, Ben. He did what he had to do."

Maggie stopped and turned, looking at the swimming figure. He had nearly reached the tower. Dee saw her squint. "I think I know him," she yelled above the whine of the engines. She ran to the ladder and disappeared over the side.

Ben grasped Dee's shoulder. He held up the detonator, wiggling it. "Do you want to do the honours?"

She smiled. "Give it to Jack. I got my revenge."

The tower shook violently, swaying like a tree in a winter storm. Dee reached out, grabbing the chopper for support. She exchanged a look with Ben. He was just as confused.

Maggie appeared, hauling the dripping man after her. Dee got a glimpse of his glasses as Maggie helped him into the waiting helicopter.

Dee jumped in and the chopper swiftly rose into the air, the movement lurching her stomach. She didn't mind; it meant they were safe, away from the horror of that place.

A satisfying calm loosened her tired muscles. Somehow, they had done it. They had faced the impossible and survived. Ben had been right. Nothing was impossible. You just had to believe it enough to achieve it. The Renegades had believed that they could take on the Trophy King and survive, and they had. Love for the boys had motivated her and Jack to summit the improbable mountain. She looked over at Jack and the boys. They all stared at each other, saying nothing. Love had motivated her to find Jack in the chaos of the Hemorrhage Virus. The feeling of love was powerful and complete.

Dee moved over and drew her boys into a hug, savouring the warmth of their bodies. She looked up and nodded at Maggie, who was bandaging Beth's eye. Maggie smiled and moved over to them, grabbing the medical kit from the seat. "Let's see to these wounds."

"I'm okay. Check over the kids first." Dee lifted George's head to show her his ruined eye. Maggie turned her head, looking at Beth. "She had the same wound. Doesn't look life threatening, but we need to clean it out. Stop any infection."

"Thanks Maggie."

"You're welcome. Sorry, but I don't know your name?"

Dee barked out a small laugh. "It's Dee. That's Jack, Boss, George and Ben. Oh, and Alan on the .50 cal.," she said, pointing to each in turn.

"Well, it's nice to meet y'all. Wish it had been in better circumstances."

Dee smiled, nodding in acknowledgement.

Ben moved over to them, holding out the detonator to Jack, who grinned and took it from Ben's hand. He stood up and moved to the window of the hold. The chopper was hovering 500 metres above the dam. Jack gasped and pointed up the lake. Dee turned, looking out the window. A huge wall of water was careening down the lake in a massive surge, taking out trees, houses, boats. Anything in its path. It reminded her of a tsunami, destroying everything. The explosives they'd detonated at Arapuni must have breached the dam after all.

Jack held up the detonator and flicked the metal switch on the side, arming it. "Screw you, Trophy King," he yelled, and pressed the red button down.

There was a split-second pause before a huge rumbling explosion echoed out over the lake.

***

Jack could hear it clearly over the sound of the chopper. He watched mesmerised as the dam exploded in a cloud of dust with a debris-filled *whump*! Hunks of concrete, steel and wood flung out, cascading into the river below.

The water behind the dam frothed and bubbled; geysers of water shot into the sky. Jack turned, looking for the tsunami. It reached the tower they had sheltered on, slamming into it, tearing it off its foundations. The tsunami then slammed into the dam, buckling the wall on top as it sloshed over in a massive wave. With the added force of the tsunami, the dam broke apart. Torrents of water gushed out. Jack smiled as the dam exploded, crumbling from the pressure. Billions of litres of water poured out over the destroyed dam and made its way downriver. Jack said a silent apology to all those towns that would be destroyed. To all those millions of hours it took to build civilisation. They were destroying it in seconds.

He felt the chopper bank and head for the coast. Jack took a final look at the wall of water smashing its way down the Waikato River. The river washed away everything in its path. Jack shook his head at what had become of his country. At what had become of the world.

We came. We saw. We conquered, and ultimately, we destroyed.

He sat down next to Dee and gazed out the window at the Pacific Ocean in the distance. It was time to rebuild. *Maybe this time we'll learn from our mistakes.* He grasped Dee's hand in his and pulled her close. Despite what the world had become, he wanted to create a life with her, bring new life into it. She glanced up at him as if reading his thoughts and snuggled closer to him. Jack grinned, enjoying her company, here in the apocalypse.

— 36 —

The sun hugged the horizon, kissing the land as it sank away, ushering in the night. Dee breathed a sigh of relief as Mayor Island grew larger before the chopper finally began its descent. Every part of her body ached from the exertion of the past few days.

She looked out at the village. Dozens of lights had been strung up along the boardwalk, linking all the buildings, trees and tents together. It looked like the Milky Way had been pulled out of the sky and laid across the village.

George pushed up off her lap and looked out the window too. He turned to smile at her. Maggie had cleaned his damaged eye and bandaged it. Dee kissed his cheek, happy that he had something to smile at after his torture at the hands of the Trophy King. The chopper bumped to the ground and the pilot switched off the engines. Dee heard the whine drop and shuffled along her seat, eager to exit. She wanted a shower, food, sleep and Jack.

She dropped down out of the chopper and looked up. Alice and the kids stood there, watching.

"Dee! Maggie!" Alice yelled.

Dee lifted George and Boss out of the chopper, then waved at them. Jack helped Boss stand and the Renegades moved away from the still-spinning rotor blades and into the waiting group.

Two soldiers handcuffed Glasses and lead him away.

Dee lost herself in the hugs and cries of joy. It was worth all the effort to see the utter delight and relief on everyone's faces, knowing they were all safe for now. A few days ago, she could never have imagined all that they had been through since then. She was experiencing new emotions, emotions she didn't have the words to express. She looked around at all the kids and adults, lost in the moment, caught up in love. After so many years of running from the responsibilities of motherhood, Dee felt that she was ready. She exchanged a glance with Jack and saw the warmth of his smile as he held George close and hugged Alice. She knew that he was feeling it too. Dee stepped over and pulled Alice into an embrace; and let the tears flow. Then she gently pulled away and hugged Ben.

"Thank you."

"You're welcome. We look after each other."

She smiled. "Still, you didn't have to. I'm worried about what Mahana is going to do."

Ben pointed at all the lights. Dee could see that several tables had been set up along the boardwalk outside the FOB. Fires were burning in the braziers.

"You let me worry about Mahana, Dee. Let's enjoy Matariki and savour this small victory."

Ben patted her arm and joined the soldiers standing apart from the group. Dee reached down and grasped

George's hand. Jack took his other hand and the trio started to move away. Two nurses had brought Boss his crutches and were helping him walk. With their aid, he turned and followed Dee and Jack. Soon the Renegades broke apart and walked with them. Dee looked around and smiled. She never would have imagined this scene. Before the Variant apocalypse, she and Jack had been hermits, enjoying their own company. Now, as the group trudged up the hill to the Walsh Villa, she was happy to have all the company she could get. With what lay out there in the world, it felt good to have human contact.

Dee sat at the kitchen table. She felt clean and fresh after her shower. Jack joined her and handed her a cup of tea. She clasped it in both hands and inhaled, savouring its earthy scent. Things almost felt normal again. But gazing out the window, she knew they weren't. She caught Alice's eye and beckoned her over.

Maggie and Alice broke away from the kids playing in the lounge and sat down opposite them. No one spoke for a few minutes. Dee assumed everyone was lost in their own thoughts, just as stunned as she was. She glanced over at Boss and Beth, holding on to each other, lying on the couch. Dee looked up at Jack. "Is it over?"

Jack sighed and ran his hands across the table. "I hope so. For now, I guess."

She watched as he took another sip of his tea. He grimaced slightly. She knew it was from the taste of the goats' milk. Cows were a rarity nowadays.

He looked back at her. "I mean, you killed the Trophy King like you were *The Bride*."

Dee smiled and stroked his hand.

Maggie plonked her cup down on the wooden table with a dull thud. "You killed that Alpha, yes, but another will take its place. It kind of reminds me of this movie…"

Dee arched her eyebrow at her. "Not you too?"

Maggie grinned, glancing between her and Jack. "Yeah, me too. So, in this movie, there's this kid in high school who's being tormented by the popular kids. They're merciless in their bullying. He snaps and starts to kill them off, one by one. Each kill is gruesome. By the end of the film, he's feared and the other kids do anything he says. He enjoys the power. He realises that he has become the bully, the one everyone fears and hates."

Jack laughed. "I remember that one!" He sobered and nodded. "There is always someone to take the mantle. To become king. If you really want to stop it, you have to break the cycle."

Alice looked between Jack and Dee. She gripped her mug tighter, her hands turning white.

"Maggie is right. After we left you, Dee, we were captured by the Variants. They killed Austin and ate him." Alice paused and looked down at the table. Maggie put her arm around her friend. "They were led by this big ugly bastard. Before I was taken to the prison, we were dragged along to this meeting. Four Alphas."

Alice glanced at Dee, tears welling in her eyes. "They ate Matt, right in front of me. They ate him, then children…kids…"

Dee reached out and grasped her friend's hand. She didn't know what to say. They had all seen terrible things. Comfort was what Alice needed.

"Well, let's hope that case the scientist gave us helps," said Jack.

Alice exchanged a look with Maggie. "Case?"

"We rescued a scientist. She had been working on a cure. Her research was in the case. It's a story for another time, I think."

Maggie cast her eyes down to her tea. "A cure would be good. This new world sucks worse than before. And I've seen the worst of it."

Dee chuckled. "Hell yeah." She glanced outside. "Let's go and enjoy Matariki. Forget about all this stuff for a while." She looked up at Jack as she spoke, and he smiled, nodding in agreement.

Dee lifted herself up from the table and moved into the lounge. She squatted and took George in a hug. Alice called the other children and they made their way down into the village.

The night air chilled Dee as she made her way along the shell path. She was thankful the soldiers and other survivors had pitched in and cleaned up the mess from the attack. The strings of lights twinkled, beckoning her to the festivities. Dee was surprised at how much she wanted to join in. She was exhausted, but she loved Matariki. Tonight was a time to remember those lost, a time for renewal, a time to pause and be thankful.

The smells of BBQ cooking wafted over the bay as Jack and Dee led the others to the tables. Ben had posted soldiers around the camp at intervals, wary of another attack. Dee reached down and patted her Glock at her hip, its presence reassuring. She sat down at one of the tables and leant back, taking in the view. All around her people stood, enjoying the company of others. Music played softly in the background. Dee recognised the song *Thank You* by Led Zeppelin. That was fitting. A microphone had been set up on the steps of the FOB.

Ben walked up to the microphone and tapped it a couple of times. An amplified thump rang out. "Good evening, everyone."

The gathered party grew silent, and there was a shuffling as people took their seats. Jack reached over and laced his fingers through Dee's.

"Good evening. Tonight, is Matariki, our new year. This year it is bathed in sadness. A few weeks ago, the Hemorrhage Virus changed the world forever. Yet it was amongst this chaos that you survived, found refuge and each other. Yesterday we were attacked, and we lost a lot of good people. But even then, we found hope. Let us take this time to honour those who sacrificed their lives, so we could go on."

Then Ben pointed to Dee. "Dee killed the Alpha that killed so many of us."

Thunderous applause broke out and a huge cheer erupted.

Ben held up his hands and the party grew silent. "Tonight is a time to remember all those we have lost. I know we have all lost loved ones, and so much else besides. Let's rise up from the ashes of this world and make a new one! A better one." Ben stood, smiling at everyone, and applauded back. "Thank you to all those who pitched in to make this night happen."

Ben turned away from the microphone and made his way to Jack and Dee. Applause broke out again and the music went up a notch. Dee stood and hugged Ben, indicating the seat next to her. She turned and watched as plates of food appeared, carried by soldiers and people from their small village.

Dee smiled and looked at Jack. "I love you."

Jack grinned. "I know."

Dee chuckled, reached over and speared some steaming pork and heaped it onto her plate. Ben was right. They had to make this new world a better one. They had to right the wrongs of so many. Dee had hope, but she also had doubt. They had escaped the horrors of the mainland. They had survived. But at what cost? How soon before a country with more firepower looked to New Zealand and decided to take it away from the remaining few?

She brushed aside her fears and dug in to the food on her plate. Time to enjoy their victory and remember all those they had lost.

— 37 —

Jack sat at the table with Dee, Alice, Ben and Maggie. A week had passed since Matariki. The mid-June sun shone weakly, casting long shadows over the well-worn timber table top.

He and Dee were enjoying the relative silence of Mayor Island. Patrols continued, looking for any Variants. So far, no more had been found. They had pitched in and helped build fortifications, adding several machine gun nests, fencing and a few trenches. Everyone was expected to help.

Colonel Mahana had not been happy with the Renegades' actions, especially at the loss of men and the chopper. He had visited the island and reprimanded Ben and the Renegades. Luckily Jack's handing over the scientist's case had placated the situation. No punishment had been dealt out, for which Jack was happy. Thankfully, Mahana had given them permission to liberate the camp that Maggie and Alice had escaped from.

The day before, the Renegades and a squadron of soldiers had flown to the camp to find it unguarded. They had ferried the women and children to Great Barrier Island, much to the delight of Maggie and Alice. The absence of the guards had confused Jack. Dee thought that maybe they had left after hearing the explosions at the destroyed dams. He hoped the flooding of the river valley had killed thousands of the Variants. The sight of the flooded plains had stunned him. Most of Hamilton and Cambridge were under water. He hoped their efforts would help turn the tide in this war for humanity.

Jack looked up from his tea, pushing aside his worries. "You guys ready?"

Maggie and Alice both nodded. Maggie rubbed her hand through her hair. "Almost. A few supplies to go. Should be ready for high tide."

Jack grasped his chin in his hand, feeling his stubble. He glanced over at Dee, George sitting in her lap. Doc had cleaned out the wound and, with Maggie's help, made sure it didn't get infected. He would never see out of it again, but he'd taken to wearing an eye patch. Jack had told George about his favourite childhood movie, *The Goonies*, about the pirate captain One-Eyed Willy and how he'd built these elaborate traps to test your worthiness to claim his treasure. He promised George that he would do his best to find a copy. George asked if he could build some traps for the monsters. Both Jack and Dee had agreed to help him; he just had to invent them. George had loved the idea and with the help of Boss and Beth spent hours drawing.

"Shall we go on our patrol?" Jack asked Dee.

"Yeah." Dee turned to Alice. "See you guys down there."

Alice smiled at her. "Okay. Thanks guys, for everything."

"No worries. See you soon."

Jack grabbed their go-bags, handing one to Dee. She opened the gun cage and handed him his rifle before taking hers.

Jack arched an eyebrow. "You ready?"

"Nearly. Just need Kingslayer." Dee grinned at him before pulling her katana off the hook next to the gun cage.

Jack couldn't help but grin back. He felt nothing but love and pride for her. Dee and Kingslayer had saved them all. Jack waved at Ben and the others before holding the door open for Dee. He looked up the hill, searching for the gun placement that was their first stop. Jack heard the door slam and, turning, smiled. This might not have been how he'd imagined his life turning out, but he was going to make the most of it. He moved his rifle off his shoulder and followed Dee up the hill.

***

Maggie lifted the last box of bottled water off the jetty. Despite the chill of the early winter, she could feel the sweat dripping down her back. She handed the box to the waiting soldier and wiped her brow with the back of a hand. She glanced over to the cabin of the catamaran. She had convinced Ben to allow her to scour Tauranga Harbour for a yacht. After rescuing Glasses from the Karapiro Lake, Ben had imprisoned him for his crimes. Maggie had visited him a few times. After finding out he was a seasoned sailor, she had asked him to sail her to America. He had readily agreed, especially if it meant not being locked up.

Glasses had gone with her to Tauranga. He had

spotted the catamaran — he called it a Victoria 67 — saying it was reliable and should get them across the vast Pacific. Together, they had plotted a north-easterly course, up through the islands of Tonga, Samoa and Kiribati, before striking out for Hawaii. Maggie had tried to contact any American Naval ships, but without success.

She heard footsteps on the wooden jetty. Turning, she raised her hand, blocking the sun. Alice stood next to her, looking at the sleek lines of the white hull.

"What do you think? Are we going to make it?"

"I hope so. I'll keep going or die trying."

Alice wrapped an arm around her.

Maggie enjoyed the sign of affection. "We're going to have to keep an eye on Glasses though."

"Do you think he'll try something?"

"I really hope not, but let's be prepared. Especially with Becs, okay?"

Alice nodded and smiled. "This is going to be an adventure. We have no idea what's out there. But I'm happy to help you get home after what you did for us, Maggie."

"Thanks, Alice. I'm glad you are here with me."

Maggie broke the embrace and stepped over the gunwale. The boat rocked slightly with her weight. She was going to have to find her sea legs quickly. According to Glasses, the waves out in the Pacific could get huge. She was taking a big risk, but she needed to find out the fate of her Texan family. She and Alice had discussed the pros and cons of taking Becs. In the end Becs had insisted on coming. Part of Maggie felt guilty for taking her from New Zealand, but she had grown attached to

Becs and, although she could never replace Izzy, maybe by saving Becs she could feel like she was doing something positive.

Maggie walked up to the wheel and stared again at the nautical maps spread out on the table. It was going to be a hard, crazy time out there on the ocean. She knew she had another fight at home, out on the plains of Texas.

***

The sun's strength surprised Dee as it beat down on her face. Even though the wind blowing off the Pacific Ocean was cold, the sun still had some kick to it. She glanced out over the bush-clad hills on the north side of Mayor Island. Apart from the bird life, she saw no movement. The other patrols had reported no signs of Variants in four days. Dee breathed deeply, waiting for the rotten fruit smell to invade her nose. Smelling nothing, she turned to Jack standing a few metres away.

"I can't see anything. Can you?"

"Nothing, thankfully."

"Okay, I'll radio it in. Let's get back to see the girls off." She watched Jack fiddle with his selector switch. "You okay?"

"Yeah, why?"

"C'mon Jack, I know when something is on your mind."

Jack stared out at the view. Dee followed his gaze. She watched the distant waves smash against the volcanic rocks, frothing the water.

"I'm sorry, Dee. I just don't know how to say this…"

Dee wrinkled her brow. A hint of worry crept into her

mind. What was he going to say? Something bad? Jack never had trouble expressing his feelings to her. He was an up-front guy. She glanced up at him, doing her best to keep her growing worry out of her eyes.

"I guess, I'll just come out and say it. I think we should try for a baby."

A flood of relief washed over her. She squealed and bounded over to him, pulling him into a strong bear hug. "You bastard! You had me worried there for a moment." She laughed at his stunned look. "Of course I want a baby with you!"

Jack cast his eyes down and shuffled his feet, then looked back up at her and smiled. Dee hadn't seen a smile like that since their wedding day. It was a smile full of love. Full of contentment. Full of joy. "I just wasn't sure…how you would feel about it…with all this craziness…"

"Jack, I think it will be wonderful."

Jack squeezed her tight. Dee lost herself in the hug, feeling like the weight of the last few weeks had lifted off her shoulders.

Dee pulled away and sighed. "C'mon. Let's go and say goodbye to Alice and Maggie."

Jack laced his fingers through hers and smiled.

***

Jack stood on the wooden jetty with Dee, Boss, Ben, Beth, George, Leela and the kids. George and Leela hugged his and Dee's legs. Jack was sad to see Maggie go. She was a fine soldier, and they had chatted long into the nights about different movies. Jack had discovered that

Maggie had read his favourite post-apocalyptic series too. He had discussed different theories with her for hours. He felt Dee nudge him and he wrapped an arm around her. He watched as Glasses unhooked the painter from the bollard and Maggie started the engine, pulling the catamaran away from the jetty. Ben had managed to contact an American outpost in Hawaii. They had promised to look out for the yacht.

Strangely, the yacht had no name. After much discussion, Maggie had christened it *Samwise* after her favourite character from *Lord of the Rings*. Jack thought that was an apt name, as Sam was strong of character. He watched as the catamaran moved out into the clear waters of the bay and out into the Pacific Ocean.

George tugged on his hand. "C'mon Jack. Let's watch from the rocks."

"Okay," he said, laughing.

Jack lifted Leela up and placed her on his shoulders. He pivoted and followed Dee, Boss, Beth, George and Ben around the rocks, watching the catamaran grow smaller.

Jack stood on the rocks as the catamaran sailed into the setting sun before tacking north, and finally north east and around the tip of the island, slowly becoming a speck. He smiled to himself, a tear forming in his eye. He hated goodbyes. They seemed so final. He really hoped that he would see Alice, Maggie and Becs again. Leela leant into him, sobbing. Jack crouched down and watched as Dee knelt down beside him.

"What's wrong, Leela?"

"I wanted to go to."

George turned from waving off the catamaran. "It's all

right, Leela. You can live with us now. Because, we love you."

Jack smiled as George hugged Leela. He glanced up at Dee. She wiped the tears from her eyes and joined in the hug.

Jack wrapped his arms around the three of them and smiled. In this new world, he was going to savour what he had and enjoy the little moments.

Epilogue

The stench made Captain Koto wrinkle his nose. He pulled his perfume-soaked buff up and covered it. He tried breathing through his mouth to escape the putrid smell, but to no avail. He hadn't even entered the hold yet and the stench was threatening to overcome him. He moved over to the rail and breathed in some fresh sea air. He could taste the perfume on his buff.

Staring out at the twinkling lights of the village, he felt a pang of guilt. Colonel Mahana and the New Zealand people had been so welcoming. They had fed them, treated the sick and given them land to settle on. They certainly didn't deserve what was awaiting them in the hold. Koto had loved the festival of Matariki, had spent the evening enjoying the company of Colonel Mahana, listened to beautiful songs, watched the captivating haka. It made his decision even harder to carry out, but Colonel Mahana had been right. They had to fight back. Take back the land from the monsters called Variants. He couldn't leave it any longer, it was time. Time to act.

Captain Koto gripped the rusty handrail, his knuckles turning white. He let out a breath and turned, facing the door in front of him. He had relieved all his men of their duties and commanded them onshore to join the civilians. The ship sat empty and silent, a dark shadow in the harbour. Koto tugged down his jacket and reached out. With a last glance out over the water, he spun the handle and pulled open the door. The stench was even worse in here.

He stood on the small metal landing above the vast hold. Stairs plunged down into the darkness. Hundreds of yellow eyes glowed back at him. The way they did that freaked him out: even with just a hint of light, their eyes glowed. It chilled him. In a morbid way, it reminded him of the lights of the Matariki festival. He bit his lip as he descended into the hold. He could hear them shuffling around, watching him as he approached.

Koto reached the bottom of the hold and held his breath. A giant winged Variant crouched in front of him. It arched its back and spread its wings. The rotten fruit stench that emanated from it was putrid. Koto swept his hand across his sweaty brow and flinched at the sound of the beast moving to face him. He had called the winged beast Leyak, after the demon stories his mother had told him to frighten him into behaving. Never in his wildest dreams had he imagined them coming true.

Leyak glared down at him and grunted. He raised a clawed hand and pointed up, grunting again. The meaning was clear. It was time to feed.

Leyak had captured Koto and his men on an Indonesian island, when they were searching for food and water. The monster had consumed most of the men. Koto had pleaded for his life. Leyak had, through grunts and basic speech, granted his wish — as long as he provided fresh meat for Leyak and his tribe. Koto had spent the last six weeks sailing from island to island, first winning the trust of the islanders, and then releasing the Variants into the night to feed. Each time he'd done it, a little piece of him had died.

Koto looked up at the hulking winged beast. He breathed out and took the detonator in his pocket. He held it up so Leyak could see. "Do you know what this is, you demon from hell?"

Leyak glared down at him and bellowed. He pushed off with incredible speed, his wings flapping, stirring up the putrid air of the hold. Captain Arif Koto said a silent prayer, and thought of his wife and children. He looked up at Leyak trying to escape, and pushed the button.

Phase One: Impact.
Phase Two: Recoil and rescue.
Phase Three: Recovery.
Phase Four: We fight back.

END OF BOOK TWO.

Continue the adventure with

THE FIVE PILLARS

book 3 of the Extinction NZ series

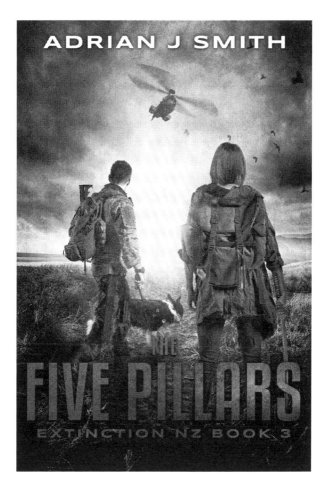

Available at Amazon Books

Glossary

Gallipoli: World War One battle fought between the ANZAC (Australia and New Zealand Army Corp) and Turkish forces in 1915. The ANZACs suffered heavy losses, but fought with sheer determination for little gain.

Haka: Tribal war dance performed to intimidate an opponent. Famously performed in modern times by New Zealand sports teams. Each tribe has its own version of the dance.

Hongi: Translates to "The breath of life." A greeting, where the two greeting each other touch noses and foreheads at the same time. Serves a similar purpose to a handshake.

Iwi: Translates to "people" or "nation", but it has come to mean tribe. In pre-European times, Maori identified more with a Hapu or sub tribe. Iwi can mean a confederation of tribes.

Kai: Simply translates to "food".

Kaitiaki: Term used for Guardianship of the Sea and of the Sky. Kaitiaki is a guardian, and the process and practices of looking after the environment.

Kaumatua: Elders in Maori society, held in high esteem. Being the storehouses of tribal knowledge, genealogy and traditions

Kawakawa: Small tree endemic to New Zealand. Used in medicines and traditional practices.

Kehua: Translates to "ghost".

Kina: A sea urchin endemic to New Zealand. Considered a delicacy.

Koru: Translates to "loop". Used to describe the unfurling frond of the silver fern. Signifies new life, growth, strength and peace.

Kumara: A species of sweet potato grown in New Zealand. Traditionally a staple food.

Maori: Indigenous population of New Zealand.

Manuka: Small flowering tree. Famed for its oily timber and, in more recent times, for the honey produced from its flowers. The honey has many beneficial properties.

Mere: Traditional Maori weapon best described as a club. Could be made from a variety of materials. Chiefs had mere made from a hard semi-precious gemstone called "pounamu".

Moriori: A peaceful indigenous people of the Chatham Islands to the west of New Zealand. Thought to have populated parts of the South Island as well.

New Zealand Flax: Endemic grass plant found throughout the country. Used for variety of reasons. Mainly for weaving traditional Maori objects. Europeans used it as a source of fibre to make ropes, etc.

Pakeha: White or fair skinned New Zealander. Specifically of European descent.

Paua: Endemic species of abalone found around the New Zealand coast.

Pohutukawa: Species of large coast dwelling tree. Often found clinging to cracks and to the side of cliffs. Called New Zealand's "Christmas tree" because its red flowers bloom in abundance during December.

Powhiri: A Maori welcoming ceremony involving, singing, dancing and finally the hongi.

Paka: An expression of annoyance or anger. Can be used in reference to a person as seen in the film *Whale Rider.*

Taiaha: A traditional Maori weapon. A close-quarters staff. Made from wood or whale bone. Used for quick, stabbing thrusts and strikes, with fast footwork by the wielder. Often found to have intricate carvings near its tip.

Tangi: A traditional funeral held on a marae (meeting place)

Ta Moko: Traditional tattoos of the Maori.

Tekoteko: Maori term for a carved human figure or head. Sometimes attached to the gable of a house.

Te Reo: The Maori language.

Whanau: An extended family or related community who live together in the same area.

About the Authors

Adrian J Smith is the author of the Extinction NZ trilogy; The Rule of Three and its sequels, The Fourth Phase and The Five Pillars.

He has had a couple of careers, He started his working life as a Painter before switching to Landscape design and construction. He switched back again, and for the last decade he has run his own successful Painting and decorating business.

Adrian lives in Hamilton, New Zealand. A self-confessed book and movie geek. He admits that he is obsessed with Star Wars, Aliens, Lord of The Rings, Harry Potter, Studio Ghibli, and Game of Thrones.

When he isn't working his day job or writing, Adrian can be found wandering the mountains, hiking, swimming, quizzing, watching movies and of course reading. **Website:** AdrianJonSmith.com

Nicholas Sansbury Smith is the New York Times and USA Today bestselling author of the Hell Divers series. His other work includes the Extinction Cycle series, the Trackers series, and the Orbs series. He worked for Iowa Homeland Security and Emergency Management in disaster planning and mitigation before switching careers to focus on his one true passion—writing. When he isn't writing or daydreaming about the apocalypse, he enjoys running, biking, spending time with his family, and traveling the world. He is an Ironman triathlete and lives in Iowa with his wife, their dogs, and a house full of books. **Website:** NicholasSansburySmith.com

28081013R00175

Made in the USA
San Bernardino, CA
05 March 2019